ALSO BY PAUL WEST

FICTION
Love's Mansion
The Women of Whitechapel and Jack the Ripper
Lord Byron's Doctor
The Place in Flowers Where Pollen Rests
The Universe, and Other Fictions
Rat Man of Paris
The Very Rich Hours of Count von Stauffenberg
Gala
Colonel Mint
Caliban's Filibuster
Bela Lugosi's White Christmas
I'm Expecting to Live Quite Soon
Alley Jaggers
Tenement of Clay

NONFICTION
A Stroke of Genius
Sheer Fiction—Volumes I, II, III
Portable People
Out of My Depths: A Swimmer in the Universe
Words for a Deaf Daughter
I, Said the Sparrow
The Wine of Absurdity
The Snow Leopard
The Modern Novel
Byron and the Spoiler's Art

PAUL WEST

THE TENT OF ORANGE MIST

a novel

SCRIBNER

NEW YORK LONDON TORONTO SYDNEY TOKYO SINGAPORE

SCRIBNER
1230 AVENUE OF THE AMERICAS
NEW YORK, NY 10020

SCRIBNER AND DESIGN ARE TRADEMARKS OF SIMON & SCHUSTER INC.

DESIGNED BY SONGHEE KIM

MANUFACTURED IN THE UNITED STATES OF AMERICA

  3 5 7 9 10 8 6 4 2

LIBRARY OF CONGRESS CATALOGING-IN-PUBLICATION DATA
WEST, PAUL, 1930–
THE TENT OF ORANGE MIST: A NOVEL/PAUL WEST.
P. CM.
1. SINO-JAPANESE CONFLICT, 1937–1945—FICTION. 2. CHINA—HISTORY—
1937–1945—FICTION. 3. NANKING (CHINA)—HISTORY—FICTION.
I. TITLE.
PS3573.E824T46   1995
813'.54—DC20
95-9077   CIP

ISBN 0-684-80031-4

As they were chatting, lights were brought in, and the servants spread the desk with wine, rice, chicken, fish, duck and pork. Wang Hui fell to, without inviting Chou Chin to join him; and when Wang Hui had finished, the monk sent up the teacher's rice with one dish of cabbage and a jug of hot water. When Chou Chin had eaten, they both went to bed. The next day the weather cleared. Wang Hui got up, washed and dressed, bade Chou Chin a casual goodbye and went away in his boat, leaving the school-room floor so littered with chicken, duck and fish bones, and melon-seed shells, that it took Chou Chin a whole morning to clear them all away, and the sweeping made him dizzy.

Wu Ching-tzu, *The Scholars*

It comes so soon, the moment when there is nothing left to wait for, when the body is fixed in an immobility which holds no fresh surprise in store, when one loses all hope on seeing—as on a tree in the height of summer one sees leaves already brown—around a face still young hair growing thin or turning grey; it is so short, that radiant morning time, that one comes to like only the very youngest girls, those in whom the flesh, like a precious leaven, is still at work.

Marcel Proust, *Within a Budding Grove*

During World War II, as many as 200,000 teenaged girls and women from Korea and other Asian nations were recruited to the Japanese war effort. They were forced into brothels and ordered to have sex with Japanese soldiers. They were not prostitutes but victims of serial rape.

By way of atonement, Japan has now decided to commit $1 billion to programs ranging from youth exchanges with other Asian nations to a vocational training center for women in the Philippines. Furious at what they regard as "symbolic compensation," some of the surviving women recently conducted an egg-throwing, slogan-hurling protest in front of the Japanese Embassy in Seoul.

The New York Times, September 14, 1994

THE
TENT
OF
ORANGE
MIST

NANKING

The young man, having made a firm resolve,
    Leaves his native home;
If he fails to acquire learning,
    Then even though he die, he must never return.

POEM CIRCULATED AMONG CADETS AT ICHIGAYA MILITARY
ACADEMY, JAPAN, IN THE 1920S

WARLORDS, UNLESS THEY HAVE SUNK VERY LOW, DO NOT SING
anthems, aubades, or odes of dithering farewell. On December
12, 1937, Tang, the warlord in charge of Nanking, fled the city,
and Japanese troops poured in, raping and looting. No child, no
woman, was safe. The remaining Nationalist troops withdrew
up the River Yangtze westward, toward Wuhan, while Scald Ibis
found herself being questioned by weary, sedate men of dis-
cernible cultivation. She nonetheless retained enough of her
wits to be astounded when she heard Japanese speaking Chinese
almost as if they belonged here, too, and had lived here in spirit
all along.

Where was her father? She had no idea. At war, she said. She did not know it yet, but her brother lay in a dry well in the garden, beheaded. Nor did she know that her mother had run into the street, looking for her, only to be snatched, defiled, bayoneted, and thrown aside like so much offal. No, Scald Ibis said, she had no idea where her brother and mother were. Surely hordes of invaders ought not to be asking such questions of a sixteen-year-old. If they upset a country, they should know where the pieces landed. Or let them go ask Tang, if they could catch up with him.

"We," one of the officers told her in pitiful Chinese—though he spoke it best of them all, clearing his throat repeatedly—"will tend you. Look after you. Save you from marauding Chinese soldiers."

I am not a garden, she heard herself thinking. I am not a woman either. Just a child trapped in the bud. Just an elementary me.

"Nothing to fear," he was telling her; instructing her, rather. Unanswering, she signaled her aversion by wrinkling her nose, eager for almost anything different: an apron, a handful of soft duster, a windup toy speedboat.

The soldiers kept looking at her as if they had shared a good joke together, as if her ravishment had been a prelude to good-humored reverie, a whiff of opium, a bite into succulent plums. They must be officers, she thought. They did not seem men who took orders. But then, they didn't seem like men who fell upon young girls and delved into their most secret places, making them—her—feel transformed, somehow distorted, no longer eligible for the finer things. Where was her mother, the Confucianist? And her brother, two years older than she, the language prodigy?

Who and what were these Japanese? As her father had recently said, they were an anxious people who, unable to act as individuals, went mad en masse. It was as simple and gruesome as that. If only she had been able to live outside history, able in a country so vast as China to face away from headlong invaders;

alone and aloof in the western mountains, accessible only by bomber, and devoting herself all over again to art, literature, and the other kind of history: the one somebody else had lived before her, in distant pain.

She clung to the sight of wealthy scholars gathered at weekends in her parents' garden, as if in a painting poring over antiquities arranged on tables and floating platforms. It might have been the Ming dynasty painting by Qiu Ying called *Eighteen Scholars Ascend to the Ying Zhou Isle of Immortality*. Her home life was a life of art. No dividing line. That was what she had always been ready for: the movement upward of measured, orderly life to the Isle; an absolute without epithets.

Again and again she had perused that painting in her mind, predisposed to believe in levitation, float, and soar. To be impelled upward by brush was not so raw a fate, she decided, grazing a teahouse roof on your way, making temporary contact with an ascending unbewildered horse. From that to soldiers who, with pent-up fury, bayoneted the furniture, made water in lazy yellow arcs onto the rugs, and spat against the walls. She could not complete the thought or the construction. That the uplifting, tender side of life was so far from atrocity upset her no end, and kept her trembling. She went from one to the other in no time at all, unable to reconcile the two, wishing she had been trained for this kind of clash. She had always adored the image of a table with dishes and linens, little beds of cast iron in which food slept until tenderly roasted. She was a sane girl back then, she thought, and looked forward to a sane world.

Was this why she did something so reckless, after the Japanese colonel draped a thin rug over her where she lay on a couch after he had finished? Instead of speaking, she got up, stumbling, and looked for her inkstick. Feeling she was dipping her brush into darkest midnight, she painted in that magical modicum of animal glue and pine soot a message as ancient as her writing tools: "I give myself to you," and completed it as poetry:

To be treated like jade.
To place me among gold and
grain would be to insult me.

That was all. Caviar to the colonel, Hayashi, who deciphered it
feebly anyway, although, to give him credit, he did remember
and utter something distant and unverifiable about plum blossom, between which and the fruit from a horse's anus he no
longer knew the difference, being that censurable species, the
man of taste turned savage without quite losing the formulas in
which he used to take pride, on which he prided himself;
Hayashi, the ruptured connoisseur, eyebrows like brushes,
mouth a bulbous taupe domino marred by cold sores in several
different conditions. He saw that she had communicated something to him, to her own satisfaction at least, and swallowed the
rebuke, wishing he were not a man but a freshly painted trellis.
No organs at all. No innards. No rank. No crime.

No fool until recently, he knew enough of China to wish
himself on the way back to his homeland. China was too vast for
any narrow nation to seize. A portion of his schooling had ac-
quainted him with just such personages and images as flowed
through the mind of Scald Ibis. In a famous painting, long-
nailed and at the squat, Emperor Kangxi sat at his studies, his
look one of forbearing disbelief as he read his Confucius. In
their hundreds, candidates for scholarly degrees fretted the hours
away, awaiting their exam results in the time of the Ming dynasty,
milling about ornate halls of learning that smelled of celery and
scented smoke. Against this backdrop Hayashi and his men had
savaged Scald Ibis's home and her body. She felt she had been
desecrated in the presence of China's greatness, whereas Hayashi
was aware of echoes only, foreign fixations, uncomprehended
tropes. An outsider, but a backslider too, letting his men go on
the rampage to calm them down for military use later.

But what happened in Nanking that day was not altogether
systematic. The army had expected an easy win, after fighting

for months and taking heavy losses. Weary, flummoxed, and hungry, they saw a city denuded of its menfolk, a city full of victims, so they ran riot, making of themselves a huge, bloody punctuation mark. Nothing and no one protected anyone, though Scald Ibis in later years rebuked herself for thinking highfalutin ancient classics would somehow interpose a phalanx between the marauders and herself. Yet perhaps not so blameworthy after all—what she remembered numbed her mind, anesthetizing it with aesthetics.

She had survived only because desirable, usable, helpless, the plaything of a Hayashi. Now he wanted to start all over again and appear before her in fresh-laundered white tunic with pearl appendages and gold aiguillettes. He wanted to bow, to click heels like a German, to disembowel himself in front of her; but he was no paragon of mercy and heroism, though brave enough in his way.

"And so?" He almost yelled.

She did not respond, though she opened her eyes.

"What did you mean? Speak to me."

Her eyes closed. Her stomach rumbled.

"Why *write* to me?"

Her indifference told him she had not written to him, but to herself, to Emperor Kangxi, the Ming dynasty, any Japanese horse's ass save him. Blood had crusted all over her. She sounded as if she were choking. Her hair was an oiled tuft. Only her hands twitched, however, as if the act of writing had worn them out.

"And so?" he whispered.

"No," she murmured. She was waiting to die, half-suspecting the junior officers he had dismissed would soon be back, ready to start on her again, a woman of the world new-made.

When questioned in class, a Staff College student at once sat to attention and shouted "Sir!", firmly grasping each arm of his chair, and fixing his eyes on the back of the person in front of him. He then bawled out what seemed a carefully rehearsed answer predicated on the taught doctrine that the Japanese were a race morally superior to all others and that the soldiers of this race, their leaders above all, were a thing apart.

INFANTRY SCHOOL AT CHIBA, JAPAN, BRITISH WAR OFFICE
REPORT WO 106/5494, AUGUST 25, 1931

MARGINAL THINGS PLUCKED AT HER MIND. WHERE HAD THE Japanese come from? One minute they were not there, no doubt pursuing their studies and attempting first poems, and then they were, with less than a street vendor's relationship to civilization. They must have come by sea. Or had they marched? Perhaps they had been here all the time, already spartan and cruel, and so many, as if some giant had spilled a sackful of them. From this kind of visitation, she thought, you begin to have no future; so much damage done so fast changes your life forever, even forty or fifty years away, so deep does the horror strike. Would they use revolvers as well as swords? Why did the Japanese love swords? Could such a nation not invade ancient history instead, vainly stabbing the past in the eye? In five seconds, she told herself, a change can alter day into night, into which it is impossible to peer.

She was not thinking, which is to say she was not remembering. She might with reason have forgotten: early in August, Peking's defenders had simply abandoned the city, and in November Shanghai's had decamped fifty miles toward Soochow. All that remained for the Japanese invaders was to decide whether or not to advance on Nanking, which in fact took a month, thanks to a tendency in the Japanese army to hear at length anyone professing to be sincere and to try achieving a consensus. Yet they preferred action all the same and, after protracted talk, always attacked.

Scald Ibis knew none of this. Her mind was steeped in the arts, in sunlit quadrangles and hushed museums. By November 25, however, evacuation of civilians and government officials had begun; even Chiang Kai-shek and his talkative wife had left. On November 26, Tang, ostensible defender of the city, had seemed bemused at his press conference, perhaps even doped. All foreigners must leave, he said. Next day, he swore he would defend Nanking to the last man, and erected barricades and machine-gun redoubts. Underground telephone wires were laid. More than half of Nanking's police deserted; doctors and nurses left their hospitals. And here, relentless as syphilis, came General Matsui's army along the south bank of the Yangtze, except for one force diverting south and west to cut off the retreat upriver. American and British ships carrying their own nationals to safety were shelled.

All this eluded Scald Ibis and her family: aware of war, but not believing in it, not even crediting the fug of smoke as Tang set fire to all houses outside the city walls, as if hoping to discourage an army that yearned for accommodation. Nor did the doomed family hear the sounds of heavy artillery. On they sleepwalked, certain of their invulnerability, being of a particular social status. War was excrescence, art was eternal; war was old, art was ever young.

What can be said of such people, the blithe aloof, the righteous oblivious, the rapt blank? They are the salt of the earth. They do not panic. And then, like Scald Ibis's father, they get swept up, informed of the worst against their will. The launch that awaited Tang and took him up the Yangtze did not take *them*, or the American director of the Red Cross, or executives of the German electrical company, Siemens, or certain selfless surgeons.

Anyone appalled by such Neronism may well attempt a comparison with the Japanese army. If the Chinese arty set were sublime, then the invading army was commanded by slowcoaches. Did the esthetic oblivion of the Chinese match the dilatoriness of the officers trained at Ichigaya? Was this the last flash of fastidious hauteur in both nations? One wonders, but only until a supplementary theory comes along: did Scald Ibis and her doomed-seeming father act as they did because they thought the invading army would bring some esthetes with it? Had they almost succumbed to that vainglorious hope of Brahmins in all nations that the well-bred and refined always look out for the well-bred and refined on the other side, among the foe? This exquisite snobbery, tinctured with flagrant finesse culled from the samurai and the raffish honor boasted by fighter aces of World War I, is the true death knell of those who, without ever being so vulgar as to use the word "aristocrat," think of themselves as the best, or among the best. The implied divine right of the cultivated to survive mocks the crude oafs who actually do war's dirty work; good taste cannot halt a horde of riffraff, but good taste honors itself in dreaming so, as if the great days of superior beings on this planet had yet to come (though the shape of things to come was clear).

Hong paused, proud of his ability to compress. His headline shorthand had a certain finesse, he thought. Impelled nonetheless to go further and sum up the Japanese complex in yet another pithy sentence, ever gaining more control, he found it was easy. One deep mental breath and then—In the 1920s, Japan had felt obliged to choose between a British system and a German one. There, that was that. He felt a certain intellectual relief, then resumed. The British kept their empire together through a mix of goodwill and creative disdain, and the Japanese version of this was called (pompously enough) "Co-Prosperity Sphere in Asia." The Germans seized territory and exploited it. And Japan copied them. So, Scald Ibis's father reckoned, there was no need to think further on the issue. He understood.

Japan had been trying to avoid war at all costs, but the officers' rebellion had tuned up a national belligerence, and, in the end, a Communist-devised incident near Peking sparked hostilities. Chinese troops had fired on Japanese infantry, or so the story went. The Japanese fired back, and Chiang Kai-shek told his diary the time had come to fight.

Scald Ibis's intellectual of a father, creating explanations like someone rolling his own cigarettes, told himself *German Japan blundered south*. The matter was settled. The Japanese would come and go, sweeping through from Shanghai in yet another predatory move nonetheless falling short of war. His eyes burned with disappointment, as if finding the right sentence would canonize him as a seer. The Japanese had come south, yes, but only because there were thirty thousand Japanese in Shanghai, two of whom had already been murdered.

So the war began, exactly what Chiang wanted. Eight thousand Japanese marines confronted three German-trained divisions, fighting gamely with their backs to the sea, showing so much more courage than some of their Chinese counterparts that several hundred Chinese soldiers were put to death for lack of moral fiber. When General Yanagawa landed his force in Hangchow Bay, behind Chiang Kai-shek's lines, one soldier kept his senses alert, later recalling the pitch-darkness on deck, the tide running fast at five knots or so, the whole fleet of some

ninety boats defended by light machine guns in the bows. Some
went ashore in fishing boats, some in landing craft; all were
jammed together. Then over the side they went, into knee-deep
water, their feet sinking deeper and deeper into mud. Japan had
seized a dreary expanse of creeks, salt marshes, and paddy fields,
all behind the main Chinese line.

That most of this escaped Hong attested to his high-minded-
ness, his unworldliness. He came to catastrophe late, with initially the wrong emotions. If he had thought about the matter at
all, he would have wanted Chiang Kai-shek to hold his hand,
luring the Imperial Army south. Hong would have thrown an
enormous cocktail party for them in the Temple of the Jade
Buddha and left the war, or the chances of it, to peter out in unc-
tuous aftermath.

Scald Ibis now realized that her family was no longer there.
Something dreadful had begun and ended without her, but she
still could not sit up. Where had the other officers gone? Who
was this older man, Hayashi? Had he really violated her? She
had heard the word from other girls. What had they told her? It
was when men stuck their fingers up your nose. It was when
they peed into your rear end, aiming vaguely. It was when they
throttled you while kissing you. It was when they shoved into
you, all the way from your groin to your eyes, a long loose-
jointed steel prong.

She had never known such pain, like a silver acid wafting
through the inmost recesses of her slight body. It would never
happen again, she was sure of that. Whatever drove these men
to such frenzies, it would be gone for good now.

Reading poetry, she had marveled as layers of inhibition fell
away one by one until all that remained was her pulse, attuned
to everything but sundered by it. Surely what happened to her
today had not been an act of poetry; it had skinned her alive, an
initiation raw and curt. All she was certain of was that what had
happened was important.

A ghoulish, well-lit meal began, prepared by private soldiers with torn uniforms and hopeless eyes. Pork, duck, and fish sat on the floor with wine and tea. It was a vampire's dream, she told herself. It was that scene in Wu Ching-tzu's old novel when the meal went wrong: a rat fell from the rafters into the bird's-nest soup; the cook kicked at a dog and his shoe flew off and landed on a dish of dumplings. Outrageous. She refused food, though Hayashi offered her some, even volunteering to feed her by hand as if she were an invalid. A meal of mud and feathers would have been appropriate, with sharp vinegar to drink and sand for salt and the galls of the fishes slit to make the repast bitter. That life went on was grotesque. She expected them all to keel over, writhing, and die within seconds. Truly proper meals, she had heard, went by rules: *wu-huo*, military heat, was fiercer than *wen-huo*, literary or civil heat. If you have just cut scallions, then use a different knife for bamboo shoots. Eat geese by all means, for geese were of no earthly use to humans, and shrimp or fish because they laid so many eggs; but do not eat cow or dog, friends to humankind. She knew all this by heart, and found it coming back to her, changed.

If her parents were here, to succor her after so savage an event, they would know what to do, arranging deep white porcelain dishes around the center to resemble a star. There would be word games and Canton litchis, bear paws and sea slugs, black beans and fried lamb. Somehow thinking of these matters eased her, but she quivered with indignity as she realized she had just learned a whole new set of emotions for which there were, as yet, no words.

Who am I, she thought? Where do I go?

The unsaid answer was that she would stay where she was while Hayashi and his subordinates turned the villa into a head-quarters-cum-brothel, dragging in other girl survivors whom they tried to feed like animals for slaughter. It was Hayashi's world, where juniors lolled with penises exposed, some of them inundating their organs with warm sake right from the cup, others lying in their own vomit. It was important to behave like victors, but just as important to degrade the Chinese, to befoul their places and spoil their wives, daughters, children of either sex. China, whose male poetry had been full of odes to virgins ("sweet and ripe as a melon for cutting") had now come full circle.

Scald Ibis began to discard an old idea of hers, which saw culture as soft loam into which abominable experiences would sink and vanish; so long as she held fast to her culture, nothing would harm her. Now she saw culture falling like ash upon the uproar and mayhem of Nanking, 1937, and leaving her behind. She felt exposed and dismembered, and afraid to ask about her mother and brother. From time to time she was rudely set upon by one or two Japanese whose lusts had rekindled themselves, and she noticed that the sigh they emitted when entering her was the same sigh that people the world over made when they sat down after walking or straining: after almost anything. It was the sigh of feigned exhaustion, done more to impress than to declare relief.

She heard herself singing in agony, though not a squeak escaped her. She writhed without moving and wondered what was this terrible urge the men had to open and pummel her, back and front, as if ramming home an inferior argument. The objective, she decided, was to lay her waste until she was no good for anything; the more defiled and disheveled she appeared, the more they pestered her, inflamed by her mess. Swarms of bees would alight on her corpse, and she would soon become a source of honey given back to nature, far from useless.

Hayashi remained a morose and tricky man, with a feral cry deep inside him; when he climaxed, he let it out like someone being disemboweled. That was it, she decided: he needs it out of him and therefore inflicts upon himself a repetitious pain. One day the pain will fall silent and he will leave me alone forever. I am a hutch and he is trying to take up residence within me. I am a kennel and he is the dog. I am a coffin in which he wants to die.

Hayashi, however, thought otherwise: he wanted to be incandescent, able to demolish and pleasure women at a distance. That was the theory. The fact was that he liked Scald Ibis and tended to favor her, though without lavishing upon her any consistent kindness. He allowed her small considerations, thus baffling her for days with a pat on the cheek, a smack on the butt.

100 meters—16 seconds
1500 meters—under 6 minutes
long jump—3 meters 90 centimeters
grenade throw—over 35 meters
march—25 miles a day for 15 days with 4 rest days

REQUIREMENTS FOR SECOND-YEAR ARMY CONSCRIPTS,
JAPANESE ARMY

Their short legs give Japanese soldiers lower gearing and
considerable advantage on steep terrain.

BRITISH OFFICER, 1906

LIVING AS SHE HAD WITH FATHER AND BROTHER, SCALD IBIS HAD
seen the male organ in all its undeviating monotony, and had
shrunk from it with only the faintest desire to know more. It
made boys boys and men men. Now, within the space of hours,
she had seen this offending apparatus in all sorts of modes, and
it had been applied to her without apology. She was still trying
to connect the appearance to the sensation, the one's drab re-
dundancy to the other's neural punch.

Back to violation her mind went, homing, shuddering. Life
required its being forced upon women, so much so that those
few who resisted it successfully were held to have betrayed life,
turned their backs on it, never having been forced or broken.

No wonder she and her schoolmates exchanged horror myths about this ghastly event. Why were they not born violated in the first place, if the life force was so eager for it? Why give men the so-called *plaisir de rompre*, which she knew meant *jilt*, but in her private demonology *rompre* was literal, meaning *break*? So: she was broken, broken into, broken up, one of the numberless elect.

There were other girls in here, she finally admitted to herself, though she had taken little enough interest in them. All of this would end someday, and she knew she would be led back into a garden where everyone would be healed, with Hayashi taken away in chains to be tried and hanged.

For the moment, however, Hayashi, the expert in geography, had his men instruct her in what to do with mouth and hands, making of her a sleeve, a groove, a clamp, a bag. After a time she allowed herself to be bathed and scrubbed. She even showed them where the best soaps were kept. When there was no water, they washed her down with sake and poured perfume on her from her mother's upstairs vials. She was not allowed outside, but they did urge her to read, to calm her down. She still, however, without warning let out cries akin to those of what came to be known as Tourette's syndrome; she barked and yelped even when not being interfered with, and she ate her food sloppily: feeding had become vicarious and sketchy. One lieutenant was so nervous he drank all the time, and when he attempted to use her body he could only hug her tight, having lost his virility. Another officer, more senior, took her several ways, one after another, without even looking at her. Such paperwork as went on was conducted during lulls, passed from hand to hand and routinely inspected by Hayashi, who sent his officers out at regular intervals to check the streets.

Scald Ibis had seen war in history books, but usually counterpointed by exquisite reproductions of art. Neither was noisy or painful, and she had developed the habit of aligning war and art as compatible pages in the book of life. When she closed her book, both stayed put, shrunken to a page's thinness, humbled into black and white. She wanted to long for something, but longing was too narrow and specific a thing (she felt gigantic heaves of emotion bundle her from one state of mind to another in which she knew, she just knew, everything was going to be all right). She would go backward to where things would be again as they always had been. Yearning was praying, and she prayed.

An image of her father, wafting and wavering through remnants of memory, helped her a little, not in a sentimental way, but for being a parallel enigma. Well-to-do, and inclined to smoke in a certain robe, read in another, and to wear both when doing both, he nonetheless gardened in his oldest clothes and shoes, even rubbing them against rocks and railings to age them further. One day they would be powder and fall back into the soil. One minute he would be hoeing, the next he would be naked, an emperor of earth revealed and clean. If she ever got to understand him, she knew she would be close to understanding the world into which he had brought her. She had especially loved the gaps in the soles of his shoes; a beetle or a worm could have crawled in and made overtures to his sock.

She had little chance to note the routine of the Japanese officers, if by her standards they had one at all. Now it was night, when the girls downstairs had fallen asleep. The Japanese, however, seemed not to need sleep at all. The sake and smoke must have kept them awake. She tried to doze, but even sheer fatigue gave her only a short respite. She saw the most junior officers carrying boxes of papers upstairs, perhaps to get them out of the way, perhaps as the first act in a general reorganization. Who knew what these guttural mutterers wanted; spoken Chinese seemed to her so lilting and lyrical by comparison, not so much a language as a twangy hymn. Miracle: she was being left alone.

Now by lamplight they nailed to the wall a Rising Sun battle flag, inscribed with Shinto prayers: a huge crimson disc surrounded by writing. There was a fist-sized rent in the upper-left-hand corner, and the center sagged for lack of a nail. The lights went up again, with no blackout over the windows, a sign of confidence. Nanking was a Japanese city now, in which triumphant hordes squatted, devoured balls of rice, and compared field postcards by the light of braziers stoked with furniture. Usually, each soldier had two kinds of cards, one the bravado battle scene with appropriate war cries drawn in bubbles or clouds poised above soldiers' heads, planes in the sky and more distant clouds exploding. Anguished surrenderers poured out from earthen bunkers while banzai shouters roared from a hillock. In the other kind of card, birds perched consolably on lovingly tinted branches, mountains loomed through the mist, lanterns bloomed amid chaste chrysanthemums.

Scald Ibis's officers had no such cards, or at any rate did not bring them into the open. What they did expose was more intimate: the *senninbari*, a soldier's belt of a thousand stitches, made for him by his family to wear in battle. Worn about the waist, it brought luck, courage, and immunity to enemy fire. She saw one in the shape of a tiger done in red stitches, slid lovingly from beneath a shirt and brought to the mouth for a kiss. It resembled a much-used bandage, and she decided it was the poultice of ferocity, longing to apply it to some naked waist loaded with scalding rice. Astounded to have come up with a thought so violent, so contrary to her parents' teaching, she mentally cooled the rice, but just as fast heated it up again to plant on soft unpublic skin, there to make a blanched scar. She wanted revenge, but shrank from enacting it; most of all she wanted to lie still, unaccosted, unabused, for almost ever, still a girl of precocious poetic response, going to be a painter, perhaps, or a calligrapher like her father, who was an amateur soldier at best.

From a pocket in his tunic, Hayashi produced what looked like luggage labels, no doubt for the boxes going upstairs or out the door, as they now were. She was wrong, however. In the faltering lamplight he brandished them at her, and she saw front and back views done in red of a short man, muscular and naked. Now Hayashi took a pencil from his side pocket and shoved it through the card, as if wounding the outline figure in the stomach. Wound tags, he shouted to her, though the double room was quiet. "You thought I had dirty postcards! See, from behind he is alive, from the front he is a dead man. We do this to all shit-eating Chinese." Had her parents and brother wandered in at that moment, she would have been just as wordless.

Oddly, with the room cleared of boxes, papers, and maps, Hayashi seemed more genial; it was as if he suffered from a special claustrophobia brought on by printed matter. Walking slowly, he came to where she lay and fastened the wound tag to her finger, smiling ingenuously at the pencil hole. "Now we know what wrong with you. Big hole in you for Japanese officer. You sleep this night." Oh, no, she would not. Anything might happen during sleep. Hayashi's nose was too small for his nostrils. He might come for her at any time. Would he be more frightening if she were alone in a bedroom, covered by a blanket, or down here, in the open? Was it better to be cocooned or defenseless? Which gave the greater shock?

Now, with an importunate sigh, he reached behind and produced another box, smaller than the others, not wood but metal. She could hear his hands making an almost melodic battuta on the sides. It looked like one of those big biscuit tins the British introduced to the Orient: Peek Freans, Huntley & Palmer or— she lost the other names as Hayashi opened the tin box by wedging it between his arm and chest and tearing at the lid. Surely a gun would appear, or some prized morsel of food now rancid, or a starving pet animal? Instead, he extracted a fat book, clearly an object of chronic admiration, and opened it gently, fishing at the same time in the box for his magnifying glass, which he then held close to his eye, making a sound of husky approbation. She could not see what he was looking at, but the book seemed distended, like some family albums or scrapbooks. What was he picking at with his fingers? No, with sheenless tweezers? He made a lifting motion, almost a surgeon adjusting a flap of skin, and then she knew.

Colonel Hayashi, stamp collector, had brought his collection to the rape of Nanking, to soothe him at night and quell the shiver in his hands. Did she hate him all the more for this little flash of the pacific? Or did it mellow him, giving him a human fascia? It did not humanize him at all, not even when he beckoned to her, wanting her to stagger bleeding across the room and peer at his treasures. She did not go, but he lurched toward her, raising the album with almost an outright gasp and tapping a page of triangular and diamond-shaped stamps. It was clear they pleased him, though they were not Japanese.

Now he was shining a flashlight on two pages and she saw something gentle and beguiling at the bottom of his insistent gaze: stag, mountain goat, camel caravan, Mongol and tent, bow-and-arrow hunters. On a miniature map of the country called Tannu Tuva, she saw horses fording a stream and was unable to resist linking the sublime Chinese gardens she doted on with the tiny country whose stamps this introverted warlord cherished. This was the lamb within his lion.

Was she like him, then? She was astounded to think they had anything in common. She feigned attention, interest, nodding and shaking her head. Calmed, he withdrew, closing the album with ritual motions, seeming to whisper a prayer between the pages before he solemnly brought them back together.

The way, she told herself, is to beguile this oaf with culture: gardens, peach blossom in spring, teal-painted pavilions, flags flying above the Canton factories; the emperor Wanli—that do-nothing—seated affably on his royal barge; the refitting of the observatory on Peking's eastern wall with sextant, quadrant, and astrolabe. With Chinese patience unfurling, she would bring him to heel, growing familiar with him, almost as if he were her father saying, "You're very quiet today."

And she to her father, "Yes, but I *am* peepeeing loudly." It was a family joke. She might be able to get by, she thought. On the other hand, Hayashi might construe such efforts as overtures and vent his gratitude on her body all over again, aching to possess her by stamp-lamplight, then urging his men to do likewise before she passed out. It would be safer, maybe, to refer to the stamps only. She would have to fend him off in his own terms, saying his name again and again, miming to him to bring the metal box to her and tap out its hollow, unmemorable tune.

Better that tune than talk since his Chinese was poor and her Japanese nonexistent. She had not spoken to him since she had told him no. If only she did not ache so much; if only she could return to the problem after a solid meal and a long night's sleep, with a table to negotiate over, a set of clean clothes on her body, and nobody else around. But what use was communication, of any sort, in a world whose everyday language was the screech? At any moment, one of the lieutenants would jump one of the other girls, hearing welcome in her panic.

On the next day, the sixth of her initiation, she was escorted upstairs, back to her room, and the other girls were assigned rooms of their own as well, except for one full of documents and maps. She locked her door. Hayashi heard and slammed his boot against the panel, breaking it. His sword came through as he yelled. She opened it and waited to be beheaded, her eyes pink and sore. Then he beckoned to her to accompany him to the kitchen, where he swept through the cupboards, rummaging for something, tasting every white powder until at last he found salt. Upstairs they went again, this time to the bathroom, where he mixed a crude salt solution in a chamber pot he found and then yanked down his pants, motioning her to bathe his penis. She began, at first holding her breath, trying to smile up at him while working, but he shoved her face downward and grunted that crud-lined noise of the Japanese. Get on with it, he meant; this is hygiene, not an overture. On Scald Ibis went, splashing and bathing, wondering if she would have dared do this with her brother, if asked; the limp noodle in her hand grew not at all, not as she had seen and felt it do only hours ago, and she saw that the salt was making him wince as it seeped into his foreskin's cracks. Now she was a nurse, hoping to blind him with pain, but he became more and more accustomed to what she was doing. It did him some good, evidently, and he soon commanded her to stop, hauled up his pants and clumped downstairs, grumbling and seething. She soon heard him bossing the others about, thwacking his sword on the few remaining chairs. Then out he went, leaving, she presumed, someone of lesser culture in charge, no doubt the dumpling-faced major whose breath was Stygian and whose hands were pocked with outsize pimples. She closed the sundered door without locking it, able to peer through the panel at the floor, wondering who was going to come for her next, and for what. To fortify her, she repeated in her mind's ear some lines by the poet Moruo, written in 1919 on his excited return from Japan, of all places:

> I am the light of the moon,
> I am the light of the sun,
> I am the light of all the planets.
> I am the light of x-ray,
> I am the total energy of the entire universe.

For lack of anything to do, but wishing for something somehow purgative, she took her nail scissors and began trimming her pubic hair, abstractedly blaming herself for doing something that, observed, would egg him on, as if she were honing herself for the next assault. Do not, she instructed herself, give him the clippings.

Her own room, which she privately called "The Treasury," looked out onto the garden, that long sinuous exercise in soil bewilderment, so she could see nothing of the outside world except bins, sacking, bottles, and paper wrappers. If she could cross the landing, however, when the documents room was unoccupied, she could peer into the street. Several times her nerve failed her, and she sprang back into her room. She glanced again at the garden, coated as it was with night snow, and wondered at an old coolie hat spread on a stone slab, failing to identify her brother or anything human.

She was, she decided, that useless thing: the young woman who had been left behind. Passive and drained, she stood at the room's smashed doorway and listened to the yells of Japanese soldiers, the crash of guns or grenades, the underfueled screams of men and women. Something hideous was still going on in the street, much worse than had taken place in the villa. If she did not find out, she would burn alive; she yearned for context, which soothed and dignified.

After *seven and a half years* of the most strenuous, the most exacting and the most spartan of all military training, infantry officer-cadets at last reach the rank of second lieutenant. During these impressionable years, they have been walled off from all outside pleasures, interests or influences. The atmosphere of the narrow groove along which they have moved has been saturated with a special national and a special military propaganda. Already from a race psychologically far removed from us, they have been removed still further and scarcely still belong to the humanity they came from.

PAPERS OF THE BRITISH WAR OFFICE, 106/5494, AUGUST 25, 1931, REPORT ON INFANTRY SCHOOL AT CHIBA

WHEN SHE SAW THE CARNAGE, SHE SAW IT THROUGH A WINDOW, unable to decipher human bodies in unspeakable predicaments: dismembered, then roasted on open fires, or just being roasted whole. Or buried alive in trenches dug into the road. The people she loved, she told herself, were far from this, quietly going about their business in the south. When she at last allowed herself to take in what was happening outside, she became the girl to whom nothing bad had happened. Japanese soldiers were taking bucket baths in the December cold, bathing in loincloths out of some decency that defied the bloodletting around them. They did not even shiver, these soldiers, and those without a bucket bath big enough to get into used smaller buckets one after another, almost flaunting their bodies before they redressed into cheap-looking tunics. Some of them astounded Scald Ibis by donning mackintoshes or overcoats, or both, having been well-equipped, as if there were some provident decorum to invasion. People who had just taken a squat bath in front of her had little shovels strapped to their backs, map cases bouncing against their buttocks, and swords, daggers, tucked here and there all over them. Each man his own pack animal, she thought.

Hayashi tapped her on the back of her head and, when she turned, pressed his finger against her nose and, all the time maintaining that pose, shoved her across the landing to her own room, whose useless door he closed. "Be still," he commanded. "Not for you to see, Chinese girl."

They had come to Nanking with wooden bathing buckets, she thought, with ladders and bayonets and tattered flags, as if *we* were an enemy. She tried to define what an enemy was, whose city you would ravage even while being intimate with its daughters. There were combinations of feelings unknown to her, cultivated in the barren offshore islands where these creatures came from. Too small, she said: the islands, the people, both too small.

Some of the soldiers had been wearing gas masks when they arrived, and she wondered if the thick-ribbed tubing and the in-built goggles of the masks were protection against gas of their own. The real stench came from Japan, she knew, from the dung spread on Japanese fields: human waste at that. So they stood in the middle of an alimentary round, defecating to eat, eating to defecate, until it became time to march into China after first bombing it to smithereens. What earthly good was her father to a country attacked by such people? He might as well come home from wherever he was—to see the ocher and green tanks, the amateur butchers amid the anonymous-looking rubble, the red snow at the front door, and, yes, the colonels in his villa, lording it and wrecking. Come home, Father, she whispered, the tomb of Sun Yat-sen is a Japanese trophy.

She was being logical, she thought, but her mind kept alter-
nating between reasoned ideas and reckless escapism. Not all
that was happening could be happening. The scrolled ironwork
on the telephone poles could not still be intact while houses had
just melted away or become a mound of shattered bricks. Surely
there were limits to what could happen in one day, one night,
but who decided? Perhaps some primitive-looking sergeant on
a bicycle, his lower legs encased in puttees wound round and
round, his eyes covetously examining an overturned rickshaw,
its cargo of cartridges spilled all over the road. Surely there were
some things that would never be done, defined by an all-seeing
sage to whom wars were as commonplace as sneezes and colds.

Scald Ibis sat on her bed and cried for nothing more to happen, for the house to heal itself and empty out, for the snow to
recede. She wanted cessation, a return to poetry and decorum.
The notion of revenge came to life in her mind like a grub in a
flower, the invasion of Japan itself executed by Chiang's German-trained troops. She gave up warmongering, awed by the
bangs and howls outside, the clatter of boots on the stairs, the
staccato barks of orders beyond her broken door, the creak as it
opened. Hayashi's unsmiling face butted in, motioning her to
stay put. "Safer," he told her. "Sometime you learn Japanese,
then we have long talks." She closed her eyes, lowered her head
as if in a bow, and joined her hands across her bosom, wishing
she had a gas mask to disappear into, goggles, nozzle, and all.

She now realized what the painter Gao Jianfu had been getting at in his *Flying in the Rain*, in which seedlike biplanes flew a
ragged formation above wisps of islands, minarets, and misty
ponds. Something in this painting gratified her: the attempt at
completeness, at holistic statement, with the biplanes appearing
to have come from behind the mountains, friend or foe. If only
the hills, the islands, the minarets, the ponds could invade the
world of biplanes. She wanted a two-way world of discordant
reciprocity, as in 1929, when Zhang Xueliang had two of his fa-

ther's old cronies to dinner, then excused himself to get his daily morphine injection while his aides shot them. The Japanese had been hoping to influence him through these two. She could do something similar to Hayashi, did she but know how, having at hand no poison, although she might manage to lay hands on a dagger, a pistol, giving her own life to take his.

She had never studied history, but from time to time her father had trotted samples out for her to ponder, sensing that a daughter with a twitchy rump, a pair of perpetually trembling hands, and a habit of reciting to herself improvised poems should know something of history, of the chronic tableau she was trapped in. She responded well, provided he kept the samples short and focused on some salient event. She took no interest at all in minutiae, regarding them as so much fluff to blow away. Highlights and headlines for her. She wondered if she had not been right all along; not because amassing details was hard work, but because the minutiae were too much to feel responsible for—the more you knew, the guiltier you felt for being alive to know it. A history that organized itself and sifted its saliences: that was what she wanted, even after her father told her she had a snob's, an aristocrat's, vision of the past and would one day pay for it. She was a clever, snooty girl.

Hayashi had become busier, appointed by the brass to create a legion of camp followers. He went into the streets to pursue terrible, flagrant tests, directing ordinary soldiers to strip naked any female between twelve and thirty or so, then stick a bottle in her rear while lighting her pubic hair with a match. Anyone who withstood this test without a murmur was exempt from service and shot at once. From this day forward, Hayashi the stamp collector struck terror into all women by having at his side, on a small table or held aloft in the street by a private, the bottle and matches. The women of Nanking would remember him, and seethe to reach him in later years or in an afterlife, eager to reciprocate, but with broken bottle, acetylene burner. Why he did it he could not have said; perhaps because he had never seen a chance to do it before, and because he could get away with it, gentling his soul afterward with a smile at Scald Ibis, and a look at his stamp album.

After wiping Scald Ibis's belly dry, he licked hinges that fastened stamps to her, indicating that her belly was a country. He blew faintly against the hinged stamps, making an effect of lifting butterflies, fetching a big mirror for her to see herself in as he puffed and cooed. Then he peeled the stamps off her, mangling some hinges in the process and cursing so vehemently that she trembled. Then he drew an outline of Tannu Tuva on her skin and affixed a few duplicates that, once he was home, he would sell or exchange. There she lay with rustic scenes on her stomach, for all the world a pantographic replica of the eight-ruble rectangular that showed Tuva between the U.S.S.R. and Mongolia, the country shaped like the silhouette of someone supine in the act of yawning, with crow's-feet rivers scattered about and a few black teeth that were lakes. At comparative, intimidated peace she lay there, emblazoned with goat and stag, hunters and tents, almost the entire iconography of a remote, beleaguered country unique for throat singing. Why Hayashi doted on it would be hard to say: perhaps on account of its vulnerability. He liked the idea that he and his hordes could go invade it any dawn; but he thought that of just about any country. No: he cherished innocence, which he so easily ruined; he prized its aloof uncooperative helplessness, and sticking its postage on a ravished girl appealed to his sadistic sense of counterpoint. He fanned the little tinpot country on her skin and nodded at its frailty.

For her part, Scald Ibis was glad he was not drawing maps on her with his dagger point, or favoring her with bottle and matches. She had heard about what went on in the street. Several girls had been brought in after their ordeal, babbling of fire and glass, out of their minds with indignity, pointing at singed hair and brutalized rears, but with sterner stuff to come, as Scald Ibis told them in language terse enough to set them weeping all over again.

How, they asked her, could they be hurt worse than they already had been? Some of them were mature women, imagining torture rather than rape; some of them were Scald Ibis's age, able to imagine nothing else, and shrieking with hunger on top of fear on top of monumental loneliness. They turned to her as one who knew, and who, as a potential favorite, could tell them how to get out of things. She began moving about the villa with more confidence, helping herself to rice and candy, distributing much of it, not quite becoming the conscience, but the matron-in-waiting at least: a sixteen-year-old governess with one or two postage stamps still affixed to her stomach, which she felt but dared not remove for fear of driving Hayashi into a fury.

Hayashi had gone up in the world since arriving in Nanking: not for conquering the city, but for his flair with women and hangers-on. The epitome of the cultivated man, he became savage because of it: so fine-honed as to be a razor when he chose, yet so refined he knew refinement was always there to come home to. For so long restrained, he could now express himself fully. He ran Japanese Nanking so earnestly that a court of miracles, a tabernacle of comfort, emerged from the ruins, a haven to those destined not to drive on with the army to Kaifeng, the old capital in the west. Years down the road, for dedicating himself to vast civil and military amenity, he envisioned himself wearing the Order of the Rising Sun at his neck. If not that (it required some act of bravery), then the Order of the Second Treasure, fourth or third class, perhaps, awarded for meritorious service. Not as comely a medal, but more colorful and exquisitely suspended on a subloop of the main ribbon, with in the center a star-shaped leaden asteroid. The first problem, he recognized, was to remove all those boxes of papers to some other commandeered house; only then could he turn the villa into a palace worthy of Japanese officers, with clean women and appropriate music. It was becoming a hard, long war, and the military elite would need succor.

He foresaw generals and admirals visiting his establishment, whispering to him about which girls he recommended, and what had not yet been done with them. True geishas might follow, though he doubted it; in the meantime, he would have to train the local talent. Silks and decent food would help.

It would resemble being at home.

Except that his life at home was routine, that of a married man with three sons. Here he was, posing as a man-at-arms when, really, he was more like a wedding organizer, though admittedly with a perverse taste for others' pain. That was it: if he failed to keep his stern front up, his fellow officers would think him a sissy. So, he had decided, best keep them busy with beheadings and interrogation, not getting his hands dirty, but taking part with autocratic relish. He was planning for Scald Ibis, determined to keep her here in Nanking so that she would be precociously gifted in the years of peace, when Japan ruled China and Chinese was a sequestered dialect, fit only for ruffians and street sweepers.

As he understood things, a man of his caliber was free to create something useful, and buff it into indisputable splendor. Not only must those remaining in Nanking have some appetite for the sedentary life; they must also have a sense of humor, not too much self-consciousness, and a well-developed sense of play. Only then could his establishment prosper, in its quiet way becoming indispensable: the Pavilion of Muted Firebirds, perhaps, or the Pavilion (he liked the word) of Impossible Peace. They would not understand all they were getting, but they would feel the benefits. He could hardly wait for the marauding army to leave Nanking so that those left behind might become a kind of civil service. We may be monstrous, he thought, but we have etiquette to spare. We of all peoples know how to evolve a ritual, how to take a paper house seriously, how to dispatch a life no longer honorable; we do not go around sulking and whining, we pledge ourselves to the hilt.

Dumbfounded, Scald Ibis found herself being stripped and bathed by a hefty Japanese woman who might have doubled as a cook. Hot water was ladled from outside, heated on one of the nonstop bonfires in the street. Soap, face cloth, towels, perfume, heel pumice, toothpaste and mouthwash, talcum powder, and shampoo all came up the stairs to the bathroom and entered her life as—well, not quite trophy or reward, or incitements to a different style, but as reminders of a propriety restored to someone whose needs had bloomed again.

She swallowed soap to make herself choke.

She dabbed soap in her eyes to make herself weep.

She soaped her rear end to ease the entrance of the bottle when it came.

She soaped her bush to make it softer for the conqueror on his next ride.

She squeezed the soap until it bent out of shape, then softened, and she fashioned a crude soldier from it, drowned him, and snapped off his head.

Other girls were waiting downstairs, alive with panic and rumor, swapping news as best they could, mainly in whispers. The Japanese were withdrawing eastward. Peace had been declared. No, Russian pilots sent to China by Stalin, equipped with supplies brought over the old Silk Road, had bombed and machine-gunned the Japanese force to shreds. No, Chiang Kai-shek had commanded his engineers to dynamite the dikes of the Yellow River, flooding over four thousand villages, drowning thousands of peasants. The Japanese could not march across a flood. The river had suffered a permanent change of course. No, the Japanese had halted to wait for reinforcements. There would soon be a whole series of air raids on Chinese cities. China, the Japanese said, would burn before it was resown.

Scald Ibis wanted her brother to return, her mother to rub her with a coarse sponge, her father to burn his uniform in the garden. That was life, or using her queue of sleek black hair to measure the radius of a circle drawn on the blackboard. Frail as banana strings that most eaters pick away from the fruit in bemused, offput reverence because they mar the contour of the

meat, she felt strings of life being plucked away from her daily.
She was all strings and no meat. Soon she would vanish altogether. It was not true that a person could assimilate whatever
happened to her. The day came when there was no longer
enough of you to take things in, and experience fell away into
the void from the place that used to have a you in it.

She ached unbearably.

Something her father had said, perhaps when trying to assist
her with schoolwork, came back to her and almost consoled her.
As he put it, identity was a process, an impropriety of the noun;
the name was ever still, the process seethed from second to second, open-ended, shapeless, undependable. Of this, her version
was more direct: I will never know who I am again. I will always
be told. When they put my pieces together again, I will be somebody different, not as bookish or as nice, still engaged in the enterprises of life, yet unnecessarily modified. A duck. A peony. A
piece of special paper to burn at a shrine. Born and dead and
born again, dealing with life like someone heartrendingly jilted.
She was going to become an empress dowager who commis-
sioned a marble boat from which to view the lake near her summer palace. A snowflake hardened in her heart and made her
wince.

Meanwhile, Hayashi, smoking his black-paper cigarettes, felt
so pleased with his future as a designer of pavilions that he
barely noticed something minor, lower down. When he pulled
it out to wash it, palping it and stretching it like a strop, he noticed that his penis had now begun to swell, the glans especially,
that sanctimonious plum. Was it a little redder than usual, too?
Was there a tiny split in the top? Who had given him this? He
poured sake over it, smiling at the sting, and put it away. You
never knew about the simplest schoolgirls. Pox was everywhere,
especially in China, where no one washed. He vowed to find a
piece of finest twine and measure himself daily. It was not the
kind of problem he had anticipated; but, he sensed, the slight
distension increased his desire, and this improved his humor.

Young officers were schooled for death, not for stagnation in a peacetime army; but most of the Japanese Imperial Army had fought little in the past thirty years. Their officers despised socialism, which they thought effeminate, and burned to reinstate the sword as *the* heroic insigne. Only a military dictatorship headed by the Emperor would suit them, and this they proposed to achieve through a coup d'état mounted by junior officers. Hence the Blood Pledge Corps of 1932. Sword-making once again became a cherished art while communism became a favorite target (3,000 arrested in 1933 and 1,500 in 1934). Japan began to buy aluminum, lead, nickel, and zinc, tin and chrome, spikes for barbed wire, tank engines, ball bearings, and, from the activated-charcoal industries of British Malaya and the Dutch East Indies, filters for gas masks.

GARTH FAIRBROTHER, *BLOOD CULTS REBORN*, 1961

WHEN A SQUAD OF CLEANERS ARRIVED IN THE VILLA, SCALD IBIS thought the war had ended, but quickly thought again. Perhaps this was the extermination crew. All they did, however, was empty out the documents room, clomping up and down stairs with cartons held against their chests. If these boxes held the plans for the invasion, she thought, they were very accessible just now, and some young heroine was missing her chance of saving the rest of China. They padlocked the documents room and marched downstairs again, she following at a safe distance and watching them begin to dust and scrub. Awnings appeared and went up, as if the room were spinning its own silk. In came couches and occasional tables, divans and cushions, a couple of new mats. The ultimate effect, some hours later, was gaudy and muddled, but she guessed what the room would be used for, and knew she was right when the cleaning staff ushered the girls out of their bedrooms, downstairs to luxury and work.

Along with half a dozen others, all of them afraid to even whisper in the presence of so many soldiers, she stood and watched the renovation of upstairs, dreaming she saw carpenters and electricians, plumbers and paperhangers, bustling from room to room. Up went newish-looking bed linens, newly commandeered soft toys, vials of perfume, chamber pots, shallow basins on rickety stands, and pots of cold-cream ripped from the palms of the dying. It was simple: Hayashi was transferring dry goods from one part of Nanking to another, creating a haven from the debris of other havens, all in the interests of happy officers. A happy officer was happy in his war. A happy war was a war won.

Cohabiting with a man so cruel, so perverse, so callously flighty, even though he was a long way from being a rough-and-ready swordsman, she felt tempted to think him better than he was, somehow misconstruing his handiness with home comforts and brothel trappings. Anything not outright vicious gave her hope, and that was the sad part. Her body was available to him, but her good sense was beside the point. She needed to know more about him.

So, for lack of anything better, she rejoiced at the sight of a clean ceiling, a patch of scrubbed linoleum, a fussily curtained window (but arranged by whom?). A samisen began, twanging her half to sleep even as she stood. Everyone save the girls was smoking cigarettes. The whole place had an air of bumptious prettiness, befitting a colonel's notion of a whorehouse; but it soothed her, and within minutes all the girls were seated, or slouching on the rugs, with only Hayashi and two other officers present. The reek of cleaning fluids remained, however, and that of disinfectant. My goodness, Scald Ibis thought, the place was a mess to begin with. We have just witnessed a piece of

Japanese make-believe intended to make them feel superior. We will be here months, until Chiang Kai-shek drives them out for good.

Outside, the telephone wires had been restored. Hayashi tried his military phone, nestled as it was in a canvas sheath, almost a gas mask. Nothing happened. He spun the ratchet and tried again, this time lucky, and reported his establishment in order, all units functioning. Distinguished guests were more than welcome. He fawned and simpered, expressing his delight, but not the delight he felt at being far from the savage uproar of the front line, where two nations ground themselves to bits.

All he needed, to make his offering irresistible, was a film projector and movie reels, providing an additional air of coziness and intimacy, the corners of the enormous former living room in darkness as the flickering epic unfurled. It would come, he was sure of that. One or two successful visits from the generals, and they would grant his every wish. He would never lose face again. Thinking this, he kept squirming around in his best uniform as his penis failed to settle down in his pants, making him pitch and flick about, not in pain, or even crisp irritation, but in response to delicate twinges hard to tell from the prelude to delight. Was it desire or microbes' tiny teeth?

Hayashi could not believe what he saw. Had he been blind before? Birthed from the full munificence of that room, Scald Ibis's mouth pulled at his eyes and drugged them, a mouth wide and slack, certainly for a nation of rosebuds, but not hanging open. There was so much pulp to it that gravity pulled it down and even sideways, keeping it out of control, ready to be bitten or tugged. If he tugged it, he thought, it would remain out of shape, a leering pout, a velvet pucker, game for a score of sportive plays. Why had he not noticed it before? Watching her closely, he noticed a series of pulsations run through either lip, as if she were making up her mind which expression to assume, in the end choosing none. She had virtually no control over that mouth; that was what excited him. Her tremors caught the light and stirred him abominably. He liked her mouth because it was like China, helplessly vibrant, his for plucking, day after day, as if the whole end of war was licking and sipping. There she sat in a purple housecoat decorated with silver embroidered birds, scarlet buttons all the way up to the high neck. He was pleased with his handiwork.

He had become the dresser at a theater, turning sows' ears into silken purses fit for Japanese gentlemen. But he wanted Scald Ibis for himself, neither sated nor affronted, worn down by randy old men who demanded obedience and a great deal of preparation. Inevitably, though, *qua* colonel, he would have to accept others' leavings, sliding himself into their sperm wherever they had left it.

And so the first hint of his own disobedience floated through his mind. The general and the admiral would get high on sake, become too engrossed with mah-jong, or even quarrel about the way the invasion was going. He would fob them off with the other girls, dressing them with grandiose extravagance, shoving Scald Ibis into any old frump of a dress, putting plain-glass spectacles on her nose, a big blob of dirty drying rice squashed against her rear end. It was feasible, was it not? But how disguise her mouth and eyes? She was too much of a gazelle to be much masked, and the venereal droop of that mouth revealed the nascent nymphomaniac. She would be throwing herself at them, far beyond his capacity to restrain her. He would have to act soon, but what would he do? Somehow, merely by being herself, she had gained potential ascendancy.

An aroma of cooked rice wafted in from the kitchen. The villa smelled lived-in again. Polish the ashtrays, he told the soldiers. They straightened the flag, set the rugs parallel to the walls, and brought in heated sake. It was only a matter of waiting now. On went the samisen. Hayashi had heard that refugees from Chungking had already eaten bark from the trees in Nanking; they had no food, and the residents of the city would give them none. Worse days were coming. Given time, though, he would

turn this average villa into a household of lascivious plenty,
never mind what went on in the world outside. Yet they would
have to pay—oh, not much: one yen for a Chinese woman, one
and a half for Korean, two yen for Japanese. So far, all he had
were Chinese, but he had only to send two soldiers into the
teeming streets to round up unwanted women, all storming
about with their mouths full of bark. It would always be wise,
he thought, to keep a team in reserve: a half dozen, say, mixed
nations. They could be given basic necessities until needed,
then spruced up and prettified.

The need for complex, devious organization appealed to him.
He liked killing, but he could live without it, as indeed he had
lived without sex, food, love, sleep, company. That was what
had drawn him from the study of law into the army, which had
room for his kind of languid savagery. On the surface dapper,
spry, and adroit, he was little of a lawyer underneath; as an officer, more interested in the places he saw than in the men he
bossed about. Now, colonel in charge of comfort women, a
masculine madam, he did not disparage the role, not yet, gen-
uinely wanting to be of use in the future. Young Hirohito had
been emperor since 1926, brainy and bookish; his very presence
promised brilliant things, and Hayashi saw himself plucked out
of the army to join the diplomatic service.

It was important, therefore, if he was to stay on here in
Nanking, to come up with a suitable name for the villa and its
offerings. Today he thought Altar of Heaven would do, though
a shade vulgar. He was in a vulgar profession, only somewhat
better than riding a horse in triumphal procession past hordes of
disheveled Chinese biting their lips. There would be others like
him in other parts of the city, engineers of the amenities, but he
was the first. Not for him the victor's braggart swig at the Ther-
mos slung over his shoulder while the horse neighed.

It went well. The general was rowdy, overweight, and had just
eaten a consummate dinner. Two of the girls swept him away as
the samisen plonked, and he got hardly a glimpse of Scald Ibis,

who never once looked up, but kept her eyes on the art book in her lap, full of maroon temples and well-lit horses. The admiral was a different matter, however, at once seizing the book, exclaiming, then lifting her up bodily. He had not eaten, he said. He was a torrent of nervous energy. He chain-smoked and had the hiccups. "Look at that mouth," he sighed "What has she never done? We'll see." Bitterly, Hayashi went to give the order for the admiral's dinner while, upstairs, Scald Ibis reexplored the amenities upon which her life depended. How soon, she wondered, would she become a pillar of granite?

A samisen had never played in this house before; at least not in her time. She knew enough to be pleased that it had begun as a Chinese instrument, *san-hsien*, not that the Japanese cared, they who had come to seize all things Chinese. Should a three-stringed, fretless, long-necked Japanese lute with a cat-skin front and a curved-back pegbox, played with a large plectrum, be moving her as much as this one did, even as she removed her mind from the ordeal of the admiral having his way with her? I am like a zoo animal, she thought: in my place, I know everything that's going to happen. What men want varies little.

The admiral was weeping now, in Japanese, out of shame or fatigue. He would probably come back, fortified with liquor, not a single part of his mind on what lay beneath or beside him.

One of the other girls padded upstairs, heard Scald Ibis heaving in the bathroom, and held her forehead as she crouched over the floral bowl, talking nervously.

"Isn't it awful? Aren't they dreadful? They killed my parents. They dragged me in here. They did awful things to me. I am going to kill myself. Will you kill me? Why are you throwing up? Will they go? Will they leave us alone after doing all this to us? What can they be thinking of? I'm thirteen. If my parents were alive, they would thrash me for all I've had to do. They grunt and shove at you, they smell of tobacco and old shoes. Why don't you answer? Can you show me where to hide?"

"I used to live here," Scald Ibis said, then realized she still did.

"It's all different now. I am so ashamed, so degraded."

The admiral moaned and bellowed, not five yards away.

"You go to him," Scald Ibis said quietly. "He'll want his head rubbed or his back. Go in and stab him."

"You stab him."

"I'm going to stab somebody," Scald Ibis said with a deformed sob. "It has to stop."

"No," the other told her. "We have to get away. The trouble is, if we do we'll get murdered in the street. They kill everyone on sight, have you any idea why?"

"We are Chinese."

"As if that were a reason."

"Let me explain to you young ladies," said Hayashi, who had come to check on them, "that you have duties. Do not forget how gentle and delicate a Japanese officer can be. We are a fastidious people. Beneath the toilet of a certain lady we dig a long, long shaft, which we fill in forever once the lady has died. She never sees her own feces. One day, for both of you, if you behave yourselves, we will dig you each just such a shaft. And then you will never see your droppings anymore. You will be like the highest-bred Japanese society lady. On the other hand, if you refuse to behave yourselves, you will be sent down the shaft of some highborn lady, with a shovel, and there create an endless wall of all she puts beneath her. You will be there forever, ultimately sealed up to breathe that terrible air."

They understood not a word, and put upon his speech a quite different construction, discerning threat nonetheless. He shooed them downstairs, then went in to minister to the groaning admiral, having left a passed-out general downstairs.

"So," Scald Ibis called to the other girl, "it was you who put paid to the general?"

"I put my finger down his throat. That's all."

"I am Scald Ibis."

"Call me Lin," the other said. Her name meant forest. How exciting it was to use their own language, uttered so fast that

Hayashi's modicum of Chinese was hopelessly inadequate. Soon, of course, he would forbid them to talk. "My nickname," Lin was adding, "is Moth Wing. That's what they call me at school, because I'm so flighty and so thin." She was garbed as a geisha, in robes much too big for her that billowed and also drooped.

Scald Ibis could sense it coming, the constriction through which activities at the Altar of Heaven would become better organized, with fewer demands on Hayashi's time, a proper schedule of who went upstairs with whom and who played games over snacks and sake. For the moment, things were untidy and a girl might get away with one or two things, but not for long; Hayashi had that stern introversion of the man with a pattern mania. Soon, young samurais would replace generals and admirals; the place would become a club for ecstatic immaturity, and she and Moth Wing might fare better. They were going to wake up transformed into little geishas with toilets that led down to the center of the earth. No more singsong Chinese, but the quinsy of a choking dog, which was the sound of Japanese. Unless the Japanese lost, and their army went racing homeward just the way it had advanced, bowing where it had strutted, and pleading not to be beheaded by a team of sword-wielding schoolgirls.

The meditations of a traumatized girl do not have worldly width, summoning from all points the fullest reverberation of an insult, a kiss, a mouse. She is more like a stationmaster, making sure the trains arrive and depart on time, than like Montaigne or Marcus Aurelius. If in doubt about something, she reviews a series of hypotheses and makes a decision; she does not practice reverie for its own sake. She practices love, though, so-called, amazed that she has learned everything in a matter of hours. Was *that* what she had been holding her mental breath for? Now, after *Ars Amatoria*, thumbed and stained, she yearned for love that was incessant admiration with no physical match at all.

Ortega said men invented love, and women invented work. It would be as true to say men invented brothels and women invented men. Scald Ibis recognized that whenever she had time free she began musing, not in the old speculative way about pavilions and emperors, about the airiness of the first, the comparative benignity of the second; but, in the mood of the scientist, about solutions to problems. Hastily, she reviewed escape, mindless commitment, point-blank refusal, and feigning illness. Burdened with loads of phenomena she did not understand, she tried to improvise a kind of substitute knowledge: thoughts of future grace that would see her through and serve her well in her dealings with Colonel Hayashi, with whose deftness and energy she had to reckon. He was going to stay to run things. No fly-by-night amateur, he was going to give the invasion a touch of silk and velvet, half-persuading Japanese officers they weren't as far from home as they thought. Yet far enough to conquer China by opening its legs wide on a divan and looking keenly into its women with high-quality magnifying glasses, their minds attuned to exquisite variations of pink. The vision thus gained would be something to take home with them. Sapping a country from within by perverting its educated young was superior to hanging them on street corners.

Scald Ibis wondered in her perfunctory way if certain girls would be dropped after a while, once they had become jaded and bad-tempered, and, if so, what would happen to them. Nothing good, she was sure. It would be better, then, to oblige Hayashi, perhaps by asking him to teach her Japanese: a specialized vocabulary, appropriate to the precious Altar only, unusable for anything else. A vocabulary for philosophical and literary discussion, say, or calligraphy. The question, as ever, was what to do with her intelligence, not always something people welcomed in a friend or a lover, or a colleague. She would have to make intelligence defend itself by ducking its head, by aiming low.

When other girls were taken away to be hanged, beheaded, or burned, she would be there to mourn, to reassure Hayashi that his duty was paramount. How close to him she might get, apart from sexually, she was unsure, but she had convinced herself to try. He would never suspect. Since he could learn some Chinese, she could reciprocate, and each, caught in a slovenly routine, would laugh at the other's blunders. They might even stage a poetry party for the staff officers, but only in Japanese, of course. She half-expected real geishas to show up, but none did, and she saw now that she and the others—Moth Wing, Dé, Meng, Cixi, and Qiu—were what the Japanese called comfort women. She could teach the others what she knew of the geisha way, talk them into it. Polite conversation over sake or tea; a little judicious flirting; a long poem recited as slowly as possible: these would smooth out her days until the Chinese army retook Nanking with trumpets and drums. She would become the girls' impromptu tutor, involving them in hour-long discussions of a fan's fragility, the scope of its draught, the style of the silken tape within. By the same token, she would become a fanatic of philately, treating Hayashi's stamp collection with religious zeal. In the end, no one would dare to bring up the matter of sex; or, if they did, it would have nothing to do with her since she had become the sibyl of amenity, likelier to counsel you about a kite to fly or crickets to breed.

If pushed, in later years, she might counsel a very steady customer about heroin and opium: how they sustain male erection and delay ejaculation. But those were prophetic rumors about herself to herself, the equivalent of nursery stories in hell.

In order to ingratiate herself with Hayashi—having given her all, she must now give something else—she would hide in her silks a neatly gift-wrapped little doll such as a nice Japanese girl would give to someone whose ways pleased her. This was what he tried to tell her, seizing her mind only to have it slide away like a carp. She failed to comprehend, so he pantomimed the whole thing, using his fractional Chinese, telling her the Japanese words that mattered, pulling on the split white socks for her.

He would have been quite happy managing geishas. She would have been content to grow into the role. It would not work, however, since the army was making fleshly demands and wanted comfort women, not epitomes of twinkling finesse. One minute they wanted geishas, the next they wanted comfort women. They had no idea what they wanted except time to dawdle in. In Tokyo, Scald Ibis would have been a riot—legs thicker than spindly, breasts not conspicuous but sturdy and pointed, face that of a starlet: expressionless, pale, and sly, caressing his stamps and holding them up to her face like vignettes of the future.

She made officers chafe for something simpler. They left her afterwards, groveling and bowing. If they wanted a quick screw rather than culture, she now knew how to provide it. She simpered in unsteady Chinese and floated her hands about as she thought a geisha might. She had almost overnight turned into that time bomb, the anticarnal bluestocking, fit only for her procurer, Colonel Hayashi, who had begun to wonder how long he would last as officer in charge. By now, a mere major would have been removed and sent to the front.

Yet, for all the hindrances of war and the lack of amenities, Hayashi managed to conjure up for his customers a world gorgeous and distant. Into this they stepped, and at once were viewing cherry blossom in Tokyo, sitting nimble and compact in a tearoom flooded with elegiac airs, invisible behind bamboo screens, nibbling roast taro, hard-boiled eggs, and dumplings, drinking Masamune, inhaling, and then holding their breath to make themselves even more light-headed.

One evening the admiral and the general stayed for a treat fresh-caught in the Yangtze. On the low table, a black lacquer box bounced about as if determined to go somewhere, escaping the invasion. Then a mess corporal sliced the fish up with some difficulty, and it became calmer. Scald Ibis looked away from the knife, wondering how the two bleary officers could eat at all. The other girls were dozing in various parts of the room. Tonight was special, with less traffic, less wear and tear on the stock-in-trade, as Hayashi thought of them.

Waking, the somnambulistic girls fell on proffered fish, not even trying to be dainty, no idea of how exalted in rank the visitors were. Scald Ibis took no fish, though. She could not rid her mind of the fish as it thudded and jerked in its kennel, making a death rattle against the fancy table. Panic would have spread blood throughout its tissues, improving the taste, no doubt; that was the purpose of the box.

Murderous planet that we live on, she thought; we keep needing to prove how godlike we can be. Japan didn't really want to possess China. It wanted to do some killing, and now China wanted to do the same. Men could not forgive one another for being alive, she thought; each victim yearned to contemplate a landscape full of corpses; each corpse is in the ideal condition for history. What, she wondered, was the exact pleasure of carving into something that was working remarkably well?

"China in a box," the admiral blurted, his mouth full of liquor and, now, fish.

"A few more months," the general answered.

"We needn't bother learning the language," Hayashi said diffidently.

"Oh, we shall stay; some will." The general burped softly and the dank, acrid smell of it floated around the room, looking for a place to land and infest.

"Speak to the Chinese with a sword," the admiral sighed. "We are moving so fast we shall soon have more of China than we want."

Caught between homesickness and his desire to make a go of the brothel, Hayashi asked for geishas. He needed skilled help.

The other two laughed. No geishas were going to come here.

"Then there will be no singing, no poetry," he said.

We will have to make do, they told him; so long as the song was evocative, plaintive, sensual, who cared what the words meant? When they were sober, some other night when they had less to celebrate, they would return, they said, and have the pretty young Chinese girl between them. A threesome. Hayashi bowed. Not if I can help it, you morons, he thought. There must be ways of keeping you off. Fugu fish, perhaps: a contest in which each dares the other to eat a little more, taking the tongue from a slight buzz to death. These two bantam cocks might finish each other off out of sheer vanity. So: requisition fugu. Fugu shall be requisitioned. Hold all for fugu. Fugu the deadly is coming. It cometh. And I, the abbot of this insane monastery, the blinking firefly of this darkness, will attribute the whole disaster to pique, ego, and obtuseness. How many of them could I kill off before being removed? Fucking them with a fugu would not harm them at all. It has to get in the blood-stream, does it not? No, into the digestive system, no more than that.

> *Only an outright duffer*
> *Eats too much puffer*
> *Whose excessive toxin*
> *Puts you a box in.*

Where had he heard this murderous, awful ditty? A little fugu poison would go a long way toward exterminating the Chinese, of whom, as the wisdom has it, there were too many. With fugu, a man playing chef might commit judicious murder and get away with it.

Scald Ibis watched his sardonic smile, misconstruing it as pride of ownership, feeling giddy as she reminded herself that this, her family's home, had become a bordello overnight. She was the only rightful occupant left. Now Hayashi was addressing her in his tortured Chinese: "Go to bed. Sleep. Another day comes."

Orders given in her own home. She refused.

He waved at her. The general and the admiral waved.

She sat still, waiting for her father to arrive.

Outside, her beheaded brother froze, and somewhere in the Yangtze her mother rolled lightly on the silt of the river bottom. The father, still alive, let the Chinese retreat sweep him from all he loved, knowing only that he had to move.

Under too much pressure from the real, her mind lunged sideways toward newly arrived young samurais, green as jade but murderous, who, born to terror, nonetheless maintained a stern exterior, with visions of themselves mutilated, burning, turned to dust in a flash. They had it both ways, these killers, afflicted with fatal urbanity, hypnotized by slogans and headbands, ritual touches of sake (a drink was never merely a drink to them), and endless talk of ancestors. All they had ever wanted, she thought, was not to be snubbed by women, but all they ever got was a death among hot steel. Were any of the samurais girls? She had no idea, but she would not have minded harsh training and then the ultimate gift of the long cool blade designed to halve those who had made her fatherless, motherless, brotherless. She decided to invent her own emblem, something complex like

which meant "troubled." She alone would know its meaning, hostile and angry. She delighted in the truculence of indecipherable insult, recalling how Hong loved to devise characters that did not exist and had a small box of them inscribed on cards.

Wishful thinking grew to white heat as she imagined in preposterous detail an admiral and a general, dyspeptic with raw fish and feisty from sake, scowling and leering at each other, wordless at first, then bellowing harsh accusatory barks she could not understand. She saw their blood pressure rising, each pair of hands reach for the belt and untuck the white gloves of remonstrance. The caps followed, then the swords. It was all so convenient for her imagination. They stood, swords drawn, still reviling each other, and then raised them, the admiral left-handed, the general right-handed. The one swung away to the left, the other to the right. She heard a pause, then a pistol shot, and, in slow motion, two swords fanned the air, two heads began to peel and lean away from the trunks, and suddenly there were two beheaded corpses spouting blood so high the two jets mingled in midair before falling. The two trunks toppled, Hayashi rushed forward, too late, and the newly entered young samurai dragged the remains outside, then reentered and seized her with butterfly delicacy, not holding her but guiding her elbows forward to the chair of honor.

Confucius bless me, she thought, it is the Japanese who, when smelling blossom, blow down their noses, with sedulous delicacy, to empty their nostrils of the bloom just inhaled; they do not want to taint the new one with the old. And so on, all through the sniffing ceremony, she heard it again and again, that forced snuffle banishing the nasal miracle of only seconds ago.

Was it within the same dream that she and Hayashi began to speak Chinese together, he with torrential fluency newly acquired? The exchange had something warm in it, almost cordial. They were no longer adversaries, but prospecting converts, already initiated into the dark pity of amputation, the pious hard breathing of friendship.

She was becoming the tiniest bit Japanese.

Older, a little shred of him was Chinese already.

There was a bridge made of entwined hair.

When she twitched, his face did, too, and his rear when hers did.

Ceremoniously they appraised each other in the dreary aftermath of the beheading. Everyone sooner or later, she thought, made way for young samurais who, later in their careers, would come to similar blows. What was the old code? A man who has committed *seppuku* is entitled to have a friend behead him, to quell the final, subordinate pain. A loving friend must never refuse. What a considerate people, she thought: chummy in everything, even last things. And *he*, she thought, will put paid to *me* when I am not looking, out of sheer friendship; he will pour cold water onto the blade and carve away while I am washing cabbage or something sublime like that. There is no break between the flower arranging, the tea ceremony, the geisha's banter, and the passion for chopped heads. The main thing is to see if ideas spill out and what they look like. What does the brain think in those few seconds left to it, cut off from its source of blood? Does it know it's been cut off? Could it say to itself, I'm chopped off but I'm still thinking last thoughts? What is that last instant like? Is it apprehensible?

Or is it struck dumb from the first cut?

They invade other countries just to find out about such things. They are not butchers but researchers infatuated with spectacular ends.

Hayashi motioned her out of her trance. There were dishes to be scooped up, spilled sake to be mopped, cushions to be plumped and neatly arranged.

Out into the night went the admiral and the general, eager to bestride their waiting horses, but reluctant to have the evening end. For a while, mounted, they looked at the bonfires, the surging crowds, the soldiers shoving and stabbing. It was as if nobody could get away, not so much to safety as to a bare piece of ground empty of others, where you might collect your wits. Then the pair of them did a small gallop, swords flailing at the heads and shoulders. Slashing away in the winter cold, they felt this a more suitable finale to their night of cautious debauchery. They wanted to talk, gasping as they were with their exertions; perhaps they even wanted to see the Nanking dawn, leaking vermilion above the carnage behind the rolling smoke.

"Are you still collecting," the general asked, "or is it all career now? Nothing but the ocean?"

"As a matter of fact," the other told him, "I have just acquired a very nice *kozuk*." He meant a small knifelike dagger usually carried in the scabbard of a samurai's sword, made by a master armorer or bladesmith. From early youth, samurais trained themselves to hurl the *kozuk* into the eyeholes of an iron face mask.

"How many *kozuks* now?" The general sounded envious.

The admiral did not say, and the general told him "I do have my first *kogal*, and indeed nowadays plenty of use for it." He referred to a skewerlike implement that one stuck into the earhole of a beheaded man's head, thus making the head easy to carry when needing to carry it to one's commanding officer for praise.

"Well," the admiral said, "you old piss-knotter, what do you think of our dear colonel's Altar?"

"Shitawful."

"True. He has had no time to get it going."

"Ah," the general answered, "I don't need time myself. I have it ready when I enter. Myself, I think he is enjoying the girls too much. He has that shagged-out look, no sperm left. We should visit him again in a few days, surprise him."

They agreed, and trotted away, absentmindedly swinging their swords as they went, lopping whatever they touched, heedless of the maimed they left behind them. Some blades, the general was thinking, have cut through the barrel of a machine gun. One can cleave a body to the waist. If I had been a samurai, would *I* have mortgaged all I owned just to buy a fine blade? Would I have cared that much? No, I am too much of a hedonist for such things. I'd have been satisfied with some ornate-looking thing of poor quality: a parade sword. Saber and scabbard of European pattern, bright factory-made blade, brass wire-wrapped rayskin grips. Nothing lordly. I'm a soldier, not a samurai. "Hey, what did you make of that Chinese girl, the quiet pretty one? When studying, one must be humble."

"Good night, general," he heard as the other swept off into the early light. There was the dawn indeed, coming up in the direction of Shanghai, a pale copper bugle forming from molten metal: a kind of visual stridency becoming less and less shrill as time elapsed. Whenever he saw it, he knew he was not going to die today, or ever; it was said that you died only because, having known so many others who did it, you talked yourself into it as the correct thing to do, when all the time you had only to think *live-live* and arrest your mind with a group of commonplace objects: a sheep's hair brush, an abacus, an animal's summer coat, a toggle, some gold foil, and your fate was warm and benign. You thought positive and your ancestors released you for another promotion. Not bad. He should not have hurried away; we could have sat here among the rabble and had a morning drink together. Who the hell cares in this vile place? A man will end up fucking himself to death in the Nankings of the world. May the order please come for me to move on. I am too far behind the lines already, flopping my tool in makeshift whorehouses while a fat fish flops about in a fancy box. I am that fish. I have been eaten. I have eaten myself this night.

Scald Ibis had closed her eyes after seeing a plump young officer bend over a small corner water bucket, a towel draped awkwardly around his waist, his head swathed in a bandage. He dabbed water on himself, then dried, repeating the act a hundred times, bent against the tiles as if preparing to vomit. For some reason the tap, level with his chest, now and then dripped, so he soon had a full bucket except for what he spilled and what he dabbed against his chubby body. She at last found something to tell herself, having culled it from amidst a million memories. It contained a pun, too. Much of Beethoven's violin concerto, she reminded herself with almost chirpy bravura, sounds like wasps. Bee-thoven, silly. What had Father taught her? A gentle joke helps to create a mellow universe. So: she qualified. Now: where was he?

For the rest of her life, would she be lying there in the half-

light, on soiled pillows, watching some oaf clump through the
doorway, all his lust behind him, drying and withering even as
her next client stumbled up the stairs, cursing, his sword clank-
ing, a boy plenipotentiary? If these were samurai, she was a
Russian bear. No. These were the sons of the well-to-do, kept
back in a safe area while the war chased its own tail westward.
She was learning slowly to be a bivalve. If only her father the calligrapher were here, he would devise an elaborate chore for her:
thick paper, ready-made ink, a middle-sized brush, a hard
springy brush, decorative characters done in flying white, a red
ink pad for pressing seals, a steel ruler, a glue brush, a decorative
envelope for donating money, another brush with loose un-
starched hair, and soot made from burning vegetable oil. And,
oh, yes, some incorrectly written characters. She already knew
enough of Japanese ways, at least as far as calligraphy went. The
words she lacked were the ones young officers used upstairs
when doing to her things she banished to the Shanghai coast.
She was changing at tremendous speed, yet into someone who,
so newly come into being, had no steady identity at all.

She became aware of Hayashi standing immobile, with his
presence alone instructing her to call it a night, and she suddenly wondered if soldiers ever slept, if these were going to be
her hours henceforth. The shelling and shooting had gone on
all night. She felt like one of the opium addicts of old, a hermit
in her own home, a coolie working on the river, a chair bearer
out in the snow.

Five officers with three hundred soldiers fought their way into my official residence at five A.M. I was asleep, of course, but my brother-in-law had the presence of mind to wake me and secrete me in a laundry cupboard. In the meantime, they had killed half a dozen of our guards. When my brother-in-law returned to my bedroom, they thought he was me and shot him dead.

PRIME MINISTER KEISUKE OKADA, FEBRUARY 26, 1936,
NOON

THE GIRLS WERE AT IT AGAIN, HAVING THE KIND OF MORNING TALK that celebrated lack of clients; indeed, as their exuberance grew they began to believe they might never have to serve again because the Altar was a flop. This was a daytime observation, however, and they were unaccustomed to the routine of a brothel, always a quiet, yawny, bland place early in the day; it was almost, as commentators over the ages have observed, a nunnery given over to pondering, piety, golden reconciliations between woman and the deity. It was hard to believe—it would always be hard to believe—that, with evening, rude soldiers would come bumbling through the door in search of cheap relief. Thus far, Hayashi had not taken any money, nor had he been offered any.

The Altar was running at a loss, but so was the whole of China, whereas Japan, having seized huge lumps of China, was profiting hand over fist. An occasional loss on a minor brothel mattered little. In fact, the more Hayashi thought about it, the more he inclined to think free service was better service; when a little altruism sweetened the air, compulsory or not, there was an air of well-bred generosity. His mind had stalled between force and finesse.

Eventually he would have to unleash the girls as Chinese geishas, having them do geisha things in the Chinese way. Officers who knew no Chinese would have to imagine themselves at home. Wasn't there, somewhere in history, an instance of someone's reading a Chinese text in the Japanese way? Could such a thing be? He thought so, wishing nonetheless he had not been appointed to proctor the halocline between two competing languages that sometimes overlapped. Damn, he thought: Berlin, Milan, Bombay, Madrid, London, Moscow, and Washington were the same in both languages, and Paris, New York, and Milan were almost the same. He had learned that much at officer-training school. Either you gave up on the insoluble language problem or persuaded the girls to put on some kind of dumbshow, with an occasional Chinese word thrown in and, yes, a few halting words of Japanese. The two languages had different syntaxes, of course, and Japanese did not have verb endings, but surely the girls, Scald Ibis especially, could learn a few silky utterances calculated to please and entice visitors: "To get drunk from a cup of feathers at a moonlight feast." Rihaku. Scald Ibis would be the bilingual one, carrying the main amount of Japanese, while the others would be allowed to prattle *sotto voce* so as not to distract generals and admirals from their tea, from the flowers being arranged, from the tiny snacks and the sake. How would it go?

She must secrete an envelope in the folds of her kimono. But how even tell her that? Dumbshow again. Off he went, in his mind's eye and ear, explaining to her the envelope, or wrapping paper, with *noshi* in the top right-hand corner. The lines running across the center, and the bow, should be done in red, for happiness. Above the bow write the greeting, and below it her name. In the envelope there would be money, and within the wrapping paper a gift. She could understand that, perhaps adding a little humorous sketch to one of the other corners or twisting the bow into the form of a butterfly. More educated in linguistics, he would have been able to explain to Scald Ibis about *shōkeimoji*, those early imitative drawings that became the philological basis of characters: quick brush impressions that reproduced an elephant, a horse, a deer, the sun, when language was a baby. He wished he had been born Kûkai the priest who, when an emperor asked him to rewrite a section of a damaged five-paneled screen that Ogishi had written four centuries before, took five brushes, put one in his mouth, two between his toes, then one in either hand and rewrote the whole thing simultaneously, thus earning himself the nickname "The Five Brush Priest," or *gohitsu-wajô*. What initiative!

Again and again Hayashi felt he was not where he was, in burning Nanking, in a commandeered villa, but deep in the bosom of time, coming to a seemly halt from which he would never budge again, doing the last things in his life and so executing them with ultimate delicacy, not rushing things like Five Brush Kûkai. He had come here to be sucked dry, tapered off to a needle point, a samurai of evanescence, aided by a bevy of Chinese girls who soon would begin to giggle all day and yawn all night. If only he had been sent forward to the fighting, where he would have been of limited use. Brutality and courage were not enough to make a soldier of you; certainly not an officer. Nor were taste and perfect manners. An officer had to believe in what he did, needed to feel in his innermost being that little throb all the way from the emperor, guiding him, impelling him, until even his most mundane act was heavenly. An officer had to feel sublime.

When they invaded Russia, he would be of no use at all since that was a language unknown to him. Better that he should be another Kûkai, who once upon a time had executed characters by flicking ink across a swollen river to land on a plaque at the other side. No mistakes. Perhaps a Hayashi would have made a few, but then he was no Buddhist priest. He, too, though, would have written in jet-black ink, gradation and finesse being no more for him than for them—priests were always slapdash with the brush. If only he could introduce calligraphy into the tea ceremonies in the villa, whose old salon was now a four-and-a-half-mat room. Sen no Rikkyu, who founded the tea ceremony, always thought that priestly writing rather than ordinary calligraphy was vital to all tea ritual, not only injecting into the atmosphere a touch of gravity and restraint but also, for a knowledgeable tea master and his guests, recalling ancient China's late twelfth century, where priestly calligraphy had begun. None admired the work of those old priests more than Japanese priests of the thirteenth and fourteenth centuries. Mystics, all of them, amazed at being alive in any given second, as if several other trances had gone by the board, classically ignored, although just glimpsed in the white heat of awe. The more astounded, indeed affronted, you were to be alive, the keener became the glimpse of the other conditions you might have been in: twigness, albatross-ness, being a flame.

On a more humdrum level, Hayashi was known as the man who, seated at a typewriter, at which he had a certain skill, refused to make corrections with typing-eraser pencil, instead retyping the bungled word on a small slip of paper he then trimmed to the exact size required and glued to the page. Sometimes his finished pages had several levels, from all the slips he had glued into place, and the story went that he made deliberate mistakes for the sheer surgical pleasure of typing, clipping, and sticking little correction slips. Hayashi liked handwork, never going quite so far as origami, but sometimes in the dead of night caressing the surface of the page, noting with delicate motions of his fingertips the minute plinth he had made for the words of either his choice or his mistake. He loved isolating them, honoring them thus, and thinking about their etymology as he stuck them down.

He was a superb proofreader and had been recommended for training as an expert in coding and decoding. The lunge into China, however, had swept him away from cryptic pursuits, although he still hankered for some such career: a young colonel with many strings to his bow. He doted on names and often thought he had prospered because of the almost superstitious regard in which the military held his name.

7

At that time, Count Makino, adviser to the Emperor, was living as an invalid in one wing of the Itoya Inn at Yugawara, sixty miles from Tokyo. It was snowing hard. He was seventy-four, you see, and essentially an invalid, an easy target. Not the sort of man to go charging at them with sword and revolver as they burst in, shooting one policeman dead, and me in the hand, which hurt less than I thought it would. But, then, I am a nurse, accustomed to others' pain. Perhaps I assigned my pain to Count Makino, my charge. Anyway, they could not find him, so they ran outside and tried to set the hotel on fire, shooting at anyone they saw. Then they machine-gunned it, screaming "Penalty of Heaven!" Count Makino got away in the confusion. My hand has never been the same, and my freedom of movement, in that hand anyway, is restricted.

SUZUE MORI, NURSE, TO A JAPANESE NEWSPAPERMAN,
FEBRUARY 26, 1936

THROUGH THE NIGHTTIME STREET A BATTERED-LOOKING MAN, swathed in mud and lime, moved along the crowd's fringe, trying to evade the raucous soldiery tending their bonfires but from time to time swatting or transfixing a wandering Chinese. The uproar stunned him. Away from the front he had walked cowed, past one shambles after another, witnessing the most appalling sights of bullying and atrocity, yet somehow managing to keep out of the way, mainly by minimizing himself as he went, hunched and contorted, a duplicitous average, the complementary opposite of the man who had gone insane in the street and yelled complaint and accusation at both Chinese and Japanese, venting a heart-stopping indictment in a weird assortment of such words as blood, Friday, lightning, death, skin, popular, custard, radish, hibiscus, brokenhearted, and so on, utterly raving to the neighborhood, sometimes felled with a clean shot to the head, more often left to entertain, talking to himself of course, doomed to a career of indiscriminate obloquy. His life and brain had gone all wrong, and there was nothing he could do about it.

He whispered gently to himself, sometimes having trouble finding his direction because whole streets had turned to rubble, corners had vanished, cut clean off by some giant hand of artillery. In effect he steered from bonfire to bonfire, aching not to be noticed by shivering Japanese soldiers whose putteeed legs reminded him of racehorses. There was no music, but much screaming, together with assorted yelps from maltreated dogs, bone-deep howls from tormented women, shouts of defiance or entreaty from men being stood against walls and shot. He shrank along close to walls, behind vehicles, moving toward rubble even if it meant a detour. He wondered why so many Japanese remained in the city, not so much policing it as dismantling it, dehumanizing it, and also wondered when he had last eaten or made water. I am finally meeting the twentieth century, he thought; this is what all of it is going to be like, China or wherever. Then he saw the street that mattered, in pretty good repair, and quickened his pace, moving around to the back of the villa, his breath held, his eyes squinted so the whites would not give him away. He toed soft ground, then wrenched open a little door and stood inside a man-sized cavity, like a sentry entering his box. Above him sat the secret framework he intended to use: a trellis built into the villa's skeleton, leading directly upward within an invisible and unused chimney whose fireplaces he had sealed with toughest paper and cow glue years ago. If you banged your fist against the paper, you heard a drumlike sound, but nothing gave way. Up he went, gasping and clawing, now and then missing his hold, or slipping down as a piece of the trellis gave way under his feet. He had some distance to climb, but he had all the time in the world, out of the cold and the snow, away from the casually shooting Japanese. He could, he mused, have stayed here all night on the trellis like someone awaiting heat or electricity, spread out for the torture of a thousand cuts like Dr. H. L. Farabeuf, onetime physician to the French legation. He had no idea where the fireplaces were, so he had to feel, shoving his arm through the trellis and feeling for iron. How many houses in the street had such chimneys, he wondered. Some families used the chimneys as toilets, and some poor night-soil hireling emptied out the mess at the bottom and carted it away. Each time the hireling opened the little shutter, the mound fell out upon him, giving him his characteristic taint. Well, said the climber, we never used *our* bolt hole for anything such, and just as well.

The trellis was part of an escape device, not useful or even safe as part of a chimney, and rickety, moldy, irregular. Its right angles were all wrong and its wood was untreated, not of the best. Yet up he went, not a heavy man or an especially strong one, though his wearied mind was keen. It would be better to climb all the way to the top and then find the top fireplace, using his feet. Groping downward was easier than groping upward. He was too far gone to tell, but he knew that once he got off the trellis into the chimney proper, he would be able to slide into the sealed-up fireplace and rest. He knew there would be no fires to battle with as there was no fuel. There were no occupants. There was no life. He could hear nothing, but a faint incessant suction of air blew past him upward, making him shiver as he climbed. He groped all the way to the top, where the trellis stopped. He squirmed into the fireplace as quietly as he could, and lay there, spent. He had come home, a deserter, owing no more to Chiang Kai-shek than to the emperor Hirohito, but home for art and love, and presumably alone. Everyone else would have gone to a safer place. Or so he hoped, with a tiny penknife now slitting the durable paper that sealed the fireplace and peering in. It was an empty room except for some unfamiliar boxes stacked against the window, perhaps to keep shattered glass at bay.

As he listened to the silence of his own home, hoping for sounds of children, wife, he drifted off, absorbing the benefits of his first good sleep in days. In his dream, he became resplendent, turning into a visual echo of Zhu Bang's *Portrait of an Official in Front of the Forbidden City*, the man to whom the other three were bowing in the foreground, and, towering behind them, undiminished endless pagodas, temples, courtyards, all depicted in sullen pink. Trees wafted in and out of the scene, and crenellated walls sailed eastward or westward like battle cruisers. As if done in crystal, obelisks came forward faintly, like some unerased sketch from the first version. Little roofed arks sat erect on the ocean of dirty saffron cloud. It was exquisite, a bit mired and faded since 1500, but stirring for its terraced, hierarchical quality. And then he saw the other official, the one in the red kimono with white flash, and saw that he was none of the blue-garbed officials in front, but this regal, portly figure with hands in pockets, looking straight out of the painting at whatever was behind the viewer. Now there was another forbidden city, his own, and not so handsome by half.

In the dream, though, he regained his dignity; the city did not reject him; the Japanese marched backward into prehistory, where they belonged, and he felt warm again, successfully calling for his family, his voice an inebriated-sounding squawk. He and Scald Ibis had pored over this painting for years, almost as if it were a mirror whose silver nitrate trapped in a magic powder the elaborate lures of ancient China, the constant penetration of human skin by eternity.

He came down the stairs in the predawn, having sliced his way out of the fireplace, his face and hands black with soot. But he found only closed doors until he reached the four-and-a-half-mat room. Sleeping girls were sprawled everywhere: Lin, Qiu, Cixi, Meng, and Dé, frozen in undulation, and two officers, one a colonel. Scald Ibis, asleep with her face buried in silks, was snoring faintly. Nothing happened. He gazed appalled at the vulgar colors, the flag of Nippon, the uncleared plates and cups, the empty bottles, the loaded ashtrays, the pornographic pictures.

A gramophone record was spinning on the turntable, failed exhibit in perpetual motion, and Hayashi was making a snuffle-bubbling sound. This was the disarray of afterward, no longer the Altar of Heaven but the Tent of Orange Mist, Hayashi's half-sentimental invention, deemed more sensual a title, less sacrilegious. Hong stared in horror, telling himself that venery came first, not tea or conversation. He did not even recognize his daughter. With an almost random pluck, he seized the Japanese flag and left.

And now, like the wise esthete he was, Hong found the kitchen and squirreled away a cup of boiled rice, a full bottle of sake. Off he went, caressing favored expanses of wall and banister, wagging a finger at patches of crumbled plaster, reserving for later research the whereabouts of daughter, son, and wife. Then he went to sleep, having been press-ganged into an army that had given him almost nothing to do but keep awake. Many thousand Chinese had died in that same bleary, uncomprehending state, too drained to protest as the fatal round struck home. They died anesthetized, like drones. Had he pottered around a bit more, he would have found Scald Ibis, and Hayashi would have run him through for trespassing. If only he had made a noise. Back inside the fireplace, committing himself to something like acute sleep, which is to say a sleep within a sleep, the sentry's sleep, he cupped his hands together and blew into them. Cold sake made him feel colder, and he twisted back to his slumber, wrapped in the flag of the Rising Sun.

We got into the bedroom of the Grand Chamberlain Baron Kantaro Suzuki. His wife tried to interpose her own body between him and our fire. Then she begged me to allow her to give the coup de grâce to her dying husband. I saluted and left at once, as was befitting. I thought all the way back about obedience based on mindless awe, and wished I had shot the bitch in the belly before leaving. He survived to become prime minister and, in fact, was the one who surrendered our country to the Allies in 1945. You may well wonder how one of those tried in camera without counsel on March 4, 1936, can speak of these events from Outre-Tombe (I was shot). But I learned how from a certain German, Colonel Stauffenberg, who came along some eight years later, also shot.

CAPTAIN TERUZO ANDO, OPINING LONG AFTER THE
EVENT

HONG'S NEXT FORAY, HOWEVER, WAS MORE CIRCUMSPECT, NOT because he had thought it out but because, after some rest, his presence of mind was keener. After rummaging in familiar closets, he donned a frayed blue jacket, dragged a nondescript cap low over his eyes, and practiced bowing and scraping. Just as well: he ran into Hayashi on the stairs, groveled low, mumbling, and got a kick for his trouble. As Hayashi reached the landing, he flung behind him a torrent of abuse that brought Scald Ibis to the foot of the stairs. Hong, Hong heard, was a filth-caked bootlicker unfit to relieve himself in a Japanese toilet. She failed to recognize him as he was bent double, face almost on the stair, whimpering until Hayashi, with new-stiffened back, began to ascend again. Who had that coolie been? At this hour of the morning he didn't care. Now Hong began rubbing the stairs with his bare hands until Scald Ibis, ever thoughtful, reappeared and tossed up to him an old shirt, better in quality than the coat he had on. Again Hong went unidentified, rapidly becoming part of the household staff, assimilable by role rather than as a specific human. He was beginning to enjoy this; it was better than being out among the rubble and smoke, the shellfire and the atrocities. So he went on wiping down the stairs, keeping his ears open and his face down.

When he arrived back at the slit in the paper, he decided to amuse himself and reached into the defunct chimney for some soot. Using this on the faded old paper he described with awkward motions the character for Xīan, which meant "immortal" or "recluse," drawing upon his excellent visual memory for Xīan, who rises by climbing on all fours rather like a monkey. Xīan climbed a mountain, watched by an idyllic princess, but the ascension theme was bold enough, and sometimes a trellis felt like a mountain. When he had finished, needing a couple of extra soots, the character

仙

was the size of his hand, a puzzle to the uninitiated, but a clear sign to his daughter, his wife, and perhaps his son. He was willing to slave on the floor and the stairs for as long as it took. Why he thought his daughter was in the house, he had no idea, but the thought of reclining in the fireplace, out of sight, without leaving some kind of sign for her made him sick to his stomach. She would know, if she saw. Then he thought of the other characters with which Xian often combined, allowing his mind some brief ebullience.

It was a little poem, was it not?

Female, red-crowned,
paradise celestial
and cactus.

Not much, but better than the poetry being written by sharp-shooters on the other side of the city. He marveled that he had not been shot or bayoneted, slung into the river or burned alive.

All the same, he decided not to push his luck too far. When the colonel was wide awake, it would be best to keep out of sight. Around dawn and just before sunset, he ambled around the villa, with broom, bucket, and duster, his shape that of men who, having borne life's burdens such as coal or wood, in huge sacks, cannot straighten up. To cheer himself, he began to daub little poems on the fireplace screen, almost all of his own invention, and these the roaming Scald Ibis actually saw without quite realizing he was there behind the paper. On the few occasions on which he actually peeped out, he could not see who was in the room when Scald Ibis, coerced by Hayashi into performing for the evening's visitors, began to sing the poems, though in a restrained manner full of pathetic, constricted effects.

Female
red-crowned
paradise
celestial
cactus

brought tears to her eyes. Whose poems were these? Hayashi's, she decided. He was testing her, showing off his Chinese, parading the effete side of his warrior being. She sang not for him, or to him, but for China, to China, China the broken, wholly missing the notion of climbing (and so trellis) that Hong had tried to get across.

Hayashi seemed to be settling down. He had seen the signs in the storeroom, but paid no heed, not understanding them. Scald

Ibis was scribbling graffiti, he decided, composing poems up there in the attic. What else were attics for? It was good to have her out of the way so long as, when needed, she remained compliant, as amazed by sex as if she had swallowed a cloud, then as bored by it as by chewing on an old pencil. She was too lovely to ignore, however, and the general, the admiral, came back again and again for her favors. Although too analytical and intellectual to be a tea lady, she did have good manners, an aloof demeanor, and exquisite features best seen in makeup, when she looked ten years older. And became, he rebuked himself, a young matron inexplicably gone to the dogs, a catechistic flirt, a peach beginning to ferment. Underneath it all, she was still sixteen, and therefore infatuated with her own maturation, not always receptive to the mimed thoughts of elders. She missed school. She missed English, which she enjoyed. She missed being a daughter, being pampered, being streamlined by adoration.

So we have had a mutiny. All my most trusted retainers are dead and the mutineers want to rid the nation of me. A man looking constantly into his underwear will never see the horizon, but it is to the horizon I look, seeing China, its shaggy hauteur.

EMPEROR HIROHITO, JOURNAL, FEBRUARY 27, 1936

YOU MAY BE WONDERING AT THIS POINT, WITH REASON, WHY Hayashi failed to connect the characters on the screened fireplace with the new scrubman on the stairs. The answer must be that his mind was full of Scald Ibis, and he was only too happy to accept the first solution that sprang to his mind. As to why Scald Ibis did not recognize her father when she saw him on the stairs, her mind was full of shame, blame, and ripening revenge. Then why did she again not recognize him when she flung him the old shirt? She was not looking at him; she tossed the rolled-up shirt toward the upper section of the lower stairs. When you have lived in a house for a decade and a half, you do not look where you are throwing things. You throw by feel. There remains the puzzle of why Hong, climbing the internal trellis and then repeatedly the stairs, chalking himself large on the screen as the climber in their life, failed to get through to his daughter the idea that someone extra was in the house awaiting a sign. The answer has to be that sometimes puzzles exist for no purpose; things fail to work out, at least at first; but watch Scald Ibis when she really zeros in on that *Xīan* character, about which she knows one or two special things, doubtless to her cost.

As Scald Ibis herself had said, you can solve problems only when you no longer fix your mind on them. Now, even as she prepared for the umpteenth time to sing her geisha song, complete with samisen played by Hayashi, she became aware of something her mind's eye had caught: not something on the old torn screen upstairs, on which Hong scrawled his poems, but in the background, the history, of the character *Xīan*. As she sang, extending the vowels almost to breaking point, Scald Ibis divined the earlier forms of the character, going past

which told her little, being too abstract, to

in which the clue was beginning to emerge in those three-pronged forks and the lozenge between them, to in which she discerned four hands, and a human head that invited caresses. Why did four hands and a lozenge shape stir her heart so, as nothing by Hayashi could?

What had her father told her, he who taught her as much at home as she learned in school? We not only have to learn to remember, we have to learn to forget. "And then," he had said, "we have to learn to remember what we almost forgot." She saw him now, not in any physical sense, for he was never present at the tea ceremonies, but stranded in the character *Xīan*, grappling with the ancient past, he who had said to her when she was little and he had shown her a book of old-style characters: "Do you see two forks and two combs? The forks and combs are hands, really, grappling for purchase on a mountainside, although it looks as if four people are trying to eat a fried egg. That squiggle like a snake is an official seal, making the whole thing aboveboard. And the oval thing that looks like a precious stone perhaps, it's actually someone's head. It's the head of the climber. The wishbone shape to the left, my sweet, is a human being. So there you have it: a climber using four hands, like a monkey, and his head bobbing about as he goes higher. Isn't that a pretty picture?" He had smiled his benign best. There it had been, and now she saw the scene again: her father climbing, herself watching with traditional graciousness.

With as much elegance as she could muster, she excused herself from the tea ceremony and walked slowly upstairs, marveling that she could still hear artillery and bombs. Facing the sealed fireplace, she gave a small whistle, then tapped the paper, one, two, three, finishing with an urgent tattoo. Now she pried the slit open and called his name into the echoing cavity, where he was asleep. He heard her voice in his dream, contentedly turned over and did nothing else. She shoved her hand in, deep, but touched nothing, finally concluding she was wrong and had misinterpreted the whole thing. In the closet she found a discarded cane, which she then pushed through the slit, maneuvering it up and down, left and right, to no effect. But he was stirring, wondering as always why he did not fall from the narrow ledge, but always answering himself that he had learned to sleep stock-still, he could not remember why, but it might have had to do with sleeping four to a bed in the days of acute poverty. When the cane touched him, he flinched; the Japanese had found him at last. Yet the cool, tutored voice that reached him through the slit was the gentlest intervention of his life. A hand came through, a sooty hand met it.

"Father," she breathed, "is it you? What are you doing in there?" He was too overcome to answer. She smeared her mascara against the shiny paper screen, trying to hug him through it, wrapping him in paper first, but he came to life and bulged bodily behind it, entering on his knees with the screen before him like a shield. She rolled backward, onto her heels, then off them, gasping at this new apparition of the nameless menial to whom she had thrown a shirt on the stairs. Here he was, in an old jacket, with that ridiculous short cone hat on his head, a man back from the dead, or from the living whom he had chosen to visit.

"No more army?" she asked. "Where did you spring from?"

"They will manage without me. I am no warrior, girl."

"They are in the house. But you know."

"And what, pray, are you doing in a getup such as that? Wait until your mother sees you. Oh, it's an old way in, or out. Up the trellis you go, four-handed."

"Have *you* seen *her*?" No, he had not. Horses were dying everywhere. Children were falling into the Yangtze. Their mothers were cutting their own throats. Young soldiers, having failed to stem the Japanese tide, kept hanging themselves from electric poles. He could not bear it, he had fled. Instead of blood lust he saw again his wife as a student, playing the saxophone, lounging back with her naked rear in a basin of champagne, her hair bobbed, her feet in prosthetic-looking black cocktail shoes whose heels tapered to an unwalkable point. Hardly a rickshaw puller in the making, she had whetted his appetite for other similarly dramatic women, and then he had come back to her, she being the mold of all the rest. She the soccer fan and pedantic Confucian scholar had changed his life; she had given him momentum, self-assurance, at least enough in later days to climb the trellis built into their chimney.

"Go back," Scald Ibis was telling him. "They will be on the prowl." The sound of the samisen had stopped. "Then," he joshed, "bring me some salt eggs, crab roe, red bean stuffing. I am starved. It may not be mannerly to complain, but I have forgotten how to eat. Teach me again, daughter. And no more sake, please. It rots my gut."

She said nothing, and urged him back into the fireplace, creamy with delight that he had come back to them, which only, alas, made two the number who did not know what lay frozen in the cropped turf of the garden, what lay on the river bottom eerily defiled. In a trice she had found him blankets and furs, these, too, plucked from the closet in the storeroom, a closet that seemed never to go empty but always provided what the situation demanded, as if her mother had planned it. Away Hong went, hauling his wrappers behind him. She reaffixed the screen, put out the light, and made her way downstairs full of inebriate longing to shoo them all out, back to the ships of their navy. Her father was the cleaning man, and she, she lamented, was their insurance policy: one wrong move and they would all go the way of many thousands whose only crime was to have been in Nanking.

How she sang that evening, with her father secreted upstairs as an imitation of something he could never be. She thought about, and wanted as a huge toy, a full-size paper replica of a Model A Ford complete with bilious-looking chauffeur. The whole thing was to be ritually burned during the funeral of a well-to-do jade merchant, but she wanted it for her paper-enclosed father to drive away in: Hong's chariot.

Those remarking her unhabitual cheerfulness wanted her all the more, but curbed themselves as if she were a real geisha;

homesickness responded most to the surface of things, in which her linnet voice was paramount. She sang with dainty insinuation, hoping to diffuse so delicate an atmosphere that the young officers would lose their drive and, instead, yearn for polish and hauteur and the most minimal flirtation. She could have screamed for joy, even as, not many miles away, Chinese soldiers ripped up railroad tracks, denying the Japanese their use, and officers with spats showing at their trouser bottoms and Thermoses slung over their backs looked for the quickest way out of Nanking.

Scald Ibis knew that life had begun again, even as the lieutenants fawned on her, holding themselves erect as if to instructions printed on a box lid, inviting her to beat them gently with her fan. They were a *tableau vivant*, she and they, she the unattainable as long as she pretended to be geisha, they lively in that, although they pretended they would be denied, they knew they were conquerors and could have more than they wanted. They were warriors, not merely officers, and eager to see the world before the Chinese juggernaut eventually hurled them back, after suffering them awhile, letting them play with its daughters.

On she would go, while her father scrubbed the stairs, converting her form into a paper lady, wrapped in boas and gauzes, plumes and tulle, her entire wardrobe appearing to be a sculptured vapor in a veil. The day would come when she doffed the lot, restored her father to his minaret of self-importance and bricked up the chimney forever.

10:1

Because of the activities of the Soviet Union and the situation prevailing in China, Japan is going to start operations in North China. Most of the people of Japan do not yet quite understand the great importance of these future operations, and their lack of understanding, I believe, will beyond doubt bring about a really serious crisis in the nation. . . .

YOSUKE MATSUOKA

UNTIL THEN, SHE WOULD LOSE HERSELF REPEATEDLY IN THE MIrage between those who could talk to one another and those who could not. Talking to her father made not talking to Hayashi feel worse than ever; he became more of a monster now, a counterpoint to the caring and compassionate Hong, who, to be sure, had some flakes of Japanese in his speech. Language, Scald Ibis felt, made people blither, less truculent, even if, as in the joke she'd heard about the first translation machine, things went wrong: take the phrase "out of sight, out of mind," and have the machine translate it into Chinese. Then feed the Chinese back into the machine and convert into English. Out came "invisible idiot." Her father had told her that, and the two of them, versed in English, had felt closer than ever.

Hayashi, though, for all his sensitivity to language and writing, came from that dreadful samurai tradition, was an amateur of words, a professional of swords. What would he do if he discovered her father hidden in the third-floor fireplace? She was nervous about Hong's pose as scrub boy, even though it had worked so far; one day Hong would lose control and ascend into the role of father once he realized the full extent of what went on in the four-and-a-half-mat room. No man could brook the ordeal of watching his only daughter turned into a slut. He might even charge Hayashi with his scrubbing brush, or with the cane from the closet in the supply room, no more able to resist than the German-trained and German-equipped Chinese troops could resist unscrewing the spikes from their helmets when a thunderstorm began.

What then?

Keep her father out of sight? It was true that he might not be missed.

Equip him with a week's food and send him to neighbors.

Wonderful, except he would not go; the more Hong saw what was going on in the villa, the more he would want to stay to protect her, not recognizing that, to protect her, he must let her slither away down the primrose path, a hostage to fortune. If only her mother were here, full of adroit suggestion, a woman who had devoted her life to manipulating Hong for their common benefit. Hong, it seemed, was best left where he was.

She vowed to forge ahead with her new vocation, at least until she and her father could make a break for it, across the city line like homing birds. Left behind, Hayashi would curse and lament, his lips forever framing the dry formulae of possessive rage. She was the best piece of ass in China. Then he, the admiral, and some of the bristling lieutenants, would quarrel about the cause of such ill luck:

We pushed her too hard. The admiral.

The Chinese kidnapped her. Hayashi.

She is still in the house, in a secret compartment. The general.

Drowned in the Yangtze, suggested one of the junior officers. It was a Japanese tradition to disagree about evidence.

"No," the admiral said, "Ryunosuke here murdered her and cut her gash away from the main trunk for private use. How loathsome."

"No," the general said, "our friend the admiral here raped her with a hose pipe and exploded her innards. It is well-known in the south, quite a tradition."

Not to be outdone, Hayashi boasted, "I strangled her with my bare hands. She was too insulting. *Catch this*, I said as I tossed her a book. Down went her hands and I was straightaway at her throat. That's the true story, gentlemen." Then the nameless servant made his deposition in faltering Japanese. "She jumped from the window," he said. "I saw. They picked her up and rushed her away." No one believed him because he was of the lowest social status, prone to fiction and embellishment, and a foreigner to boot. A samurai would have known what to say, lying or not. The girl had something extraordinary about her; she was evasive and blatant at the same time, a person of many selves, succoring them physically but only until the Chinese returned, and then she would propose a wild pajama party with most of them in the dark in the same bed, prompting them to undreamed-of abandon, with maybe even a little lascivious dog in the room, and with hidden razor she would strike, castrating them one after the other, doing it by feel and familiarity. Now, who proposed this as an outcome? Hayashi? It had his preoccupation and his personal style. No, Scald Ibis thought of it herself, ashamed for taking to this fleshly lifestyle with such avidity: glad of having something to do, and now some purpose in doing it, such as saving her father. She had developed a new smile with a twist in it, the rictus of some clandestine lust taking over her facial muscles and tweaking; she was reveling at sixteen in something she should have saved for twenty. Oh, yes? She didn't think so, almost on the verge of developing tartlike tastes, especially as she could just about get away with her geisha pose, executing it so crudely the officers giggled, but occupying them nonetheless with her solecisms. With one hobble skirt, slit to the thigh, she had been able to plant Tokyo in Nanking. They found her act more tempting than her body or face; they talked about her to her face, laughing and braying, proffering an intimate tone that actually shut her out: the appreciative mock, the contemptuous bravo. To them she was no more real than the paper auto she had thought about, but they set aside all their knowledge of other cars and let her reign supreme.

If you are sixteen, Scald Ibis thought, you're entitled to change your mind every day. You are still a taster at life's feast, neither ingenue nor whore, neither innocent nor woman of the world. I am radiant before they touch me, and then it begins to diminish, and the radiance returns a bit shopworn, somewhat mishandled. Now I know what men want from us, I feel truly sorry for them. They care most about size, which is grotesque. What I do like, and find interesting, is this geisha stunt that has in it more of the stern mama than they know. She titters, she smirks, she waves a finger or two, swirls her silks, makes a pun or half-does a song. I am good at it, I am, I am. I dither and stammer, even in Chinese, but that is because I don't want my head lopped off, and now it's because I don't want them to find my father.

10:II

Japan cannot halt her North China operations. The arrow has already left the bow. The progress of these operations will decide the destiny of the Yamato race.

YOSUKE MATSUOKA, PRESIDENT OF THE SOUTH
MANCHURIAN RAILWAY, AUGUST 5, 1935

FOR NOW, SHE SET ASIDE ALL WORRIES ABOUT PREGNANCY OR DIS-
ease and tried to evaluate herself on the plane of postulant. To play the role badly would be dangerous. Already, gullible Dé had gone out into the night never to return, her escort the most sullen of the lieutenants, a raw red-hot coal of a man, determined to show her the sights, of which, alas, she was likely to become one, a lethal caution against who knew what, but diagrammatically arranged against a railing, her hands tied, a hot coal in her mouth as all conditions and sorts of Chinese fled from the spectacle, their hands over their ears, crying, "The Japanese, the Japanese!" Her fate was allegorical, Dé's, her name meaning "straight as tested by ten eyes." Straight-hearted, she failed to

please, and her lieutenant came back for his pseudo-geisha.

If the girls had any idea in common, apart from revulsion at their nightly chores, it had to do with love, something which, once attained, made the rest of life agonizing because love would end, and it might be better never to find it. Without voicing the thought, they came to the dismal conclusion that hope denied was better than happiness blighted. Perhaps they acquired this idea in school, or from gossips, popular literature; they now had to contrast it with prostitution, and it was as if some ferocious, abstracted taskmaster out of the blue ordered them to contrast the life of a desert Bedouin with that of a sixteenth-century monk, or that of a stamp collector with that of a camel, or that of an ant with that of blazing Arcturus. In this way, the flighty but maltreated girls became expert in incommensurate knowledge, obliged to think about things no human should have to contemplate, but skidding, slithering, day after day, toward twisted notions of both love and cruelty: love was better *in extremis* and developed new proliferations thus, while cruelty was the needed stimulant that made love metaphysical. They had all these effects without the words. Their world smelled of balsam, tasted like ammonia, felt like shagbark, sounded raucous, and looked like a badly acted scene in a vulgar play. The only love they felt was for one another, but it was a wan, bleached thing, compact of subterfuge and shame.

It had been Dé who initiated the late-night cuddling sessions that soothed the girls after a hard evening. Dé had tapped on Scald Ibis's door and entered without an answer, almost a child seeking its mother, and the two of them had wordlessly embraced, nodding their heads, hardly noticing when the others entered, too. In no time they were a Laocoön on the narrow bed, not writhing or fidgeting but coiled together in complex oblivion. If there was a sexual component to all this hugging, Scald Ibis was unaware of it; they were too tired for anything such, more concerned with warmth, anonymity, and physical proximity. Scald Ibis calmed her mind, then thought of the stars, of bushes in springtime, ribbons so new they still had a springy curl. Dé was the whisperer, the only one they heard whispering, but without ever understanding her words. Perhaps she was praying, or reciting charms. The other girls did an occasional short giggle, sighed, and cleared their throats, touching faint electricity in one another, knowing no harm could come to them combined. So it was a convolvulus of little hiccups, rumbling stomachs, and intimidated-sounding sighs: a heap of girls, untidy as if dumped there, waiting for some evil genius to pull them apart and make them attend their duties even as they got colder and began to shudder.

Since they had few conversations other than stilted ones in the four-and-a-half-mat room, the few they had stood out, most of all certain utterances that, for Scald Ibis the born note-taker and observer, lingered as characteristic:

Cixi: "City girls don't think about animals so much; they take stuff for granted—they don't say anything is like anything else. Things as they are, and no fudging."

Meng: "I feel as if my belly was full of soup, all gurgling and swampy. I must be growing up."

Dé: "Another year, my loves, and it will all be over and done with. We'll soon be all we were, all over again. If not, I'll drown myself."

Qiu: "I suppose the *Chinese* will want us next. Hey, these girlies have all been broken in for us. After you, sir. No, sir, after *you*. You know how men are, once it's rigid and eager."

When they spoke they felt they were poisoning the air with victim poetry. They talked only to confirm to themselves that, far from budding into tempestuous delicacy, as girls should, they were not only old before their time, but also uniquely deprived of wisdom, unable to do anything but survive. They were not even pets; only wallflowers at the universal dance of death.

Sometimes Cixi felt a need to disabuse Moth Wing, but refrained, certain that Moth Wing was entitled to her brief euphoria, really a form of shut-eye as the city roared skyward in vermilion flames. So Cixi would chide the sometimes mumbling, offhand Qiu until Meng intervened, lashing out from her professed knowledge of sweet boulevards and suave nightwalkers who flogged girls' faces with flowers. Odd, Scald Ibis thought, some of us are quite experienced, well-versed: Cixi, Meng, Qiu perhaps, but what difference does it make now? What was that figure we learned about in school? The Klein bottle, which enabled you to go from the inside of a vessel to the outside without passing through the material it is made of. The open narrow end of a tapered tube goes back into the wider part and then flares out. Something like that. Just like us. We went from one state to another without passing through life. Our growing up was a mere lightning bolt, no time to brood on it in little diaries locked against prying parents. The way in was the way out.

In order to remain in the storeroom, Scald Ibis had to have a reason, and one valid for day after day, so she took up there some treatises on calligraphy, battered but inexhaustible, and a thick sketch pad, inks, a pad, and brushes. She meant to set up a studio, spreading her things about lest someone else, most certainly Hayashi, try to use the room for something else. Up here, with the crackle of gunfire audible most of the night, she began to hold whispered conversations with her father through the slit, through the paper, almost as if confessing in that sly Western invention, the Catholic church. First, however, she had to wake him up, this being the first night, and the best way of doing this was to buzz loudly against the drum-tight paper. She smelled glue, mold, mouse dirt, and varnish when she pursed her lips and put them close. She was talking to ancient China, embodied there in a pretend houseboy whose dignity had not ebbed, whose right to the villa had not lapsed.

He was still Professor Hong, whose breathing you could neither feel nor hear; nor did his chest, like that of others, rise and fall, bulge and dwindle. He often seemed dead, unconscious at least, and this helped him to hear what people said

about him behind his back, which was to say to his unimpor-
tuning front. It also involved him in a hair-splitting intellectual
quest that asked if people said different things after your death
from what they said when you only seemed asleep. He had
wondered for years if, upon death, say, there developed a new
absolute dimissoriness unpermitted while you breathed. He
wanted to hear what they would say about dead Hong, but no
amount of shamming convinced them, so he was always
fobbed off with semigenerous put-downs, uttered by those
who knew he had the rest of his life to get through, although
not as a houseboy; no one would ever have predicted that. It
took hordes of Japanese to bring him to that. Yet what happened to him was as nothing compared to the city's systematic
rape according to formula: secure; seek food, fuel, shelter;
erase the vital centers; kill all Chinese on sight. He would
never forget those who, using their puttees as ropes, tried to
lower themselves from high walls, aiming for sampans and
junks moored on the river. Those who made it swamped the
vessels while others tried to cross on rafts. Even the poor
found themselves stripped of their bedding, their rickshaws;
their tenements burst into flame behind them, fired by spe-
cially designed chemical strips. Roped together in groups of a
hundred, captured soldiers were doused with gasoline and
burned. The survivors could be seen walking the streets eyeless
and noseless, moaning for help, which always took the form of
a bullet. The Japanese identified their victims by the tight in-
dentation made in their hair by a close-fitting hat or helmet.
Anyone with calloused hands was killed.

"What do you do?" Hong whispered harshly; he had been
saving up the question for a long time.

"Housegirl," she said.

"Housegirl, as I am houseboy?"

"Or comfort woman, aspiring to geisha."

He tried to assimilate that, but was unable. "Have they interfered with you?"

"Not with geishas," she said. "They're different. Too educated to be messed with. Too high-class."

"Since when have you learned Japanese?" He had reverted to his tone of the classroom, a high-handed civility no one objected to.

"I do it in Chinese. I sing, I sing."

He could not believe it, he who had invented her bizarre name, singling her out not for punishment or exposure, but managing to express his feeling at her birth: something incinerative yet magical like the Sacred Ibis of the Egyptians, white like her but with some black in the wings. Her arrival *had* scalded him; his epidermis had burned with shame and joy, and life would never be the same. She had blazed into his demure system, at once making her life more important than his. She had resented the name at first, but had grown accustomed to it, its curt novelty having sunk into her hide, adding complexity and allure; Scald was the radical, Ibis the phonetic. Scald was the basic notion, Ibis was the part you sang with a nasal lilt.

He could no more believe she had survived than he could accept that his wife and son were missing. He also thought she was lying to spare his feelings; he said nothing, but part of him began to squirm, wishing he were back with the poor wretches jumping off walls into the river mud, or the refugees from Shanghai, being robbed of their pigs and hens, their rice and coverlets, then beaten for their trouble. Any of that would be better than coming home to a defiled daughter in an intact house. The wait for vengeance would be too long, he thought; he would never live until then, they would soon find out who he was and break him into pieces, first abusing his daughter in front of him. Could it just be, he prayed, that she somehow, through duplicitous acting of huge refinement, fooled them into taking her on as a geisha without first availing themselves of her body? How often in the rise and fall of civilizations did that kind of thing happen? Providential vicissitude. Callow gullibility? Did they like her that much? No, she must have had a protector, who in his own way used her; he must have: Hayashi the cock of this walk, the gay blade of the Tent of Orange Mist. In his chimney eyrie he retched and heaved, wishing no more to be a family man, killing in his mind all extensions of himself, wishing to be curled back upon himself like a rose and then stamped on by a Japanese boot.

"Have you?"

"Did I?"

"Either."

"How could you?"

"They're Japanese."

"I'll tell you in a hundred years," she said. "Not that I mean I did. I'll tell you then if you were right. You have to have faith."

"Well, did you?"

"You mean: did *they*?"

"You know what I mean. I am your father."

"And a wonderful man, too, in your funny little chimney room, like someone in a painting," like Ren Xiong in his self-portrait, his expression one of marmoreal severity (head shaven, cheekbones pushing through like wing ribs), his robe all razor-sharp folds; the slightest motion might cut him. She imagined Ren Xiong in the chimney top, naked in his lethal robe, and sobbed for her father, who knew too much. Somehow they were going to see, coax, each other through, but only by the most adroit duplicity and the sly meshing of their roles: professor turned houseboy, art student turned geisha. The more he thought about her fate, the more likely he was to go on a predawn rampage with a butcher knife. There were too many of them, even asleep on their tawdry mats. All she and he could hope for was something else in the Japanese tradition; not unheard of for soldiers to shoot themselves in the mouth by pulling the trigger of a rifle with their toe; but how soon would Hayashi and his crew arrive at that particular plateau of shame? In a hundred years, of course.

She was appalled by how bloodthirsty her thoughts became,

crouched here, whispering in the chill to her father in one of the few houses in Nanking that had lights. Perhaps soon, an army whose soldiers had no soap, toilet paper, gum, chocolate, candy, peanut brittle, smokes, would disintegrate; she doubted it. They took the long view, could last forever so long as they had the Emperor remotely steering them, a little touch of home in the early evening.

I am going to end up—she was unable to complete the sentence. I can see it now. I am going to be something I never meant to be. I am going to be nobody. I will belong to somebody not my father. I am going to finish up whispering into mailboxes and envelopes, and cozying up to generals and admirals who might be able to find my family. When I tire of that, I will be truly homeless: just an orphan in a war tent.

11

The military is like an untamed horse left to run wild. If you try to stop it head-on you get kicked to death. The only hope is to jump on from the side and try to get it under control. Somebody has to do it. That's why I've jumped on, from the side. And soon we will jump on China, too, from the side.

PRIME MINISTER KOKI HIROTA, 1936

TRAPPED BETWEEN THE ROUGH AND THE SMOOTH, SHE MARVELED at her sudden shift, though less astounded by her gravitation toward the exquisite than by her almost categorical interest in what the men did to her, or rather how: the admiral did a fast to and fro of limited range and almost constant rhythm; the general withdrew slowly for a grand slam that rocked her pelvis, as if he were trying to propel her some distance; the lieutenants did to and fro as well as slam, sometimes achieving a sideways shimmy that had no effect on her. Did she respond? She thought not, though she did convict herself, after the initial pain and the consequent soreness, of an ache down there.

As for Hayashi, the stamp collector, he just entered and lay there for the longest time quite still, waiting for the planet to shake him, and then at last he began, slower than slow, a chronic savorer. She had no idea what he was savoring, but she could tell it delighted him from the sounds he made: engorged, congested sighs as of a cat waking up.

She caught sight of herself playing the classic disobedient daughter, lying and lying even harder once she realized that lies did not show in the face, the hands. How could her father be angry with her for suppressing something he never wanted to know? Tell him something amiable, yes; he was in no condition to withstand news of unspeakable depravity. In any case, was it that unspeakable, that depraved? It was what the whole world did sooner or later, what the planet wanted its people to do, whatever else they did: the venereal imperative. She thought of all the men in history, butting their loins forward to the fray as if a hard-on were some contribution to campanology. She thought of all the women, spreading their legs wide, all in the interests of what they could not resist. Sex seemed to Scald Ibis unimaginative, a bore built up into a huge scandal. Her father had done his share of it, so he might not take as much offense as she thought. Could he possibly believe she had not been interfered with? He had only to tiptoe downstairs in the small hours to watch the silent innovations that took place on the rug in the four-and-a-half-mat room, on the couch, against the wall. It might be better to tell him before he saw for himself and then—what? Killed his daughter with his own hands for befouling the family honor? On the other hand, he might succumb to the nature of things, the sadness like boiling onion, and look the other way.

She could not tell, but she tried to plan what would happen next.

Hong kills his daughter.

His daughter kills Hong.

Together they kill Hayashi.

Hayashi kills Scald Ibis, or her father.

Hayashi kills himself.

The junior officers kill Scald Ibis.

The same juniors kill Hayashi.

Or they kill Hong.

The admiral and the general kidnap Scald Ibis, secreting her aboard a battleship or into an underground headquarters.

Hong kills as many as he can, downstairs in the four-and-a-half-mat room, with a gun.

In spite of all this, Scald Ibis realized that the best course was to wait it out, urging her father to act with even greater caution, never to slip out of his houseboy role. Mentally she corrected herself in the orange-red ink calligraphy teachers used on student work. She was always correcting herself, hoping in the end to achieve deliberate integrity, which meant attuning herself to whatever she became. She felt like Marco Polo in reverse. Something huge had come to meet *her*. She felt tugged between a coarseness that became ever cruder and delicacies that had almost run off the map of refinement.

She wanted, still, to be left alone, by her father, too, reconstituted as a virgin and sent back to school, to its drafts and its long echoing halls, its squeaky blackboards, its constant aroma of whitewash. If she could not manage that, she would mentally re-create herself as a virgin since she had not cooperated in any way. Human feelings, she reminded herself, are thin as paper sheets; consider the paper punctured, then, and not her hymen. She made the best of her wound to keep her father out of harm's way, but she knew they would soon run out of time. Hong would come stamping downstairs, unable to restrain himself any longer.

She so much trusted in the providential fecundity of events that she was bound to discover what to do about her father, whose name was doubtless on some list of deserters to be hounded down for the next twenty years. The next day, however, large crates of elaborate kimonos arrived, closely followed by the first two geishas to enter the Tent of Orange Mist. Sup-

planted, she would soon no doubt be roughly beheaded. She
was wrong, though; the two geishas were tutors, schooling her
with aloof tooting sounds as they ministered to her, like twin
parakeets debating a worm. As they coached her in movements
of preposterous feminacy, coaxing her to sit neatly and ease her
muscles out of sight. Scald Ibis saw also that the two geishas, Aki
and Fuyu, Fall and Winter, allowed no real intimacy with men.
She wondered at two such highly paid women arriving in the
wake of the invading army, grooming girls in houses of prostitution, trying to breach the language barrier and wishing the bewildered Chinese girls well without telling them much at all.
Were they here for show, then?

That evening, Scald Ibis felt awkward and out of place, disin-
clined to sing or curtsey. Pleading illness, she sidled upstairs to
talk with her father, calling him "old mole" and "paper cutter"
through the slit in the paper screen, anxious to tell him, yet
daunted by the night's events. She remembered groping for the
light switch in the darkened villa, back in the old days, and
lurching into the wall as she tried to flip down what was already
down, or upward what was up, too lazy to feel at the little toggle first.

With a houseful, Hayashi would be on his mettle and would
settle the hash of anyone at all, just to show what a tight house
he ran. What an occupation for a colonel, she thought; but she
had not seen him clip little strips of paper and paste them in
place on a sheet already in the typewriter, angling and planting
with the mellow finesse of the master surgeon, his breath released only as the graft slipped into place and the error died.

Even while being schooled in geisha gentleness, she witnessed something else she failed to understand. After a great
deal of shouting outside in Japanese and German, a perspiring
overclad heavy-featured man of middle age burst through the
doorway, raising his arm in the Nazi salute and pointing first to
the Nazi armband, then to some order of the Iron Cross on his
front. "Do you know what this stands for?" he asked in cum-

bersome Japanese. Everyone laughed. "This is the highest dec-
oration in the country. Now, stop all slaughter outside or I will
ask the Führer to intervene personally." More laughter. Someone led him out, flattering him the whole way in a German less
than that of the poet Rilke.

"He doesn't like blood," someone said through a yawn.

"Soft-hearted Nazi," one general said.

"Wipe his nose."

"Wipe anything."

Scald Ibis wished she had stayed upstairs with her father.
What soothed her most was to creep up there and lie down by
the paper screen without his hearing her, and then sedate old
memories eased her to tears that nonetheless soothed.

Judging the present situation in China from the point of view of military preparation against the Soviet Union, I am convinced that if our military power permits it, we should deliver a blow first of all upon the Nanking regime to get rid of the menace at our back. If our military power will not permit us to take such a step, I think it proper that we keep a strict watch on the Chinese government so that they do not lay a single hand on our present undertakings in China until our national defense system is completed.

GENERAL HIDEKI TOJO, TELEGRAM, JUNE 9, 1937

SCALD IBIS WAS LIVING HER LIFE ONE RAPE AT A TIME, ONE DAY, one shock. To get away from there, leaving her father behind, was impossible; to escape with him was out of the question. The streets were fatal, and, besides, there was nowhere to go, no one to tell, no police, no officials, no lawyers, no nurses, no doctors. There was virtually no Nanking, so the Tent of Orange Mist was some kind of sanctuary, to be endured until—well, she couldn't think of the year. It did not have a date on it. She had no idea that the attack on Nanking had set a new low for moral depravity, that the signal for sudden attack was to wave a white flag, that Japanese soldiers were often stood in double file and ordered to slap each other's faces until the blood ran. The other girls took whatever was meted out to them, like so many doves in an earthquake, lucky so long as they were alive. To them, Scald Ibis was la-di-da, a fancy-school snob who deserved all she got, one who curried favor and made excuses to run upstairs. If becoming a geisha meant behaving like that, they'd sooner be whores, lying down with disease, getting up with Japs.

Scald Ibis was beginning to work things out: consort with Hayashi and slowly turn him into—a name she knew from her literature classes—her Pygmalion. A geisha was an "art person," after all, required only to converse, but all the more beguiling if she sang between recitals of the most intimate gossip. Many a young girl, she knew, started out by being sold to some organization or other that trained geishas. She would then emerge into the so-called world of willows and flowers and, bit by bit, pay off her parents' debt.

If geishas were lucky, they married well, often men associated with the theater; if unlucky, they became tutors, making love to wearisome echoes of themselves. They also laughed, which Scald Ibis had not done for days, and slept, which she had been unable to do from being fidgety. She was hardly even a beginner-geisha, and Hayashi was not the man to teach her, unless he knew more than he pretended—more than dumbshow let him say. The thing, therefore, was to practice in private in the storeroom, testing out her voice, her demeanor, her concision of movement. Up there she could sing off-tune, and they would think she was one of the few surviving birds in Nanking. It was simple once you thought things out. Although the officers would use her several times nightly, she could spend her daytime hours learning a role and a career. And her father could look through the slit in the paper.

Fretting about ways of dealing with Hayashi, she thought back to the parties her mother and father threw in the villa: high minds of all kinds, invited there, as Hong had often said, to keep the right people in touch with one another, but really to bring them together under his approving and censorious eye. Since he could not have them all to little dinner parties, or chose not to, he rounded them up every three months or so and perambulated through the throng. In this way he could gratify those he didn't want to talk to but liked to watch, and spend time with those he liked, creating the impression of having thrown a successful big party conducted as a series of long, intimate chats. Sometimes he just drifted away into the garden, leaving them all to wonder about him and worry. Hong wanted reputation, and he got it, never explaining his behavior, never changing it. At each party, when he was in the room, he would be mentally checking his invitation lists, considering whom to drop even as he put on his most charming face, balancing their gaffes with their virtues, grading them in orange-red, wondering whom to reactivate on the guest list, who had died, who had risen in the world, who had sunk. He hated parties, but he liked to be seen giving them.

THE PUCCINI
MINEFIELD

*Censorship was tight. But there is enough in the way of
photographs and even film footage (mostly taken by Western
missionaries) to give an impression.*

Ian Buruma, *The Wages of Guilt*, "Nanking," p. 113

EVEN THOUGH SHE WAS NOT FOUR HUNDRED YEARS OLD AND HER memory not that long or wide, Scald Ibis somehow fished out from the cold anecdotal isinglass of history one Sandro Somatti, a wry, astute Jesuit born in 1539, soundingly known as Visitor to the East, as if he were the only visitor ever, as if the Orient were a college. Sandro Somatti, S.J., had run the college in Macerata, in fact, until instructed to flood the Asian mission with a new spiritual zeal. Off he went in 1574, doting on the idea of a purged, extroverted, loving church, almost a vast dark animal presence into whose pelt he nuzzled, knowing that one century soon geography would be different, communication and conversion would be faster, and the source of piety would be everywhere.

"They came in hundreds," she told the other girls, "as if somebody had told them China needed to be put right. And Japan as well. The odd thing about them was that they all had to be virgins. Honest." The others tittered, then cackled, laughing with world-weary derision. They didn't believe it. "Now, this Somatti," she persisted, "he was better than most of them. I heard all about him in school, so it's bound to be true. He didn't really want to come, but they told him it would make a great man of him, and, besides, my loves, he might have thought he'd get away with some dirty sexy stuff on the side. Out of sight, out of mind. Even priests like to get it up now and then." They laughed again, less derisively. A new subject of conversation had been born, unlikely and preposterous as her Somatti seemed to them.

Intentional master of a continent's soul, Somatti took with him a number of *confessi*, Jews who had converted to Christianity, whom he regarded as challenges, grafts, misled reaspirers. Alas, Portuguese India proved a hellhole, corrupt and devious, and Somatti began to part mentally the dark Asians, whom he thought as bad as the Africans he called "brute beasts," from the paler-skinned Chinese and Japanese.

She pried him loose from where he had been, from the beliefs and people he had been involved with, and made of him something to talk about, somebody to tell about, even though, clever and precocious as she was—her father's glowing golden parrot—she did not quite have the vocabulary with which to do him justice. And of course, although she now knew something of the bustling, coarse side of masculinity, she lacked insight into the male soul, especially the soul of a proselytizing Jesuit. She nonetheless equipped him with libido and introversion, Hayashi needs and mandarin expertise. She began to tell the girls more and more about him, not so much embellishing as dragging him down to the good earth.

Somatti's mind flowed on, voluptuously comparing Greek to Chinese. She remembered him writing to his old rhetoric teacher, Martin Fornari, "There is so much ambiguity in Chinese that many words can signify more than a thousand things, and at times the only difference between one word and another is the way you pitch them high or low in four different tones." The language thrilled and appalled him, but Scald Ibis's account of his response to it left them cold; they were waiting for the sexy bits. Scald Ibis persisted, reluctant to waste her education. " 'They have as many letters,' " she recited him as writing, " 'as there are words and things, so that there are more than seventy thousand of them, every one quite different and complex.' " It was not so much a language as a population, yes. And then: no mood, no tense, no gender, no number, no cases, no articles, not so much a language as an informal music. He loved the Chinese, and *Chinese*, belittling even the recent feat the church had accomplished, converting the King of Bungo—lord of five Japanese kingdoms. Truly, he found the Japanese the most deceitful and insincere people of all, no longer white and piously simple, as he had once thought them, but cruel, depraved, hypocritical, permanent Buddhists whatever else they professed: in a way almost blustering Lutherans. All they had to do was invoke Amida and they would be saved. They just went along with the Jesuit missionaries, humoring them, knowing that the real religion lay in their own hands. The girls fidgeted at Scald Ibis's impenitent learning, wishing she'd get on with it, defer more to her audience, none of whom had been to a fancy school.

Now, nonetheless, she had Somatti deciding the Chinese were whiter, more capable, better bred: no weapons in China; they beat one another until they bled, but they never went in for decapitation. Raucous chuckles greeted this, as if the girls thought decapitation something else, far sleazier. Scald Ibis went on, getting strange shivers from them as she spelled out an ancient Italian's account of a culture they knew only too well. The laughter ebbed. "The Chinese," she told them, "tear their hair out so as to stay bald. That's what he said."

"What a fathead," she heard. "What a turdypoo."

"He said a lot of strange things," she answered, "back then. He couldn't get used to walled towns, long clothes, the usual old stuff. Stop giggling or I'll tell you no more." She knew, but did not intend to waste time telling, about how Somatti had groped for an exact contrast that dismissed the Japanese; he wanted to condemn Japanese quietude, their finicky civility, their short clothing, their preoccupation with weapons, and their indifference to learning. Back then, he had blathered on to himself, as sickened and unbalanced as if he were again making the sea voyage from Goa to Macao. "Actually," she told them, with a pretty, sensuous inflection, "he wasn't very good at condemning people, even those he hated. He played favorites, fickle as a nun. It didn't matter to him that the Chinese attitude to food was nearly European (which pleased him) whereas the Japanese one was barbaric (which revolted him), but that the Chinese language was just about as unwieldy as the world of things. You know, a language is supposed to make it easier to *manage* things." Were they getting it? Did they care? Yawns, giggles, shivers, and little abandoned farts told her no. The girls were listening to her much as they audited the birds of morning at their meaningless toots.

"From things," she told herself, knowing her audience had gone to sleep, "you go to words. That's what Papa always says. And there you are, back among things again. At least in Chinese you are. Chinese is the same flux as the flux of the world. Well, similar, anyway. Tell them that? I'd as soon explain the place of the whelk in yacht building." Back then, in the old haphazard days, Somatti was coughing his Chinese cough, beating his chest to quell the tickle, trying in the midst of his eye-tearing confusion to sort out his prejudices, reminding himself how discreet and unassuming Chinese women were, and hardly ever seen in public, whereas Japanese women were all over the place, and loosely behaved. The Chinese had little use for priests, those so-called bonzes, which made them open to Christianity, while the Japanese showed theirs the most blatant respect. The

Chinese were entertaining and lively, the Japanese verbose and dithering. Yes, a nation of ditherers until you put a sword in their hands. The Chinese, no surprise, he thought, disdain outsiders whereas the Japanese fall into a frenzy over them, inviting them in and fussing them. The Chinese are orderly and disciplined, with a reliable system of government, as far as I can see, while the Japanese thrive on muddle. In fact, the Japanese are quite willfully the opposite of the Chinese. How could I ever have thought otherwise? When I have learned enough Chinese to condemn the Japanese in it, I am going to write a book called *Western Memory Techniques: Hsi-kuo-chi-fa.*

Slave-driven as she was, she nonetheless felt she was marinating in that old cantankerous Jesuit mind, rather than succumbing to the lascivious onslaught of the monkey men. What was that old priest going to do? He was going to write a book full of Seneca and Cicero. Why was she here among girls to whom Seneca and Cicero were (perhaps) toothpaste or boot polish? Anyway, old Somatti did it, he wrote his book; and for an instant of pure gratuitous heraldry she observed him, childless, worrying about an erudite young girl brought naked into a cordon of soldiers by means of a cord around her neck and made to pleasure them. Chattering ably to her contemporaries, fudging up just about anything historical, rather than artistic, to tell them, she took advantage of that distant, touchy altruist, borrowing him slavishly against the end of her ordeal, battening on to his whims and prejudices, updating him as a savior, seeing him, so to speak, cringe toward her as he saw her on the floor, thrusting his arms behind him high as if to keep them clean, but crouching while shrinking, murmuring, What have they done to this child? As much of him wanted to go and write Greek or Latin as wanted to stay and help. The arms took flight as the body dithered in its cassock. Had he ever had a mother who warmed his cassock before he went out, wrapping him up tight against the blustery wind of the world?

She soon had him Ibisized, updated, thrust into a rough

Japanese uniform, into a brothel even, and regaled the others with compact stories of his shame and pain as the lustful side of his nature tugged on him, making him harden and turn relentless. "He stiffened, but he didn't do it," she told Qiu in the midst of a squeezing kiss that toured from eyebrow past cheek and mouth to the brow on the other side. "He didn't go that far, but he knew what an astounding thing grew beneath his tunic, not to be shown to anyone, or used for sex." And, because he had to be chaste, she made him randy, at least in her tales for the girls, who took up the theme and her lead with ease, both domesticating Somatti as their joint husband and making him into a two-dimensional roué upon whom they foisted their own immature lewdness. Kisses, hugs, strokes, pats, tickles all played a part in the compacts on the bed, usually Scald Ibis's, and a tradition grew among them of nameless groping, fingering, probing, which being nameless were inoffensive. There they lay in the putrid darkness, feeling one another up, listening to Scald Ibis's Somatti yarns and adding lewd bits of their own to his helpless performance as invalid cocksman. The stories were about Somatti and his cock: how he hung washing on it, dug vegetables out of the soil, bathed it, flogged it, and choked it with tiny lanyards to keep it down. In Scald Ibis's unruly hands, he became their lightning conductor.

WHEN HONG FIRST SPOKE TO SCALD IBIS ABOUT THE RAPE OF
Nanking, his voice quavered through the slit, almost as if he
didn't quite believe what he told. The soldiers were all drunk; it
was the army disease. There were too few military police. Too
many of the Japanese troops were peasants recruited without
much thought for the rage and disappointment they had built
up while tending their fields. "They slap them all the time," he
said, "to degrade and humiliate them, almost like breaking the
spirit of a dog. The officers smack them as if they were babies.
What do they tell them? Loot all, burn all, kill all. They regard
all non-Japanese as inferior beings, even you and me, even the
British and the Americans. These soldiers have been told death

is sublime and gorgeous, easily the best thing that can happen to them, or anybody else. They regard their own wives and children as scum, so you can't expect them to do very well with Chinese and Koreans. They will use just about anyone for bayonet drill. They believe violence is an art form. The more violent they are, the better they are serving the emperor. Some of them are insane: they began insane or they go insane. They will cut livers out of living people, all in a clinical mood, just to see what the livers look like, and the people without them. They like bloodthirsty novelty. This is why, daughter, you must keep out of the streets. You have heard the shouts, the whistles, the bugles. They never cease, they resort to water and electric tortures. Indeed they do so many appalling things that, according to the most attuned spirits remaining to us, ghost fires go on burning, never die out. Fires so intense they burn the hands and faces of soldiers." His voice sounded clogged and shrill.

"Ghost fires?" she asked. "That sounds interesting."

"Not to you," he told her, with what sounded like a thwarted kiss from behind the screen. It would have been easier to talk to him in the room proper, with his eyes to watch, his hands to clasp as he recited the truth about the invaders, and the mystifying phenomena that arrived in their wake to terrorize the Chinese who survived. "Ghost fires, daughter, are a warning. Evil is shifting over from the everyday to the transcendent. Human behavior has been so bad that phantom swirls like powdered rice blow in upon us, telling us our pain has not gone ignored."

"By whom?" She never liked it when he talked this way, hypothesizing a moral dimension to the little, dreadful events of the world.

That would come later, he told her, knowing that in the worst circumstances, when all seemed lost, you never turn your back on superstition. It would see you through and sometimes incinerate a fleeing enemy. And sometimes it acted like a samurai in reverse, as when it assumed the form of their fabled *i-ai* stroke of the sword, done straight from the scabbard and maiming your enemy from the first. "They lack nitrogen because they eat fish, canned vegetables, and too much rice. They oil their shoes; they do not speak when heading into the wind; and, if you look, especially into the mouths of the dead, you will find a leaf they have sucked on to keep their mouths moist. They are quite diabolical, so it's not much of a surprise that forces of good in the universe come after them to chastise, to cauterize, to electrocute. I myself call it avenger lightning. You have to look at them. They shave only once a week. Some of them have their uniforms on back to front and, accustomed to clogs or sandals, walk with chronic blisters caused by boots, but they keep on coming. They never stop."

Scald Ibis had some idea of what went on outside, but this was too much. She wanted to leap into the arms of Colonel Hayashi, keep him erotically busy lest he send a pair of thugs upstairs to poke around. She was only sixteen, but the notion of death began to drift into her mind, first amazing her that a nation's soldiers could be so willing to be wiped out, wholly disregarding bombs, bullets, grenades, shrapnel, torpedoes, pits ablaze, and planks with nails driven through. Then it struck her that anyone afflicted with the fear of death should fix on the eons before she was born, on the unknowable blank of all that. Before birth, you were not aware of all you were missing, of all the lives going on without you. You had utterly no sense of previousness, of having missed something. So, too, with death, she thought; there goes along with it no awareness of anything, even though you are no doubt going to be dead longer than you were unborn. Maybe not. She could not figure it out, but she knew there was no mental agony involved. Death returned you to the unborn state, but full of memory, ripe with use. Waiting for so long to be born had not affected her one way or another. Yet the idea worried her, because the newly born had nothing to be deprived of, had acquired nothing, had nothing to lose, whereas the dying person was on the brink of morbid dispossession.

"You'll be all right," Hong told her. "Just stick to the rules.

The Japanese have it all worked out. They turn green when dead. They smell so bad after being left in the field a few days that sentries have to cover their noses with rags drenched in ammonia." He had to tell her something, based on his days in the army, watching atrocity build to fever pitch. He had found out a great deal while skulking away from the gunfire, and he knew that a soldier who cannot blink his eyes will be dead at dawn; one who cannot speak has only two days to live; one who has to urinate lying down only three; one who can sit up, twenty, and one who can rise to his feet, a month. Scald Ibis heard him fall silent, reluctant to tell her any more, but shoving his hand through the slit, seizing hers, trying to make from a handclasp an almost crystalline reassurance that allowed her to advance to twenty, whisked forward by one of those ghost fires, so as to survive, able to look at things with the eyes of a mature woman. She sang something elegiac to him even as Hong wrapped himself again in his Japanese flag, safe within an enemy veneer, and once more shifted his position. The slit had begun to tear from all that use, so before she left she used glue and paper to seal it up again, at least the corners, and went away downstairs mouthing a prayer for his silence, immobility, calm.

A sixteen-year-old's version of death is likely to be generous, drawing out from that state its warmest, most genial elements, and Scald Ibis exercised her privilege of dating death always from eighty or ninety years old, as far away as possible, certainly not from sixteen. Last years, she understood, however, as being devoted to the mere consumption of time: not doing anything special or grand, but just counting breaths or heartbeats, listening to the viscous stealth of peristalsis, the snuffle in the sinuses. You waited like that German, Doctor Faust, for them to come and take you. Perhaps that was what her father was going through upstairs, trapped but looking with jolly self-denial at the slit through which a bayonet or a whiff of poison gas would come to fell him, send him rattling back down the chimney, no need for a trellis.

She wondered about a different hiding place, but there was none suitable for winter; he would have to hang on in there, and she would feed him with loyal despondency, urging him to flex his muscles every hour, and not to look for trouble. Hayashi had already asked her in Japanese where the houseboy was, and why he did so little, but she had not understood. Not that there was much to do beyond a bit of dawn sweeping, garbage to remove and burn. Hong cut the figure of the anonymous, obsequious coolie, making up in servility what he lacked in skill. He had evolved his own special kind of work: he squirmed, he groveled, he contracted his body as if his destination were a pupa, and somehow the less room he occupied the more he seemed to be working. And he wondered what they would do to him if they found out he slept in a Japanese flag, swathed in rising sun. The very notion kept him a peck warmer, but he longed for huge billowing eiderdowns, gray-and-brown stone hot-water bottles, warming pans with long handles and a lidded dish of hot coals at the end: in short, bed warmers filched from the British, who knew about these things.

Already, to keep him company, he had folded together several origami birds, and glued them to the interior brickwork: sharp white silhouettes, dovelike, announcing the end of war. His droppings landed behind the little trapdoor at ground level and froze during the night. The door was unlikely to open again, so anyone hunting him would have to start at the level above and climb the rest of the way. When roaches and centipedes crawled over him, he stroked them back, believing in befriending all alien worlds except that of the Japanese. To calm himself, he entered into cosmic speculations about the beginning of the universe. Once, he told himself, there was nothing; why then was there not always nothing? In the dark he made and remade a proto universe out of bubble gum, squeezing and squeezing it until, as he pretended, it exploded in his hands. He knew he had cheated, though: the ball had nowhere to be in, because all the space there was ever going to be was within the ball, all hunched up. Yet . . . he had heard such things at the university, or at those parties he gave. What had always amazed him was the fervor of those who talked cosmology; he had expected them to be tentative and diffident, but they all insisted as if they knew, like the Christian pope. Positive opinions in the absence of evidence amused him no end, and it was at parties that he had developed one of his most annoying mannerisms, always adding *soi disant*, "so-called," when he alluded to anyone, as in "Chu Feng, cosmologist, *soi disant*." One visiting professor, an Englishman with thick, intricate glasses and a name for writing sexy poems about women undressing, would always introduce himself by name, then pause to see if the name registered, and add "Unvivaed Oxford First," to which Hong would murmur "*soi disant*," which said who the hell cared. People with unvivaed Oxford Firsts didn't end up in China, he grumbled, unless they had committed a serious sexual offense, in which case China would make them behave.

To keep calm, he prayed in his own way, not to gods, but to forces, bidding them to salvage him and his family as virtuous, unharmful folk addicted to art, calligraphy, and good taste. He knew how unforgiving the Japanese rabble had been, brutally cutting off the heads of those whom bullets failed to kill, but never too fast or too neat. He knew he had failed his family; as soon as Shanghai was attacked, they should have gone, clambering aboard some rickety biplane, ending up in Hong Kong or Macao, like several of his friends. If only, he thought, he had been a more consequential man, with a power complex and a knowledge of military history. Yet he knew the difference between historical and ontological trauma, the first of which came from war, the second merely from being alive.

Even if he hanged himself in the chimney, he had no guarantee that Scald Ibis would escape; indeed, his death would only worsen things. There were bound to be investigations, beatings, beheadings. He decided to stay alive: a suicide needed a firm context, and besides it was too Japanese a thing for him to do. It would be like a misquotation. Nonetheless, he was not being quite rational. Hour by hour, although surviving on rice and leftovers from the officers' rations, he found himself trembling, flexing limbs hard to keep them from going numb. His penis itched. He shoved it through the slit and left it there to dry, at least until the day Cixi grabbed it and guided it flaccid into her mouth, where it hardened while she cursed the Japanese for abasing her to such readiness. Hong half-expected a sword to amputate, but in some dither between horror and hope he left himself exposed, and Cixi finished a chore now familiar to her, herself wondering if anyone would care.

"What I got," asked the stunned but pragmatic Cixi, whose speech when she was weary allowed itself a Chinese lisp, "is no rhythm. When they axes me stuff, I says Whaddya thinks I got here, a liberry? It a hair-y, not a liberry."

"Yaw berry," said Meng, the snippiest girl in Nanking at the time, "sure better-looking every day. They crazy for dat berry."

"Till it wear out." Cixi no optimist.

"These Japanese," Qiu was murmuring in her semisophisti-cated, liquor-darkened voice, "has not lost their homes. How they going to understand us? No home to go to, 'less this dump."

"You watch out." Scald Ibis snapped without energy.

So shocked by their treatment—regular but polite violation—they lacked the intellectual stamina to be surprised at being alive. They just plodded on, young but used, pretty but hypno-tized by history, their minds muffled.

"Once upon a time," Qiu began, "they was Catholic priests come and get you out of this kind of shit. They was missionar-ies. Where all the missionaries gone? Always the first to get their guts cut out." She began to rock, forward and back, then side to side, as if overwound.

"Christians!" Cixi made the sign of the cross.

Meng sneered and said, "Sleepy-time, girls. Quick."

HAIR GOING WHITE, A DISMAL WIND-SEETHE OF PHLEGM IN HIS
chest, her Somatti was brooding again, as he mostly did when
she was not narrating him direct but possessing him for herself.
His brooding was an act nobody could recall anyway: a nonce-
tic of the interim, such as his picking at his nose or wafting away
from his face an invisible wasp. He was brooding, she knew, on
a Chinese custom honored more in the breach than in the ob-
servance. A thousand cuts, she had heard, would be inflicted on
some poor devil: thief, murderer, missionary, in loathsome
crescendo, and she wondered what anyone's chances were of
eluding such a fate. To be stippled thus with knives—here came
Somatti's gorge rising, bile returning too far into his mouth and

making him go for water. What a brutal nation, these Chinese.

This was Somatti, opining.

But also Scald Ibis picking him up from sideband splashes of radio ether.

She was making him more Somatti than he had ever been before, gifting him with modern say-so, newfangled know-how: anachronizing him. All Orientals, he decided, were brutal at root; they just had a crueler sense of ceremony than other peoples.

Now she told them again, and he stopped brooding. "He had joined the Society of Jesus when he was twenty-seven, after a so-called religious experience in which fishing boats at anchor seemed to flame and bleed." That got them. "Silk trade, humoring the feudal lords of Japan, dressing his priests in the manner of Zen Buddhist monks, which they in the end agreed to." With boyish exuberance, she added mentally: "And he sent off to Rome and its Pope the four Christian samurais Tintoretto painted in 1582. Imagine that clash of worlds. You didn't know about that, did you? Never mind." It was for her, and those like her. As it had been for Somatti, it now became so for her; she, too, a missionary of sorts. It was like founding a honeycomb in the Caucasus. It had not been easy for him, nor had it been wholly worthwhile. As for her. Misgivings and irrational hatreds surged up from the seabed of his brain and corrupted him. She had felt this, too, harrowing and deflecting her. On the whole, she remembered, he would have preferred Padua or the college in Macerata. Tell the girls that? No. He did not like the shape or mien of Orientals, and he knew all this high-minded pressure to adopt an alien faith would drive them berserk. How could she tell unlettered girls, recently traumatized, about things like that? Somatti found himself padding his words with aimless conjectural phrases which she uttered for their inane delectation: "in those days," "which was when we," and (more and more often) "where will all of this end?" One of the girls had hiccups, another was farting hugely, and yet another was gasping in indecipherable pain. It was as if, she decided, Somatti had to know the inevitable context of all that happened, unsatisfied with mere events and wanting the design, the direction, the trend, the undertone, the drift. He was full of foreboding about the past, stationing himself among old crises. He had elegies galore, ready for the future, and the present was a continuous amber shock one day to be identified as the vacant doodling of God. He wanted to undo all he had done and then go home to Italy, wanting no hand in the pious mutilation of China and Japan. Slowly, he turned against all nations, at last recognizing that he wasn't going to like any of the people out here, though he found their habits and languages fascinating. He needed to give up the remainder of his life and come back between, say, 1850 and 1870, a random choice, or even 1900 and 1910 (presuming he would not survive as long—the later he came back, the shorter his stay would be). How was this possible? To whom, beyond His Holiness, did one apply? If you were butchered in this life, like Jesus (a thousand cuts), did you come back as a succulent steak? His mind had a disgraceful sense of caricature, turning piety and history against themselves, garbling them into a putrid flux. Scald Ibis had surrendered to him quite, in bliss.

"Sorry," he said to a young priest who had asked after his health out in strident sunlight amidst the lancing winter wind, "I am dreaming of the future. It has a cross-eyed fever." He took the proffered beaker of water.

"Sir?" The young priest conducted a tiny smile around his face like a pet animal, then laughed outright.

"The penalty of a thousand cuts," Somatti said in his spare baritone. Now Scald Ibis knew where she had heard of this before: rolling toward her like a war wagon.

"Only a rumor, sir." The young man was shocked. The young woman was relieved that her conjuring up of an old priest's radiant nightmares had at least a shred of accuracy.

"It's the heathen crucifixion," Somatti sighed. She heard him sighing in, what was that language he sighed in? Italian. "He talked Italian all the time," she told the girls. Then her mind played her false: I only saw him for an innocent, she thought, intending an instant; he was an operation (whereas she meant apparition). Then it was over: she was talking and thinking normally again, as demoted as a letter forwarded.

Culling the most colorful materials from his monochrome life, Scald Ibis told what she thought she remembered, not for a moment thinking there might be other rememberers who recalled Somatti differently, who would install her version of him as only so much icing on a big, slaty theological cake. Scald Ibis was his tabloid reporter, doomed to exploit him for restricted ends, an unsavable Scheherazade reciting not to save herself but to numb time and eat it. She invented all manner of trivial things, gave most of Hayashi's, converting Somatti into the bogeyman of the Tent of Golden Mist, recalled with impunity from history with its sulfurous, grandfatherly stink; he was not so much a man who had *been* as an impromptu figment, obscene yet pious: an odd mix, about whom the other girls made up their own timid stories. He was someone to reach to, someone worth making fun of, someone demonstrably eternal. Yet why he? It was he, a frog spawn of bits and pieces, who had surfaced in her maltreated mind: the only external figure she might mess with in order to purge herself while maintaining contact with the girl she had been, a fusion of embryonic pedant and esthetic fugitive. Her father had told her about Somatti, and the lesson had stuck, only to reappear as Somatti confetti, Somatti abused, Somatti transfigured, Somatti narrowed down. Somatti was a distraction.

And he was off again, back to the pump, desperate to swill his vocal cords with water. The young priest with the permanent red nose went to help, aware only of Somatti's need to drink, knowing nothing of what occupied him severely this January morning: Where would the first of the thousand cuts be, and then the second, the third? Did they begin with an eyelid, a finger tip, a nipple? Somatti shuddered at all the cutting to come, long after he had gone to his indeterminate reward among the billowing cumulus. All he had done in China and Japan would not help the future. Bloodbaths I have known and stepped into, he mused. What is this prophetic sense I have of something dark and massive hovering above the most trivial thing I do? Is it just a weather metaphor gone wrong, blown up out of all proportion, or a genuine tuning-in to God, who says not to bother: what we achieve here is a mere ripple on the unchanging face of depravity.

He could see the abused young girl no more and began to wonder in what hovel or hole she now reposed. writhing and bloody.

How much of this Scald Ibis knew, reclaimed, bumped her head into, will never be known. Up into the light Somatti came, nightly mutilated but bringing with him entire tableaux of unmitigated seriousness that she could hardly pass on to Qiu and the rest, but an erotic find nonetheless: denied sex yet sexual, not a rapist but a self-flagellant, someone worth making into a scarecrow, a patron saint, a local gargoyle. They heard her murmuring about him and took him at face value as if she had been introducing them to Odysseus or Aeneas. Somatti was sort of on their side, a professional forgiver, an assuager-revenant, a pal in subfusc and sometimes black silk. And, fished up by her for them, he brought with him countless other reverberations such as would appeal to Hong or Hayashi even. He was the man from ages past who proved that what was new between China and Japan was old, after all, just the latest variation of the old theme that Japan was derivative and China was not, that the more a Westerner saw of the Orient the more he yearned for home. Perhaps Hayashi, if he had known of a Jesuit priest inaccurately remembered but wafting anyway into the furnace of history without needing to change prejudices, would have slit his belly open, recognizing futility when he met it. A man four centuries old had become more real to Scald Ibis than anyone else, an Italian at that. Ghosts had more clout with the living than reformers or invaders did. A querulous cleric saw the terror in history long before it began, a comfort woman his catalyst.

HONG HAD ALWAYS DELIGHTED TO BE, AS HE PUT IT, IN THE THICK of things, by which he meant not mere profuseness or plenty, but at the center of discord, especially of the kind that exploded when one of his parties included a number of movie stars, Chinese ones anyway. He thrilled when those famous faces surrounded him, creating an unmade movie in which he starred, an evening on which reality and illusion fused. It was hard to tell if he was at a party in a movie or with actors at a party. Someone filming the events of that evening would have complicated the question no end. He looked at them looking at him and knew he had irreversibly changed the world, easing celebrities out of their churlish introversion down to the level of lamb and goat butchers or the lard in which everyone cooked.

Knowing how much the Chinese adored secrecy, he opened his guests up, with a word, a grimace, moving through them so fast (he was nimble, light) that a tour of the room was just long enough for him to say the word and then return in time to witness its first impact on the revered and flattered face. Sarcasm, irony, innuendo, double entendre were his little scalpels cutting home to the ego. All he had to do was gather some stars together, promising each a memento of the evening, and they would begin to work on one another, grating, colliding, one taking fire from another's overt indifference, another warming to the hostility in another's gaze. One of his favorite lines, for which an entire retinue of guests would wait, aching for him to get it off his chest, was "Now all the good-looking men have had their say, it's time for the geniuses to get a look-in." He meant he was the only genius there, of course; it was his royal plural. His guests, who loved him for his wit and gifts, applauded always. It was the simplest way to get him off his high horse.

Superb calligrapher that he was, he was a superb speaker as well, able to hypnotize an audience and make it wait him out, whether he talked politics or art. He adored movies, which endeared him to the actors; he needed that surreptitious form, to which he would sneak in the afternoons, entering the cavern like a gratified pervert, knowing that only the most acute observers could observe him observing. What appealed to him most of all was the way the reel unwound on that big windmill of a mirror, before which he lay passively. Gifts brought to one of his birthday parties had once included six mirrors. For once, then as now, he was not responsible; the brightness of the universe sagged into the putrid barrel of the night-soil man with his mule cart, and Hong knew it was no human's fault. The world depended on waning, faltering, continual painful subtraction.

Some called Hong a pessimist, but he was not a pessimist about hope, zeal, or faith; he was pessimistic only about the lack of these things and the constant appetite for mediocrity. It had impressed him deeply when he heard that Japanese troops were submitted to special tests during their training. Each man had to eat a bowl of rice while sitting under the corpse of a hanged man, alive only that morning and chosen at random to be the display piece of the exercise. China, he thought, could do with something so radical, just to get it moving. Would he himself have been able to finish his bowlful? He thought so; but that was only a test of callousness, of muscle control. What if the dangling cadaver were that of his daughter, wife, son? What then? Did success in life imply the ability to perform unspeakable acts as a manifest of self-control? He had often thought there should be Chinese samurai, less gruff than Japanese ones, less violent and more self-effacing, who kept the militaristic rabble at bay. He had no idea that the rabble now infesting his villa included a man obsessed with stamp collecting, a colonel who, despite his standing and title, was essentially an aide-de-camp to generals.

Enclosed in the fireplace, Hong relived his best parties, but always ended up saying good night to Anna May Wong, either in fact or in a dream state, marveling at her talc-white face, her characteristic expression of disinfected hauteur. His most precious possessions included several English cigarette cards of her with a write-up on the back. She was world-famous, but even more so for being at his parties, where her fellow actors bowed to her as to a goddess.

He had once told her that he survived only by resorting to what he called accommodation ploys. For instance, he had never been able to abide the thought that his mother was dead since she seemed always alongside him, opining and soothing. He had managed to save his wits by slipping two photographs of her grave into the long envelope in which he kept an assortment of stamps. Each time he selected one, he would glimpse the photographs and so steel his mind, associating his mother with the mail, always going or coming, thus according her a mode of return, or, if not that, some role in the nimbus of farewell that surrounded the envelope. Because he had had the courage to set her among the transient, he reaped the benefit of having her among the unexpected arrivals: letters from the British Museum, the Metropolitan Museum of Art, the Louvre.

When he told Anna May Wong this, she cupped his face in her porcelain hands and kissed him on the brow, murmuring that with such sensibility he should make films. He did, he told her, in his calligraphy, murmuring in return something on the brink of incoherence about a mouse's having only six whiskers and a springy brush's requiring scores of them, and hence dilution of the brushhead with hairs from raccoon, sheep, sable, deer, and cat. They agreed to shoot a movie about calligraphy, which they never shot, but the intention always glowed in her face, and he could detect it in the aroma that came off her of mulled salmon swathed in a potent scent from Paris.

"Such tenderness in a man," Anna would say.

"Gone to waste," he'd answer, eyes brimming.

"We must work together," she told him.

"In heaven," he answered, "so long as we remain on speaking terms."

She would scoff and add, "We always have this conversation. We always will. If we keep saying the same thing to each other, just like this, with nothing extraneous allowed, we will never quarrel."

He would look for her in heaven, he said, and she demurely concurred.

As a child, Scald Ibis had been as unlike her father as possible, not so much social as a miniature natural historian, gently seizing a spider as it ambled toward her and cupping it captive in her hand, showing it to friends and strangers, often caching it in a pocket. She doted on insects, but was forbidden to bring them into the house; those she found indoors to begin with, however, she was not forced to evict. She kept them by her, fastidiously retained, and invented names for them. Baffled by her father's way of greeting children—a cuffed ear followed at once by an embrace—Scald Ibis waited and waited for the cuff, but he exempted her from it, though not her brother. A born transcendentalist, she excelled at seeing the good in things, and she developed the knack of making everything work to her advantage, at an early age assuming a mature point of view that saw all as useful, even colds, bronchitis, measles: part of nature's deployed radiance, though a little threatening. She seemed indiscriminately grateful. If Hong had managed to learn these things from her, he would have been a happier man, less dependent on the factitious.

A personage less likely to put up with life in a chimney's top would have been hard to find, but he had enormous self-discipline, to a point; he would endure almost anything for the sake of his two favorite art forms, calligraphy and film. About the perpetuation of life he was less sure. So far he had persuaded himself he was a mountaineer, stuck in an ice chimney, or an aviator frozen into fixity with his parachute. He would stay put, but not forever, and he might refuse Scald Ibis's advice, she who knew how the villa ran and how the Japanese patrolled it. He had to break out only once, and he would be counted among the Nanking drunks he had noticed while out serving in the army. The drunks were in their usual postures, lying there as always, but dead. Somehow he could not get it through his skull that his being in a room proper was more dangerous than being in the chimney; he wanted to be living normally in his own house, even if without wife and son. It was enough that he had survived so far; his survival proved he had a right to one of several rooms, a comfortable bed, some books, the usual meals, one of the better washrooms. It was not *written*, he told himself, that he should have to do without for so long, not when his daughter had the run of the house. He had been evicted from heaven, and he was running out of initiative, especially having to live through a slit in varnished paper. After popping his penis through it for the first time, he had not dared to do it again: you never knew who was in the room, you never knew who might seize a penis or do what with it. Clearly he was out of control, much as the whole of China was, and he had enough self-importance left to want to put things right, even if it was out in the street counting the dead, choosing an unknown civilian for the ultimate peace: analogous with the unknown soldier.

Life, though, as he had heard, put itself right from the center outward; so he ought to arrange family affairs first, and only then emerge into the streets, perhaps flaunting himself as a Japanese officer, slapping the faces of soldiers, yelling a falsetto imperative at them. He might get by. Perhaps he, too, would have to slash a few hapless Chinese with his sword, just to create illusion; but that couldn't be helped, not if he was to save Scald Ibis, her mother and brother. A long foray might be possible. He might smuggle her off with a lot of bluster and sword flashing. Yet where to? Where would they go? There was no transport to speak of. Most of the public buildings had gone up in flames. There was no food, fuel, light. Nanking was worse than a ghost city; it was a cipher, warm in memory, but no longer an address. It was hard to imagine Anna May Wong in such a place. If the end of the world began in Nanking now, he was bound to be part of it, perhaps recording it like a Chinese Nero on best-quality paper.

All very well, he decided, to think of heroic deeds in the streets of Nanking, where he had seen old newspapers used to stanch a bleeding abdomen; he fantasized a similar use for the most exquisite screens of calligraphy, art a blotting paper in the heathen turmoil of twentieth-century ideas and their carnage.

"I have to get out soon," he told Scald Ibis. "I will soon be the shape of a chimney."

No, he must not, she said, or they would both be done for.

"So what?" He asked with petty bravado.

"We'll wait them out. They're bound to go soon."

"Why would they go? They have Nanking—why leave it?"

She did not know how she knew, but some kinds of irrational knowledge were flawless.

"A room," he pleaded. "I need to stretch."

"Hayashi would find you. It's no good."

"As you love your father, find him some other place."

"Father, it would be a grave, if you were lucky."

"In the garden, isn't there an old well, partly filled in? Am I dreaming? It has a lid flush with the ground."

"You'd freeze, you'd die. Be still."

Hayashi wondered why the officer in charge of street dead didn't clean up outside the Tent of Orange Mist, which was after all not a clinic in bloodshed but a parlor of sexual elegance. The Tent was such a place that an officer took pride in how he entered it. Hayashi felt he was missing something, that things were not quite right in his establishment: perhaps not enough flamboyance or not enough music, though one samisen ought to suffice; or not enough servility on the part of the girls, the junior officers, the houseboy whose comings and goings looked far from straightforward. At any rate, he wanted the carnage out front removed, the whole area sluiced down, and armed guards stationed at the entrance as if the Tent of Orange Mist were at least as respectable as a railroad station.

While Hayashi mulled over his military and sexual fate, Hong the uncomfortable tried to recall something he had heard about the entire university's removing itself not only from the Japanese advance, but also from the possible range of Japanese influence. He fondled mentally the conga line of academic refugees headed for the mountains, the future of the university in the tonic air of high altitude or deep in caves, and didn't much like the idea. The entire community would march away, bearing the tools of its trade, talking learnedly week after week, actually making new discoveries en route or at least hitting on new angles, new stances. It was a lovely, scenic notion, but a poor swap for life in a chimney. Was there no way of modifying the curriculum to suit the Japanese? Not with a view to inviting them in, but merely to persuade them that what went on wasn't seditious—which of course it would be anyway. Yielding up a campus was not Hong's way of maintaining tradition; he had already lost a villa, it seemed, and the right to be seen as himself. Besides, there was something lowbrow and overdemocratic about tramping all over China with a university locked firmly in your head, to be resumed later, as the jargon had it. Hong was too empirical to tolerate any such thing, one of his tenets being that the laying on of eyes and hands mattered most: splendid the eidolon abstracted from erudite talk, but better the constant invigilation of the thing admired, peered at until the end of time, until eyes burned out and the brain declined into a chunk of glazed duck. For Hong, abstraction was a dreaded terra incognita, unusual in a man devoted to calligraphy until you recognized that, to him, calligraphy was warm and wet as gravy, a living monofilamental ectoplasm not so much to be read as journeyed through by the hungry mind, ever unreeling the thread that led back to the center of the written labyrinth. A complex man, Hong was a connoisseur's connoisseur who knew that inksticks sometimes resembled ingots of black chocolate but, even in a poor light, could be told apart from chocolate by their musty aroma.

The best ink always came from China, and bore rings showing the degree of blackness: five for blackest. He knew how the eminent calligrapher Cho Shi saved on paper by practicing on cloth so that he could wash things out and start afresh. It was said Cho Shi turned his garden's pond, where he washed his cloth, a black of five-ring caliber. It was said he began left-handed, but switched because in the left hand the brush points the hairs the wrong way and correct pressure cannot be achieved during the strokes. Through diligent practice, he became a right-handed calligrapher, but still used his left hand for ordinary chores, almost like a desert Arab using one hand for his rear end while keeping the other pure. Hong was a self-made man who had gone to his own smithy, his workshop, and re-created himself as if he were a project his mother had ill-started, she having no particular end in mind.

Hong no sooner realized that calligraphy was all than he cut himself a new destiny with a few brave, impenitent strokes, leaving behind him on his self-taught route such practical, cryptic banners as this, cast as poetry but really orders to the young:

> Wet a third only. The sucked-in ink keeps the tip springy. Soft tip, stiff at the shaft, in between mellow. Two degrees of torque, if you please, my masters, are not enough: no spring. Later an unstarched brush. The Chinese *bunjin* could depict himself, compose a poem to match, and make a seal to clinch the job.

Sometimes he thought like that now, hunched up in the warm chimney, arguing with himself that a man with a concise mind deserved a tight bolt-hole in which, just to show his mettle, he executed some exquisite calligraphy in the dark, cramped, and profoundly spent. Metaphorically speaking, he had stood guard over his piece of China, red-tasseled spear in hand, and had then quit his post, but only like an artist abandoning a work not going well—Zhuo Shi washing the design away into his soot-black pond and starting over. You could not kill a man for doing that, surely.

He was not so sure, though they might murder a man who slid his organ through a slit in the paper that sealed a fireplace. He had not been behaving well lately. Odd acts kept sprouting from the stalk of his being, no doubt in response to a Nanking without water, food, power, mail, and Englishmen, who had slipped away Empireward. There were Germans still, though, like the loudmouth with the armband, about whom Hong did not know. He considered immolating himself, administering a little cut every five minutes, so it would take him fifty hours— two days—to arrive at the desired thousand, at which point he would have all the dignity of marmalade, but would certainly have expressed his feelings about invasion, Japan, and Chiang Kai-shek, sometimes known as Chiang Cash-my-check.

Bounders and rogues were going to inherit China: not the Japanese, who had no staying power, but ideologues, lovers of abstraction, fathead fanatics. Everything had ended, and he wondered if there were anything still worth doing apart from enduring with the mind shut down, the wholesome and heavenly contribution of each individual to his so-called experience rendered null and void.

Never give in, he said. It thwarts them.

But, to be thwarted, they would have to know.

How? One could hardly announce it in the newspapers.

Skywrite it, then, using a convenient biplane.

They would shoot him down and his literate smoke would vanish into a different smoke, terminal and swollen.

When next he wiped himself, he would use pebbles instead of paper as a mark of abasement.

Then he cheered up, realizing he had broken through to a new domain of response in which he still had a choice: between killing two Japanese and killing three Japanese, his own life a mere feather, blown upon, blowing away, blown. These were the unsavory joys, he told himself, the final pleasures, though you still had room to maneuver in the small space left. Yet he could attempt nothing while Scald Ibis remained a hostage downstairs. So long as she survived, he was not a free agent, and the Japanese would poach both her and him alive in the boiler of a locomotive, just for having lived. Well, it was a Chinese tradition to arrive at everything early, as at his parties; so why not, he wondered in delicate bewilderment, do whatever you are going to do before they expect it? Fact: they expect nothing, not from a fawning houseboy. So whatever he did was all earliness. He had the Japanese completely at his mercy. Or he and his daughter did, if the two of them were willing to sacrifice themselves in the interests of a sign, a symbol, a show. Now he withdrew, shuddering, from his own thoughts, recognizing the futility of gesture, acknowledging the sense of making do. Another week, anyway. Two. A month. Good God. Surely they could hope for death before that. He should find his wife, his son. But where begin amid the carnage of a hundred thousand or more? Sit here and guess? How did one look? With hurt heart he settled into place and tried to freeze.

A scholar and a cavalier, he had already rehearsed his deathbed speech, informing those present that he had stared into the petals and branches of a tree on a summer's day, subdued his being to that mild gorgeous thrashing of boughs, and announced himself ready to be taken by the destroyer of delight, even as he inhaled the beauty of uncoordinated blooms tossing mild and gentle against the antler tracery of twigs, beckoning him, teasing him to get off his duff and melt into anonymity. He would, he told them, he truly would. "You reach for me, my dear friends," he would say, "as if we were going to play a final game of croquet on the grass, you as entranced as I by that doldrum foreign game. You come near and cart me off. The ball nears me, I strike, I miss, the ball rolls away into the cabbages, I fall, I feel that sharp pain like a sword shoved right through me, and then something monstrous and inevitable begins to suck my marrow, and I know the time has come. I vault from the greensward, lovely old poeticism, and burst through varnished paper into that ovation of newborn flowers, tossed by a little wind, but wholly undisturbed. Is it time? Oh, it was. I overstayed." He might get through some of this speech, not much, but they would know he was mindless-beneficent, dwelling on them and their names kindly to the last, whom he had loved to see at the parties he hated. He gave parties because he was on the side of life and dared not do otherwise.

ONCE AGAIN SHE CAUGHT SOMATTI'S THOUGHTS IN THE ACT OF
trailing away into the undifferentiated sluice of time, aimed (as
she liked to fancy him thinking) in the direction of incessant
newcomers, to whom history would seem no larger than a
peachstone. A gentle, corrosive, and effacing wind blew from
him into the backs of their heads, chiding, nudging, telling him
he would influence people centuries hence, merely by having
been what he had become. In her closed eyes he became greater
and greater, yet ever earthier, too. He was already, she knew, a
propelling force, an agent for change, a perpetual presence, forever shaping Japan and China. She conceded he may not have
known the names of all those in generations to come, but he

knew their texture, their cellular eccentricities, their smiles, their scowls, their shrugs, their yearning for completeness and perfection. In getting to know him at such a distance, she also created him, inventing more than she told. To her, he was not merely a priest, a cleric, but an ancient of days, as knowing about the future as he was interested in it: a prophetic devotee. As she saw him, he was the Resident of History, the Prefect of Mutability. The thousand cuts he fussed so much about were mental; she knew that; and came from too much worry, too much rigorous anticipation, too keen a yearning not to have been wasted. I am a weathercock sibyl, she got him telling himself: I am the cock that crows at dawn as well as the nightingale that says good night. I would love to know the life stories of, oh, perhaps a thousand of those who will come and go during the next five centuries, in China and Japan.

Instead of dominating history, however, this rapee's eidolon turned to his old favorite, zealous as any Zen Buddhist, doing for himself the *Cha-no-yu,* or hot-water tea, there in Japan in a borrowed teahouse, something between cubbyhole and kennel, separate from the main building, with the pendent scroll at one end, a flower arrangement at the other, and the tiny deep-set fireplace that heated the tea kettle. She moved him about from country to country, from era to era, peremptorily proud of her creature. Not surprisingly, now she felt Chinese, now Japanese, now a mere Oriental nobody, clinging to shreds of history. How she parsed him and catechized him in his doll's house, she as much as he towering over history and the delicate, furtive arts of fable. Here, above them both, hovered an eternity every bit as vast as the Christian one. Somatti, she saw, came into this place through a little low door, hunched like a cat, humbled before even beginning, yet thrilled by the formulas of exotic ritual, as by something forbidden but only because too exquisite for a Westerner, a Jesuit, a scholar of Greek.

This day, it being winter, she had him decide on a heavy tea, *koicha,* metallic and bitter, giggling at him as he partook of the sweets kept in a little packet. Since he was alone he could take wry pleasure in the thought of joy kindling in a speaker's voice as a liked person entered the room. She made him take a fancy to himself, for him an act painful as twisting the wrist skin on someone's arms in different directions, with him on the receiving end. He rarely rose to such hubris, but she made the warm benison tour his throat even though he said nothing; he welcomed himself, the relished. He would never be uxorious, of course not! But he knew how uxorious men told their wives what other men kept back to tell to other men. The ways of the promiscuous and the married had not escaped him altogether and came to him from a distant planet where the innocent sooner or later found themselves in heat, making the buoyant hop of a rabbit toward the hardly known beloved. Tapping the top of his ear, he brought his fingertips to his nose, marveling at the aroma of salt and cream, yield of an insufficient scrub, he thought; had he lived later, on into the seventeenth century, he would have exclaimed "Camembert" and become fond of such tiny self-exploration, leading as it did to preposterous, tea-room-scale coincidence.

Back to *Cha-no-yu* he went, half-wishing, as always, he were in China, just as when in China he craved Japan. It was a Chinese ritual, after all, filched by a nation whose monks needed something to keep them awake during sustained bouts of meditation—if only they had had Christ crucified to gape at, he noted, the tea ritual would have stayed in China. Ah, well. He rinsed out his mouth and washed the tea things like a past master, reminding himself that the ceremony's desiderata—respect, harmony, cleanliness, and peace—were universal things attainable by all men of benign disposition, not just by tea drinkers. Having sipped and achieved a measure of diffident calm, he slid the little European teaspoon under his tongue until it reached the frenum, the slim cord that tethered the tongue, and nodded at its superb placing: just where tongue wanted it, neither too constricting nor too loose. The rustic tea things favored by some appealed to him little; his own taste was almost gaudy, and he doted on ingenuity, not so much the barely modified natural as the supremely fashioned work of the canny artificer. Human cleverness had never troubled him, not least because he thought he had a fair share of it himself, though little enough scope for it in the lands his faith and discipline had taken him to. German, he told himself, was a good language to bellow in, much as Greek was one to be subtle in (more than Latin, say), while Chinese was a language to become symbolic in, Japanese one in which to celebrate passivity. He smiled weakly at two of his favorite words, surfacing after the tea ceremony like flying fish, silver and sleek: easily younger than the universe. *Sumballein* was to put the world back together; *passive* meant spread out to dry, like a grape. When he died, he wanted it to be while he was using words with extraordinary reverence, not fussing about to make gentlemen of the Chinese and Japanese; perish the thought of doing so with the Indians of India. He would not mind if he died while contemplating one of his favorite verbs, such as the one—what was it?—the Romans invented for when you had a weepy eye, a runny one. *Lippĭŏ, lippīre, lippīvī, lippītum*: to have sore eyes, to burn, to ache, in the eyes. What did such a verb tell you about Romans, who must have stared into the sun too much or had too many freezing winds (all that coastline!)? Such words were the tabernacles of sensitivity. And *lippus* meant "having sore or watery eyes"—bleary, half-blind, blind even mentally. Then he canceled what he was just going to say to himself: the Romans had no word for dry eyes, dry-eyedness. But they did. His churning skull brought it up to him at last, a word certainly younger than the universe (a phrase he was going to have to fight off before it became a bore). The word was *siccoculus*. And they no doubt, he harassed himself, had words for feathery-eyebrowedness, for how the outside leaves of plants picked up last after being watered. Damn us all, he whispered. Damn the tyranny of human potential. Why were we not less clever, considering the dreadfulness of our final doom?

SCALD IBIS FELT HERSELF BEGINNING TO CHANGE, NOT PRO-
foundly, but in the extras of identity. She, she felt, was a little
bolder in demeanor, she who had never been a shrinking violet;
she lifted her chin somewhat higher, kept her neck a bit
straighter, set her foot down harder. This was little enough in
ordinary cirumstances, but in the Tent of Orange Mist it signaled a major shift in tactics. Perhaps she was just getting used
to things, to being a comfort woman with aspirations to geisha-
hood, and would become even surer of herself as she divined
her lack of vulnerability, hoping it would rub off on Hong,
whose complaint had now become incessant; no longer a mere
problem, he was a constant threat, perched there in chimney

limbo. All she had to do, she reasoned, was become more and more important; in other words, excel until she became almost an authority. She was still only sixteen, however, and her notions of such qualities as audacity, invulnerability, disdain were amateurish, not thought through, and certainly unrelated to immediate consequences. For her, an attitude terminated with its display and did not waft onward into a fringe of repercussions. Hayashi, she thought, could be dealt with, mainly by niceness, just so long as she did not provoke the bureaucrat in him. He was proud of his makeshift establishment, but he was even prouder of the piece of him that created it. He was the brothel's author, self-surprised.

For ways of coping with him, she tried on little scenarios of mind, first pretending he was her older brother, either come up or gone down in the world; then her father, stripped of attributes that sometimes made her feel sorry for him: he got carried away with himself, or at least he had in the good old days when life was a circus whose ringmaster he pretended to be. Old days only a day ago.

Whatever sense of time she had ever had, she the tangential dreamer touring along her own Silk Road, she had lost it now, sometimes thinking time traveled backward into unknown terrain or slung out shoots that curled away from space to an inhuman destination beyond telescopes. She was in a conduct zone, she told herself, devoid of codes, etiquettes, traditions; even ethics had become merely decorative. No one behaved as they should. You survived by the skin of your teeth, but you made the flagrant most of what you had, ripe for execution minutes ahead. Not that she had all of a sudden turned hedonist or sensualist; that would no doubt come; she functioned with numb areas being drawn along by the rest of her, no less immature for having to pretend to so many adult ways. She was flesh, she decided, as never before, and not the least grateful for her rude awakening.

Was she giving birth to herself? Was this how that would feel?

She began to believe in a dissonant universe, all clash and clatter, in which the dragons of the twentieth century looked for a girl with clear plans and mauled her to death, sundering the envisioned advance from school to university to—what?—the diplomatic service, maybe, or teaching. All that torn away from her and hers the responsibility to make the quick change from student to whore. She knew how things went wrong briefly, then righted themselves: an old door on an outhouse, warped in summer humidity, opening at the bottom but jammed at the top so the door bent open without coming free. You banged it with the heel of your hand, once, twice, and the top usually gave way with a little flurry. She could cope with such matters, but not with what she was beginning to think of as brightness defiled, promise butchered.

The first of possible changes bloomed when Hong, furious at being cooped up, emerged from behind the paper screen, limped downstairs, helped himself to cold rice in the kitchen, brushing a few house centipedes aside in taking it, and moved slowly to the room of four and a half mats, where he witnessed his daughter serving tea to some junior officers: accountants and doctors, not that he knew. In the one other lit room, Hayashi was seated at his typewriter, composing his weekly report. The machine had arrived with him, oiled and overhauled. He frowned and muttered as he worked. Hong stood in the doorway awhile, savoring the extraordinary scene. He shuffled once and Hayashi snapped something in Japanese that Hong understood. Hong answered. As Hayashi swiveled around, Hong bowed.

"Are you Japanese? Explain."

"Servant only," but he said it in Japanese.

Hayashi was stunned, at once thinking he could have used the man in a score of ways. He tested him, and the man understood, at once bending himself to work as commanded, giving his name even as he lifted and stacked boxes, picked up scattered papers from the floor, bowed, bowed, then fetched a duster and cleaned up Hayashi's working area. Then he stood awaiting further orders while Hayashi, with a dismissive wave of his hand, ordered him to stand at attention in the doorway.

Hong now watched Hayashi, intent and adroit as a surgeon, pencil out certain mistyped words and remove the sheet from the machine. Now he typed the correct versions, all in one line, slid the paper out again, and with held breath scissored a narrow strip the exact width of a line of typing. Clipping off one piece, Hayashi touched its back with glue and, breathing heavily now, eased it into place over the pencil mark, nudging it with his fingernail, sliding it a little to the right until it was in position. Then he pressed it down hard, masking it with a piece of scrap paper. Several times he did tiny grafts, grunting with satisfaction at each, finally lofting the paper to the kerosene lamp and its cloud of unseasonal insects. He was pleased. He turned, tapped the page as if to instruct Hong to bury its lesson in his soul, and began to laugh. "I never need to behead anyone," he said. "I cut paper instead. I am Hayashi the correction man."

What happened next would flicker in Hayashi's memory for as long as he lived. Hong walked boldly in, picked up an inkbrush, and, on a sheet of paper, began to describe a whole series of elegant characters with a flair that Hayashi had seen only in exhibitions. The man was a cursive genius. Hayashi looked harder, realizing that some of the characters were Japanese, some not. "Was it not Shoyo," Hong asked in his clumsy, deliberate Japanese, "who, from rehearsing characters again and again on his bed linen, wore holes in the cover? I do no such thing, but am thought a master in my own right, sir. We have seen better days. In China, New Year greetings appear on scrolls hung either side of the door, to greet friends. *Dui ren* or *tui-lien*, meaning "a couplet." Japanese paper is called *washi* and Chinese paper *tôshi* or even *karakami*! Your honorable stair- and floor washer, sir, has devoted most of his life to this gentle art. Have you ever tried to make a brush from the hair of babies? No use, sir, it lacks springiness. But if you can come by a sprig from a bush of wisteria, well then you—"

"You are making fun of me," Hayashi blurted. "I work with paper, too, but I am far from the ignoramus you think I am." Hearing the other talk his muddled Japanese had defused his military rigor, but his weariness still showed.

"No, sir," Hong whispered, "I am serious about the wisteria. You boil one end for about an hour. That softens it up. Then you beat it gently with a hammer, fanning the fibers out to make a brush shape. You should be warned it will not hold ink so well and it hardens up, so you have to keep softening it in hot water."

"I am a Japanese officer. Why tell me all this?"

It was part, Hong said, of civilized concourse. All refined people such as the Japanese cared about calligraphy.

Where did he come by such knowledge? "I was well brought up, Colonel. My Japanese I picked up here and there. Many of us know a little."

"You don't talk like a houseboy."

"I have come down in the world. Some houses you just take to naturally. They don't refuse you. You confide in them, they confide in you."

What a marvel, Hayashi thought. Here we sit in one of the great old cities, smashed and looted, but never beyond ultimate repair. We have almost no electricity, so it is like a city of the barbaric times, with everyone reduced, except the most senior officers, to some dreadful primitive level. We sit here like savages from the desert by the light of an inadequate lamp, and there arises from the earth this high-spoken houseboy with a taste for calligraphy.

And that was how Hong, the mouthpiece of tranquillity, got his promotion in the dead of night, just for having spoken up in Japanese. Whatever he said might not have mattered; he just said it in the right language to the right man, utterly justified, so far, in having made his foray beyond the fireplace, risking execution or at least a good beating. Here were two men sequestering themselves from their war, with it but not of it, one in uniform, one in disguise. Together they added up to some demurral in the face of atrocity.

"Look here," Hayashi said, "I can't have my interpreters being slaughtered the instant they step outside. Our soldiers are more than zealous just now. We will get you into uniform as soon as possible. Do you mind wearing a Japanese uniform? If you don't, you won't last long. Your head will roll away for the rats to nibble."

Any masquerade was better than life in the chimney, Hong thought; any life was better than death. Heaven knew what he was going to find when he went outside. Agree with everything, he instructed himself, until at least a month later. Scald Ibis isn't going to believe her eyes. How improbable I am, like the world. As an interpreter, I might be able to track down wife and son. Families should stick together. Invading armies should keep their distance. I am an idealist of the old school, gambling as ever, trying to get away with something. The miracle is, I have found someone who knows the role of art. I must have gleaned some seeds of acting from Miss Wong. I am now the comedian in a serious mess, and it is important not to let him know Scald Ibis is my daughter, otherwise he'll use it against us. He'll extort things from us. I hardly know her. My acquaintance with her begins now.

Already Scald Ibis looked different, having changed her appearance with the cosmetics kit supplied by the two visiting geishas. In fact, as Hong began to realize, she had modeled herself on Anna May Wong, whose round pouty face was like her own. Low fringe, rosebud mouth, thin and generously arched eyebrows, the expression between pique and hauteur. Miss Wong, however, the so-called Yellow Pearl, had been born in Los Angeles, in its Chinatown; she would do as an idol for a Chinese girl trying to look Japanese, though in some lights Miss Wong had too much of what was going to be known as Win Min Than quality—mysticism, biteable vulnerability, dreamy exotic selflessness—associated with an actress yet to appear, and Burmese. Scald Ibis was taller, too. She remembered that Hong spoke a great deal about Miss Wong, about how she had to take a back seat to such as Myrna Loy in a film in which Loy played an Asian role. Miss Wong went off to Europe, made a name for herself, returned to Hollywood, then dazed London, made her way back to Hollywood again. Scald Ibis could recall having seen her only once in the flesh, in 1936, when she visited China for the first time, going by her Chinese name, Wong Liu Tsong, Frosted Yellow Willow in Cantonese. Early this very year, she had seen her. On the way, Miss Wong had even stopped in Japan, and had told a reporter No, there was no man in her life right then. "I am wedded to my art," she said, a remark she came to treasure. The next day's newspapers reported that she had already married a man named Art. In fact, she never married, but she did, while in China, study Mandarin Chinese and bought many costumes, which she later auctioned off for the Chinese cause. Sleek, delicate, soulfully importunate, she was an epitome of sorts, and Scald Ibis could never be sure if she remembered her from photographs or that one encounter when, on Hong's arm, she had said "Yes, my art and I are very happy. I do, however, find it odd when I play a supporting role to some Western actress painted Oriental. Doesn't that take the cake? Oh, boy. Yes, my father ran a laundry and always accompanied me to the studio. Then he locked me in my room. He didn't want me humiliated or put upon."

Miss Wong's presence never left Hong's household, perhaps because as an American she was exotic without looking it, perhaps because she embodied so many of Hong's ideas of what a woman should be. He had spent much of his life infatuated with a phantom, determined to conjure her back into being from the leftovers of her presence, almost as if remaking her first movie, *Bits of Life*, made in 1921. Hong did not make movies, but they made him feel good, and, committed now to Scald Ibis's career as a geisha novice, he found new uses for old images. Father and daughter were playing into each other's hands.

When Hong came out from behind the fireplace screen, he was wearing a tattered Japanese uniform, rank of corporal.

"No, no charade," he told Scald Ibis. "I am official. Interpreter. Your friend the colonel and I hit it off. I speak Japanese, you know."

She knew, but she wished he had kept it to himself. "You might have stayed put, Father. No taste for being a houseboy?"

"I'm better off in this," he said, brimming with self-esteem, more like her father than he had been in days.

"You'll have to watch what you say."

"As ever," said Hong.

"As never," Scald Ibis sighed, blowing him a kiss.

"Now we're a team, child."

"The geisha," she scoffed, "and the interpreter. We should be able to get anything we want."

"You're nothing besides geisha, are you?" He suddenly sounded frantic.

"I try to keep them at bay, Father. There are other girls for that, who can't sing, simper, or mime."

"Then that's all right. Play it by ear."

"Are you going to stay in the chimney?"

"No, I'm allocated a room, the one we used to call Old Slimy. But when I'm in it, I miss the chimney."

A SAMURAI WITHOUT
KNOWING IT

BLANK PAGE IN NOTEBOOK
OF SANDRO SOMATTI, S.J.

WHAT, SOMATTI WAS WONDERING, COMES TOWARD US SO FAST we thrust our hands in front of our faces, to fend it off? What is this demon of manganese? It wafts toward us, gathering speed, neither sought after nor provoked, and we cannon blindly into it, destroying our faces, our skulls, our brains. What we want is a static universe in which nothing comes toward us ever. It is like two people walking toward each other, feinting sideways in identical fashion so as not to collide, but colliding anyway in a flurry of wriggled toes: what do we call this? We have no word. We do not want to_____thus, but we cannot even find the word for a mere social contretemps.

When we want to talk of disaster, we dream of something gone wrong in the stars. Having no word, not even one of my own invention, I decide the truth is as much my tale-telling as the human tale told.

HAYASHI SMILED AT THE ARRIVAL OF SOME SMALL PINK BOXES
neatly sealed with red ribbon, which, he explained to her, contained a special diet sent her by Admiral Saikaku and General
Fujimoto, the two senior officers nearly always present, to
whom she was never allowed to say no. The population of
Nanking was starving, what remained of it, but here were rations flown in from Japan; she had no idea she was pleasing
them that much with her schoolgirl wriggles. The food went off
to the kitchen, to be kept in darkness until afternoon, which
struck her as an odd time to eat; but in Nanking nothing was ordinary. People ate when they could, dogs and rats and rice. She
was learning how elites ran themselves, war or no war: they

claimed their pleasures and so, in one sense, were never at war, or away from home. Grace and favor traveled with them, and the means of pleasure, but for officers only. Now she saw some other boxes, much larger, being carried in, indeed one borne by Hong himself, his demeanor quite different in corporal's uniform. All over again, he made up his own mind, and prompted Hayashi into important decisions.

Tonight, for instance, Saikaku and Fujimoto were bringing several other senior officers to the Tent of Orange Mist, with obvious intentions, and Hong had offered to do calligraphy for them at some point, just for the pleasure afforded them of his pliant, swirling hand and his commentary on his work mingled with humble erudition, from round fans and the sheep's-hair brush to mallets and *mokkan*, old strips of bamboo that had characters drawn on them. Hong was useful as a social leaven; Hayashi vowed to make full use of him, having him tidy up, but also lift the conversation beyond the crude and erotic.

How, Hayashi wondered, does he come to know so much, almost as if his entire life has been spent preparing for Japanese invasion? Hong took to the goings-on in the four-and-a-half-mat room with solemn alacrity, perhaps because it seemed to him yet another party, small but cultivated; Hayashi usually managed to usher the drunkest of the junior officers out, propelling them upstairs or into the street, secretly hoping they would never return.

Scald Ibis knew something was amiss when Hayashi, with many bows, beckoned her into the kitchen, where she saw an elegant wooden tray laid with a crisp white cloth and, in the center on a silver plate, a seaweed omelet whose fragrance— cloves?—reminded her of childhood games coming to a weary end while cooking aromas wafted out from the house. She was to eat this with reverence. Hayashi clicked his heels, bowed, and left, leaving her to wonder. On no account, he said, must she leave the kitchen; when he left, he posted a guard at the door. "Safer that way," he said vaguely. "I don't want you interfered with."

When he returned, a couple of hours later, he began to speak to her in Chinese, doing his best to impress upon her the role chosen for her that evening. She burst out laughing and in rapid Chinese scolded him for being so juvenile. "Not really?"

"Oh, yes," he sighed. "Important guest have special request." Then he rattled off the Japanese name for what she had to do. They always had a name for it, uttered with grave intimacy. "No more?" she said.

"Just this," he stammered in that alien ancient language.

Now she knew she had a future. It was all a matter of knowing your enemy, his kinks and twists, and then you could make a career of necessity, sending them all back into the night with egos aglow.

At the tea ceremony the table seemed loaded with toys. She lifted a cardboard picture of a house front, popped open a shutter, and saw a couple weirdly contorted on the bed, a small group watching them and feeling one another up. In one teacup stood a fey geisha, right under a cherry tree. Saikaku poured and her kimono faded away, only to reappear when the tea cooled down. Ah, chemistry, Scald Ibis decided. Another toy consisted of a dainty whore with the tiniest of mouths, a lipsticked puncture, glancing away from a gigantic mushroom of a penis around which she had an arm, her expression one of jubilant lasciviousness. The senior officers fussed over these blunt little baubles, but hushed when Scald Ibis walked out, paused, then came back in, walking with oiled suggestiveness, slowly inching up her black silk kimono. Up to the low table she walked, a slithering sleepwalker, the kimono around her waist so they could see she had nothing on underneath. Poised over the gleaming silver tray on the table, so as to reflect her parts, she strained a little, coughed, and relieved herself into the center of the tray. Then she left with a somewhat hasty stride and the assembled officers exclaimed and shouted, laughing and arguing as the tray passed from hand to hand. Then each received a silver saucer with a souvenir plastered in the middle by a silver cake knife. Inhaling the bouquet, the senior admiral commented on what he called its pink boudoir aroma, suggesting which herbs it derived from, and which foods. Then it was time for the silver spoons and the tasting, at which the youngest officers quailed until shamed into partaking by those whom they dared not affront. It was a scene of preposterous delicacy and exemplary submission. The senior officers appeared exquisitely to feast, the others performed as if being executed, heaving and gasping, their eyes pouring, their faces savagely distorted. Scald Ibis saw none of this, or the sudden final recourse to sake, in which relief partnered bravado. She would never want to kiss them again, not even when ordered, and she marveled at the arbitrariness of taboos that made tonight's ritual revolting whereas what she had been subjected to—licking the finger that had just been deep within her—was supposed to turn her on. What on earth had thumb-sucking and stink finger to do with her almost adult life?

It was all so algebraically far from what she read and dreamed about. She had already encountered the paradox that, although ordure was dead and death, it brought both Chinese and Japanese vegetables to abundant life. That was why you cooked them in a *very* hot wok. These officers were not vegetables, however, so they were giving themselves to some deathly component in what was on the shiny tray: something that was death only, and not resurrection in the field. Were they demonstrating their submissiveness to the universe or paying homage to the death-bound part of themselves? Could such a pantomime fan their urges? Or were they just playing the naughtiness game, being bad big boys, each loathing the fact that he had to behave like this at all? She left the topic alone, knowing her next seaweed omelet would reek of what it was going to become, but this was still to be alive, in the midst of the mess. If they found out that Hong was her father, he would be given a silver spoon of his own and made to eat. And then he and she would be made to reverse roles. Life could soon get ghastly for the sake of one wrong word. She was learning, but not how to forget. More sake went down that night than on any other, and Saikaku and Fujimoto wondered when Admiral Saguchi would perform his party piece, dancing naked with a long string of pearls around his neck and lighted cigarettes stuck up his nose.

Next morning, while Scald Ibis slept in, Hong began his chores, first collecting the debris from the four-and-a-half-mat room, into which he trod with ever-increasing pride. He tried not to make a clatter as Hayashi was working on accounts and reports, but the silver things from the special evening foiled him and set him stooping. He did not object to manual work, able to relate the dexterity and gift of calligraphy to something as mundane as dishwashing. A hand was a noble device, he thought, whatever it did; imagine all the evolution that had gone into its opposable thumb, its ability to cup and gauge, its deftness at the pianoforte. As usual, he did the dishes in cold water, first scraping the remains into a small zinc tub. As he did so, a strong odor quite unlike that of decomposing food struck his nostrils. He sniffed the saucers and the silver tray, recoiling somewhat, at once deciding the Japanese were every bit the barbarians he had always called them. His nose told him what they had been eating, his mind fumbled for the reason—surely food wasn't that short, not yet, and certainly not in the Tent of Orange Mist. What was that old English saying? Liberty Hall here, gentlemen. Nothing denied you. So: they had been eating human waste, these devotees of his daughter, and it was clear that he would have to withdraw her from the fray. She was mingling with self-degrading men who had no future. Yet wait a moment: were they coprophages, or had they simply relieved themselves onto their plates, as foul and inappropriate a deed as he had come across? In his weary mind's eye he saw the scene, the guffawing sycophancy of the junior officers, the elated nods of the senior ones as Saguchi grunted to a squat over the table and began. Scald Ibis looked away, frozen in a frenzy.

Had that been it? This ostensibly suave evening had degenerated into a shambles of filth, a masque for modern heathens. It was a form of bravado, surely, like the man who chomped on a sandwich beneath the dangling corpse of a hanged man. Showing off, he called it, *pour encourager les autres*. Yet, strange to relate, these men were the brains of the invasion; not for them the savage rigors of front-line combat, from the disemboweled to those neatly punctured in the forehead, any of which could drive a man crazy—as some calligraphers, press-ganged to the bloodbath, had discovered. No: these were the planners, the savorers, the ones who in the midst of carnage kept a severe, straight head, drew the lines and flagged the map. In that case, his nattily reasoning mind informed him, they did this bestial thing—some dogs had done it, he knew—to liven things up. They needed extreme experience because so much safety was intolerable. That must be it, Hong: they were the fetishists of abnormal calm, at home wherever they went because they never did what others had to. Like Scald Ibis, who had dubbed them an elite not many hours earlier, Hong gave that knowing, conclusive look, launching a slight nod to his right that said I know, I've got it now. He bulged his lips, glad to have settled so taxing an issue, and began the job of plate-cleaning, but unable to shift the smell, even as he rubbed with the old shirt, ground away with a handful of sand and soft soap. The silver had received the taint. Ah, now he saw: they used them only once, for reasons of hygiene, and each time they staged the perversion they used new plates, which poured in from Japan. He burst out laughing. *Hygiene!* Why, they'd eaten the stuff, unless indeed they had just taken a dump. No: the silver saucers and little spoons told him all he needed to know, and for reasons unknown he thought of the Japanese general who, in wildest Manchuria, had managed to have Philippine beer, a private air-raid shelter, a lavish bathroom, a prayer room, and a four-poster bed while his men camped out, frozen and hungry. That, Hong told himself, was the Japanese way. Such things happened in Baudelaire, didn't they? But that was Baudelaire, the dimension of literature and nightmare. This was China, where carnage was commonplace.

And therefore whatever else happened did not matter, never mind how appalling. The demoralizing notion had struck him that the butchering of women and children was somehow not as evil as teatime coprophagy. Murder, extolled by the sibylline Englishman De Quincey, was only murder whereas the consumption of human waste was an affront to God. How could this be? Was he, Hong the refined, not enough of a human to be a representative witness? What was wrong with him that suddenly murder slipped into second place and the prime abomination was filth? Rubbing his fingers in dry sand until they bled, he tried to puzzle out his aversion to human dung beetles, as he decided to call the officers, and his comparative adjustment to wholesale bloodshed. There were so few dung beetles. That must be it. They had not had a chance to become trite. His daughter sat down with them at their grotesque feast, retching and looking away. Even if they only touched the tip of what sat in their little spoons, touched with tongue, they were doing the equivalent of murder. They were denying life. Or were they? They were only poisoning themselves, therefore doing no harm to others, and therefore—well (he straightened up as if to receive an honorary degree in humane letters), the only thing you might object to was their lack of taste. He cackled. No: their excess of taste. All they were doing was breaking a taboo. They were disgusting, but not murderers. What kind of beings are we, he nonetheless went on wondering, to whom an esthetic peccadillo mattered more than an atrocity? Am I alone in this?

The more he pondered it, the more convinced he became that his dung beetles were practicing only a form of dandyism, better pronounced as *dandyisme*, that would eventually sweep the world. After a few years, dung-beetling would be as routine as beheading. His head spun, his body twitched internally. Thank goodness he did not have to render his verdict this morning as he paused, lounging over the dishes, with last night's laundry from the four-and-a-half-mat room in the offing in its wooden tub. Of all the base practices he knew, this was by far the least. Not that he had the slightest desire to partake, although mentally, he supposed, millions had done so, humiliated and degraded by those in power. An old proverb gleaned from who knew what waning civilization came and went: you'll eat a peck of muck before you die. What had a peck been? An English unit of weight, he thought. Was this not an ancient punishment for prisoners? A sometime torture? Making people eat their own and thus converting them into a perfect life cycle, never needing to eat again after the first tuck-in. How came it that someone as sophisticated as he should be taxing his brains with a puzzle so picayune, backing away, then charging on as if his life depended on it? He did not know, and he suddenly failed himself in the examination for self-knowledge, certain that a man should know himself better than he did, or he should not be meddling with dung beetles at all.

It was only a step to the crude rope strung out in the snowy garden, where clean laundry froze. He sighed as he pinned rectangles up in the December wind, shivering and coughing. A diet of almost nothing but rice was killing him. Now he collected the plates and cutlery of the night before, the silver still shining, and dropped them into an old small box, using a page of newspaper as a mitt. Out he went again, determined to bury the evidence, hoping he would never have to do this a second time. His own contribution to hygiene or decorum was that he would open the dry, filled-up well, and drop the box where it belonged, so that long after the war and the occupation he could return and burn it. Up came the lid after the fifth or sixth tug.

The well was full to the brim. He reached, shoved, and saw a white, blood-flecked face, there inexplicably, and now Hong knew what it was like to die without falling. He waited for a sound, a sign, then replaced the lid, leaving the box of silver on top of the snow. The bourgeoisie, damn them, were always tidying up.

NOTEBOOK OF SANDRO
SOMATTI, S.J.

OR IT COMES IN A SHOWER OF SOOT, NOT IN A LUMP OF OVERHANG at all, but millionfold black iron shot. Peppering us, leaving us with a thousand scars. Yes, *that* again. I cannot but assume we to some extent want this to happen. We wish ourselves no good. Human energy on the move switches from side to side, witness the tergiversations of Somatti, S. vis-à-vis the Chinese, the Japanese. Atrocity is only another form of busyness. History trembles invisibly, like the bed of the sea. Like the tenderest flesh beneath the prepuce, once seen and scrubbed neutral, now sealed forever. What a man does not use atrophies, and what atrophies itches, burns. One hour to drag it backward, two to push it back in place. The hood, as of a headsman.

Now Hong was telling Scald Ibis about the goings-on in
the four-and-a-half-mat room.

"Kinky old men, Father. You end up feeling sorry for them.
They're looking for something keen and final, but *that*'s all they
end up with. There's something childish about it. Don't you remember being childish?"

"Not that sort of childish." He wanted to tell someone about
his son, but he could not tell Scald Ibis. He desperately wanted
her not to know certain things, perhaps never. If his role was to
protect, then he should guarantee her a safe adolescence in spite
of what had already gone on. Yet how could he go on being se-
lective, holding back this or that? Once the mind had been

slammed by something gross, it bent back, didn't it? Minds were resilient. Children's anyway. Otherwise he would have to wipe out the entire Japanese army, even the general who had handed a scout his one jealously guarded can of sardines, the other general whose wife had so disgraced him in London that he tried to throw himself out a window in the Langham Hotel in Portland Place. His mind kept churning its pain, its perpetual searing ambivalence as he tried to make sense of recent events, from the grotesque to the tragic, even as she kept from him her own part in the night of the dung beetles.

Trying to protect each other, they demanded too much of themselves and squandered energy they should have saved for the fending off of Hayashi. A triangle made of a rubber band stretched around three nails that moved ever outward, guaranteeing sooner or later a snap. Or did it? The three of them seemed to be moving closer together, creating a proximity that would choke them, as when, for instance, Hayashi would overhear them talking and his limited Chinese would suffice to undo them, or when Hong heard Hayashi talk dung beetle to Scald Ibis, as he no doubt would have to do the next time around, or when—yes, even this—Scald Ibis heard Hong berate Hayashi about his murdered son out in the well.

Hong tried to grovel even more, promising himself he would do the most terrible things once he got started, and Scald Ibis assured herself that, if deviant behavior were the price of staying alive, she'd pay it. If life was worth having, as an absolute, then there could be no quibbles about how you kept it. If an unworthy life was not worth having, then indeed how you acquired it was subject to all manner of critiques.

Even to live disgracefully, said Hayashi, is worthwhile.

A shameful life is always a life, even as a houseboy. Hong recited this until he could hear nothing else.

Whatever you have to do, Scald Ibis told herself, so long as you do it you're alive.

To some, three musketeers, three floaters, three survivors. To others, three fakers, three frauds. To you, dear reader and empathizer, three incomplete lives, not stitched together from within, and therefore three incoherent souls improvised from moment to moment, yet livelier than a dead mother on the bottom of the Yangtze, unintroduced in novels, than a severed brother and son in a dry well. Whose life, subject to the mindless vicissitudes of a century, does not end up disheveled and dismantled, fit for the rubbish heap yet obdurately persisted in because, perhaps, such is the way of the Creator after all? Blind creative foison, simply for the sake of motion, bustle, snap.

Strange to say, Hayashi was a pessimist, somehow knowing China would root them out, send them packing back to their beloved Nippon: not this or next year, but in time's fullness, with huge loss of life. Which Japanese commanders were to be hanged would then be the issue; but who would seek out a brothel commander, a colonel of geishas? The longer he hung on in Nanking, or kept the Tent of Orange Mist going elsewhere, the safer he would be; he was not responsible for what went on around the house as savage menials-turned-soldiers worked their frustrated will on the citizens of Nanking. By the same token, both Hong and his daughter knew China would prevail. Hong had come running back to save his family, and look what he found, look what he did not find: a son, a wife. Look what he did: became a guerrilla in disguise, eavesdropping on the off-duty gossip of the high and mighty, risking even his daughter as a spy. All he had to do was keep quiet, pretend nothing had happened, and Hayashi would continue in his fool's paradise, unaware that, with one tweak from a mere houseboy his life would be over, his bordello would fall into other hands. The thing to do, in the midst of desolating pain, was to keep on plying him with calligraphy, Japanese spoken passably well, clean stairs and cleaner hallways, until—he hardly dared define what that would be, but come it would, and then the other officers, admirals and generals, too, even the dung beetles, would have to watch out. Hayashi would vanish like a moth in the night, perhaps a deserter, a man weak enough to abscond with a woman for the sake of pussy, cash, the chance of being a kept man forever. It would not, he thought as vengeance began to boil in his gentle brain, be that hard to dispose of him once he and Scald Ibis had his confidence. Hayashi's tenure in the Tent of Orange Mist became weaker the more Hong pondered; the idolater of Anna May Wong became the crimson avenger looking for somebody to blame, just so long as Japanese and available. Fujimoto, Saikaku, or Saguchi would have done just as well. The only problem was how many to kill, he having already chosen one: some number between one and the entire complement of the invasion army. The violence that Hong had not felt at the front now became his *raison d'être* in the primrose pavilion. He knew his daughter was more than a geisha in there, but he wanted to avenge her without knowing the details.

Preoccupied as she was, Scald Ibis noticed the change in her father, who looked paler, slower, more intense. She asked him repeatedly what might be wrong, knowing how prickly such questions made him. He brushed her off, saying it was the weather, the abject role he had to play in his own house. "Our day will come," he would say, making some grand gesture toward the future. "And then we will be snapping *our* fingers."

She next saw him outside as she glanced through the window of the attic in whose fireplace he had lived. There he stood by the old well, tears streaming, his fists hammering air, his feet now and then stamping the iron ground. He made no other motion, however, and stood there talking into the open mouth of the well; the lid was lifted aside, a disc of snow and ice. Why was he speaking or praying into the well? She sighed and went downstairs to fetch him. When she neared him, she heard a sound she had once heard from a rusty door which, shoved against its stiffness, let out the yelp of an old hound.

He was enclosed in grief, deformed by it, eager to be swallowed up. Shu was the name he dared not say as he aimed his face downward. Scald Ibis hugged him, asking why, but he choked on his sobs. He did not even say "Look." At first she could make nothing out. Was it a human or some cache of dark blue clothing? She made as if to touch whatever lay in there, but he restrained her. Then he managed to say Shu. No, her brother was away at the front, honorably conscripted, surely, not of use but swept up in the horizontal avalanche that had captured Hong, too.

She looked again and recoiled. She had seen the face of her brother, and his neck; in some demented version of good night his head had come around her bedroom door, grinning, and then had continued to advance with no body behind it. Now the nightmare spewed up from the well. Some barbarian with a grotesque sense of neatness had done to him something she had always assumed could not be done to *him*. She knelt and pawed him, a side of meat in a rough winter coat. Hong was on his knees now.

"Tell Hayashi," she blurted. "I'll tell him."

"Tell him nothing," Hong said. "Who knows who did it? Who cares? Say nothing. We must close up the well."

She persuaded him to go indoors, but his head homed to the well as if he had prayed for a miracle. Without any prompting from her, he headed upstairs and climbed right into the fireplace, groaning and sneezing, seeming to grumble through his spittle. She sat there for an hour on the floor, right by the slit in the screen, saying nothing but listening hard. It would be unlike Hong to throw himself down the chimney, but she wondered if he might swallow his tongue. Her own building grief burned internal and relentless. No, this was shock, she told herself; grief came later, when her body had remobilized. They needed help, but who could help them in this Japanese oasis surrounded by Japanese soldiers and hundreds, thousands, of dead Chinese? It was no longer a city but a vast wound. Now she was sure her mother was dead, too, gratuitously killed by somebody wearing the same uniform her father had worn. She called out to Hong, who answered that he felt stronger now; he knew what to do. Would she help him?

"Mother," she said lamely, but he snapped back at her to forget Mother for the time being. It would be all right. What would? she asked, wondering if he was indeed going to kill himself right there in the chimney alcove. It would be more like him to finish himself in public, ending with a chronic flourish so as to be remembered.

Amazed to be able to formulate a thought at all, Scald Ibis discovered some part of her brain opining: so this is how it goes when your life begins to go wrong, and death shows up where you expected life. It is this painful for those who go through it, and those who don't have no idea how much it hurts, how little you can do, even with the discovery that you're glad it wasn't you. How can you hate those who have died, as if they set out to ruin you? It was just possible to think, though all of her felt overheated and choked: blood throbbing through her temples; a huge headache engulfing everything; the shakes in her hands, her legs, her rear (where she had that twitch, to begin with). Her father managed to get the pain out of his system, but she crouched around it, ritualizing. It was as if some cosmic overseer, discerning the mistake made, put it right, struck somebody dead, and brought her brother back to teasing life.

Then Hong began to speak again, slowly, but with oratorical emphasis, telling her the minimum, and she said her yesses hypnotized, eager to be rid of the responsibility of hearing him out, wanting to tell the admirals and the general all about it, spooky and vacant effigies that they were. Had they power to raise the dead? Only among their own, perhaps. Sooner or later some worthy official would come by, even a German or an Englishman, and the truth could come out, although by then she would be lying down with pigs in gray tweed suits, cigars they never removed from their mouths, little sinful boxes with a diamond mounted centrally, herself in a scarlet cloche (for having a whorish head), a green feather boa around her naked torso, and a crimson garter around her left thigh, her thrushy tongue just touching the tip of his smoky one. Only then would she be able to tell, in the Kingdom of the Silver Tray. There would be a Mister Nice and a Mister Neiss. Someone would pretend to believe her, help her, but by then her father would be dead, maybe even killed back in Nanking by a sword-bearing lieutenant. Of them all, only Anna May Wong would survive, having had the foresight to be born in the U.S.A. Scald Ibis began to cry, in 1937, having no idea what her father had in mind, yet certain it would end them both in spite of all their efforts, their self-abasements, just to stay alive, as if being alive were some great honor. She knew only that she had to invite Hayashi to her room, and then he might be persuaded to talk, to let them go, once he understood the true circumstances: that the girl had a father who was not a houseboy at all, but worthy and distinguished, with a wife to find.

Moaning in the chimney like winter, Hong felt his strength coming back and some weird relief that it was all settled: he was not going to be happy.

23

LETTER FROM SANDRO SOMATTI, S.J., TO MARTIN FORNARI, FEBRUARY 14, 1582

Magister,

The situation worsens, not in the mind, but in the loins. What had previously been open to inspection for cleansing has sealed itself away through some chronic tightening of the tip surplus, so the bálanos *remains unvisited by brush or scrub cloth. Once a week, while bathing, I heave and twiddle the skin back, causing much shortness of breath, and after a long while the little fellow pops out like a headlong grape. Thank God I have no need of him; the slit in his head matches a hole in the prepuce sufficient to make water through, or I would be in a pretty plight. Restoring the hood after scrubbing, however, is much harder as the bulb tends to swell from all such handling (involuntary self-defilement!), but eventually af-*

ter much manipulating and thrusting I manage to fold it back over the corona. When it at last sits back in position, frayed and puffed, sometimes bleeding a little, it is sore and remains so for days. I am being strangled down below, dearest friend, and the only remedies known of are Jewish. A cruel fate. For the time being, I soak and pull, soak and thrust: a vain and gruesome waste of life. If I do not, the quantity of discharge builds up, converting itself into what we prettily know by the Greek word for soap. It needs to come out, and does weekly; but it should be more often, perhaps during a prayer. Is this the last indignity, or is worse to come? I fear greater degrees of tightening, total adhesion of the hood, closure of the gap favoring the meatus, and beyond the power of prayer to mend. I remain yours amid a grueling skirmish having nothing to do with language, except for acorns, muzzles, gags— ἤ πόσθη , in short, God love us and our appendages.

Yours in God,
Sandro

It is going to be a fierce year.

HAYASHI'S CURT WAVE MEANT SHE COULD ENTER AND WATCH HIM
work on his accounts, laboriously typing something he at once
had to correct. She realized that officers who visited the four-
and-a-half-mat room paid for services received; she saw the
money on his desk and wondered why she had never seen it
changing hands. With tweezers he adjusted tiny strips to an exact place on the paper still rolled into the machine. Even as the
paste dried he jiggled the strip, sighing and breathing hard. He
must have evolved the technique a long time ago. Some strips
had handwriting on them, some were typed. A separate sheet
was the one he sliced up, and this became so ragged around the
edges, from various-sized clips, that every now and then he cut

a straight line all the way across to tidy the sheet: first one way, then another, so he dealt always with an ever-shrinking irregular oblong eventually too small to be of use. She admired his dexterity, especially with the tiniest slips of paper; one cough and they would scatter. Why did he make so many mistakes, she asked herself; was he deliberately careless? Then her mind returned to the reality she wanted to wound him with, telling him in blurted Chinese from several feet away. At last he held out both arms in distraught innocence: he was far from responsible for the whole Japanese army. She believed his wildly expostulating face, the hands tossed up and down, the look that grew tender but hardened as he remembered his station.

He shook his head, but not to say no. He meant alas.

She pounded one hand into the other, making a fist.

He half-bowed to her vehemence, knowing she was a poorer geisha for all of this.

He made the motion of tipping a cup and pouring tea into the mouth.

She spurned that and sat down, drew the well and its lid, shoved the sketch right under his nose, and said Shu's name.

Hayashi began clipping and pasting, then typing, all over again; the dead brother was already buried. What else remained?

Scald Ibis hated him for being able to resume his work, as if no one were dead, as if her grief and her father's were the merest whim of presentation, as if the wreckage of Nanking were normal. To be so single-minded argued a stunted mind, not one of your more compassionate colonels. After all, she was an employee here, in the brothel that supplanted her own home, and she had already been of distinct use. Hayashi gave her the evening off, but she cajoled him into visiting her room in a few hours with a cup of tea, conning him with misery into an almost romantic fatherly gesture he agreed to, mainly to keep her out of his sanctum, away from the lamp and typewriter, the scissors and paste, the confetti of tiny strips, the ultimate pasteup sometimes too thick, after being added to, to go back into the typewriter: the ultimate palimpsest. These were his household gods, and he wanted no Chinese girl meddling with them. Admiring them was one thing; touching was another, and she would surely touch. Then, having touched, she would presume even further in the infernal effusive way of these people who always found ways of making an inroad until they felt they understood you through and through, when all you wanted was to remain aloof and severe, perfect in your bearing, the conqueror with the heart of bamboo. Hayashi grunted, fished out his philately box and opened the album at Tannu Tuva again, his final offering. If that did not soothe her, nothing would. She ignored it, intent still on the dead brother, who should have been away in the army anyway. That was the trouble with these people. Full of noodles, they did not bother to defend themselves, had no tradition of arms-bearing, never put up a fight. In any event, casualties incurred during an invasion were hardly his concern, whereas the demigods back in Japan required of him a strict accounting, reports of venereal disease, statements of proposed changes in services offered. Indeed, he was a colonel shopkeeper. It was clear that when peace came he should resign his commission and go into civilian life as a brothel manager. He found, he reported, that the consumption of sake went up daily; that officers would come three nights running, then stay away for just as long; that the *délectation* as he called it appealed to the senior officers more than straight sex with the half-dozen Chinese girls (of no training, no sophistication, no good looks). Conclusion: his customers were getting choosy and kinky. Into the report it went. During orthodox warfare, quick purgative sex was the staple. During mop-up phases, *délectations* were more in style. You had to be ready for anything. The cynic in him was prompted to ask what the sexual preferences of his customers would be during a rout. No erections at all, he whispered.

He then realized that Ibis had not gone, had been there watching him think, was waiting to be dismissed. As if she were a soldier. What an amazing thought. She could go, he said. Yes,

yes, he would stop by later to console her, cup of tea in hand; surely, once upon a time she must have had a father, like his own children in Osaka.

Good-bye.

Good afternoon, Colonel.

Why didn't she go? She kept hovering.

She could not believe it that he didn't care, had obviously never lost a brother.

Again he dismissed her, with elaborate body language intended to usher her out with far from tempestuous graciousness.

Well, then, my Chinese observer, go away, clear off, take your hook, I have work to do, and I am all thumbs today. Now, how did it go? Ten yen for a Chinese woman, fifteen for a Korean, twenty for a Japanese? Had outrage ever been this simple? The one-night visit of the two geishas had been free, but if they ever came back on a regular basis they would charge a fortune. Best get the Chinese girl properly trained, even if she did sing in her own language. It was odd how attached they were to it, for all its cumbersome unlearnability. The fatherly side of him swam about in his being like a goldfish in a pond, sometimes visible in the murk like an ingot from the sun, but more often down in the weeds where it was safe. So he would take her tea later on and perhaps have her for one yen, which he would forget to bill himself for. *Droit de* something he had heard it called, though he could have got it wrong since it had been a German who told him about it.

Higher up, Hong was still chewing the bubble gum that had accompanied him to the front, back from it, and through his adventures in the chimney. In all of these places he had taken it out now and then, not realizing it was bubble gum, to mold it into the shape of this or that animal. He would let it harden, then chew it back into formlessness. It was his way of possessing and repossessing the uncooperative world, though he had no idea that if he blew into a thin skin of it, the world would bloom hugely until it popped.

Hayashi resumed his clerical chores, a man becalmed. The fortunes of war were the misfortunes of war. He had heard that some children got extra good-night kisses if they coughed after just falling asleep, so they coughed nightlong, making their throats quite sore. There he sat, a medium-sized man, the personification of a bureaucratic century, at ease by lamplight while outside the city went on burning, the convulsed girders buckled and crashed downward, the palls of smoke blackened, and the streets filled with the impedimenta of modern living. It was as if the whole place had turned inside out; the buildings were gutted, but their stuff was arranged outside for some colossal garage sale. Fires blazed, giving off that acrid reek of burning paint, a delight turned into poison gas. Quiet master of his trade, he sat there, controlling and answering, obeying his masters far away, reckoning ways to exploit the future without having to put his neck on the line. Anticipation was what mattered, and a willingness to look the other way when savvy required what duty banned. He could see himself growing old in this trade, grooming the best women, dumping the used-up ones, learning daily how to join the establishment's various activities together, so that it became less a collection of erotic booths than a coordinated homage to desire. He felt grateful to other officers for existing, for their boots, their open-necked white shirts, their gratuitous violence with one another in an etiquette whose most manful facet was the shout. His lips tightened and changed shape as he seemed to masticate something that had long given him trouble; his chin, his cheeks, his nose all quivered and tightened. He might have been speaking an unknown language that required no opening of the mouth. Silent oratory as the planes of his lower face changed, it belonged among the apparitions of history, a gentle enough mannerism akin to André Malraux's tic or Churchill's meow at his wife's bedroom door.

Hayashi liked the idea, the habit, of prostitution, thinking it even one of the abiding art forms. Its spectrum delighted him because he knew one end of it led straight into the keenest meta-

physical experience, as when a geisha sang something too delicate to be endured without cutting your belly wide open. When
that cheep or chirp occurred at the same moment as he, the
semisamurai, felt vulnerable, all would be over; he waited pa-
tiently for a note of a certain pitch to fuse with a longing both
ravenous and eloquent. Part of him yearned to die, just to *know*.
Another part of him yearned to know without having to die, and
it deferred to the other, abacus to calculus. The swarthy planes
of his face, in constant autonomous motion, caught the light
and turned him silver, charcoal, auburn as he sat there. He
adored her for the compact symmetry of her head and face, for
the sturdiness of her legs and arms, for her forthright gifts as a
survivor. She was the only one with promise and the right physical equipment. On his mind droned, from the missing flag to
the houseboy, who sometimes walked around as if he owned the
place. Too intelligent to last, Hayashi mused. Japanese efficiency
required several notable failures; he smirked at his own apho-
rism.

Each night, as he clipped and pasted, typed corrections onto
his slips, his mind did its tour, sifting the trivial and the banal
from the sublime, eventually returning to the perusal of eternity
after something as unrewarding as a newspaper round.

He recognized that his duties required him to abstain, to wait
until the last, to go to the end of the longest line, wishing he
were higher in rank than he was and could come swaggering in,
cracking a whip against the furniture, and be waited on by
Hayashi himself, the author and supervisor of it all. He had
made love to his employment; he need not have made the Tent
of Orange Mist as palatial as it was, but he liked to fill out the
forms that requisitioned rugs, spittoons, cushions, screens, can-
delabra, blindfolds, and chains. He loved to think of slightly
bronzed flesh opening, peeling open like a wound, a flank soft
as chamois leather being revealed and laid waste. Open and
close, open and close: he doted on clefts, aching to fill them, to
pump them out, to fill them again. His main pleasure, perhaps,

was to sit in the room of four and a half mats and ogle the sexual miscellany around him as it rustled and whimpered its way to haphazard climaxes. He was a voyeur, but also a master listener, a man with an egregious nose. His was the true hubris of the promoted greenhorn let loose upon the world because it was safer to risk losing him in battle than letting him escort desirable women at home. With war had come a dimension that sanctioned and enfolded him, whose riots matched his hankerings, whose total gross effect spoke to something destructive in his mind. He did not mind if things ended, if the roof of heaven fell in, so long as something massive wiped him out; he did not want to die for anything so puny as a bullet or a sword. He wanted, at least in the garbled geography of his petulant memory, to go down with an iceberg calving above him, so that for a second he could imagine a vast slab uncountably bigger than his mouth was going to land between his teeth.

Well, the girl had egged him on. He owed her that cup of tea, taken wobblingly upstairs. The villa was quiet, at least as quiet as possible with an inferno blazing outside and staff officers babbling in their cups. It was quiet here, in this room, with his stamp collection pent up in a box. Always carry with you, he had told himself, the fodder of your favorite grace, and you will never be lacking, you will always be able to retreat from the insensate world into a cone of tranquility. Making a mental note to require bathing in hot water heated outside on bonfires of Chinese furniture, he stood, whispering *clean girls, like scalded pigs*, adjusted his double Sam Browne, then began his glide to the stairs, arguing with himself silently about disease, pregnancy, cash received, about all of which rigorous and pedantic memoranda had arrived from HQ, reminding him he was not running his own show. It was an *army* hothouse and he its butler.

Hand on the newel post at the foot of the gleaming stairs, he realized he wanted pink, matte flesh, soft to the tooth; young biteable nipples, thick and studlike, and then his fancy would expand, he would really attend to the foreplay. Otherwise load and shoot. How did it go? Load, shoot, and aim. Aim, load, and shoot. Load, aim, and shoot. Who cared? The main thing was to stop this girl from getting haughty. Somewhere in history another man had mounted the stairs, groping a little at the landing where the flames outside could be seen, swirling and reeling. The villa was actually warm from the flames around it. He was the timekeeper of hell, the majordomo of the damned.

"Good evening," he said in Japanese. "I have brought my tweezers." He laughed hysterically because he had not and she did not panic, not understanding. Here he was, with tea and a conqueror's poise.

25

PLEA BY SANDRO SOMATTI, S.J., INSCRIBED ON THE HULL OF A PAPER BOAT SET INTO A JAPANESE STREAM

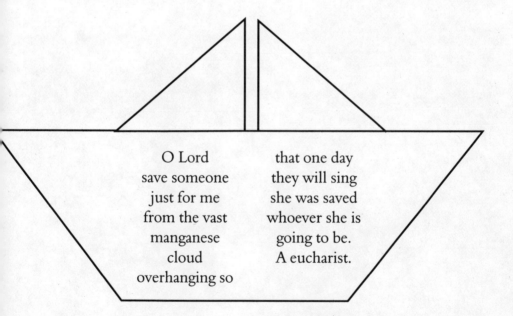

O Lord
save someone
just for me
from the vast
manganese
cloud
overhanging so

that one day
they will sing
she was saved
whoever she is
going to be.
A eucharist.

WHEN YOU ARE SIXTEEN, YOU ARE BEING SOMETHING LYRICALLY
outrageous; some girls, some boys, never are sixteen. You have
to yearn to be it, touching a foot down in your perfumed flight
to the precious stone of it and resisting further motion. Sixteen
has to be connived at, doesn't it, from within an almost convul-
sive longing to enter myth while eating petals? Scald Ibis, having achieved that age, now began wondering if even the right
disposition led to love, as distinct from desire. Having all the
right characteristics—tenderness, glee, trust in humanity, a taste
for refinement, a streak of bright selflessness, an unexplored
faith in complementarity—she had already assumed she qualified. It was only a matter of waiting. Now, however, she puzzled

about love. Here was Hayashi, and downstairs were his colleagues and customers. Her life had all the symmetry of spilled
candle wax, was no longer temperate or combed; she had so
many feelings for which there was now no place, and she kept
entering into belated meditations, hoping to catch up emotion-
ally with what kept on happening to her. Forced forward, she
had gobbled up those languorous intervals a young girl is entitled to dote upon, inscribing a face or a name in her autograph
book, or murmuring a remembered phrase while she falls
asleep, she who has just given up swinging on doorknobs over
imaginary depths of water, or talking to herself with iambic vol-
ubility on her way home from school.

On that cusp or watershed, Scald Ibis sustained a thunderbolt
from behind, commanded to assimilate what she had hardly
even seen, and to make from it a place on which to stand and
save herself, muttering when she might have giggled, groaning
when she might have let out an exultant mauve shriek learned
from literature, mentally absenting herself when she might have
labored heavy-breathed to be present for whomever, right in
front of his face, actually inside his focus, thumbing his cheek or
his knee. None or little of this seemed to await her; down the
road she could discern only smoke and shooting, nothing even
half so much fun as Hong's erudite mistakes when he was trying to trip people up at his parties, misplacing things in time,
getting names wrong, mispronouncing foreign words: the deca-
dence in the first decade of the twentieth century; Marcel
Baudelaire or Rainier Rilke; Lumpedusa. On each occasion he
intended arcane wit, but often failed to entertain as his heart was
not in it; he didn't care if they laughed or not.

So with his daughter: her heart was not in it either. Even as he
worried himself insane about her, she was being filled with sawdust, coated with lime, measured by a Japanese Procrustes
whose deviant needs at this precise moment focused themselves
in a cup of tea borne upstairs by a man whose needs were not so
fierce that he *had* to have Scald Ibis, or any of the other girls. He

could do without, mostly, when his ego flamed as host, recep-
tionist, majordomo, *viveur*-in-chief. And he knew what *viveur*
meant—a cocksman—as distinct from *bon vivant*, who was a
gourmet. This, unknown to Hayashi, was one of Hong's old
party traps, source of many a well-bred guffaw as the maladroit
guest confused his penis with his palate. Hayashi was not as devious or cunning as Hong, but he had worldly aspirations, not
to rank or polish, but to recognition. He wanted the world to
know what a worthy man he was, that when he took something
on he applied himself and came in a winner.

There he hovered, peering at Scald Ibis's moonlit form, half-
inclined to go back downstairs, stupefied by her slimness and
stoicism, wishing he had had a daughter to make him gentler,
less percussive, more of a hero in his own home. Girls made a
man mild, he thought. Was that it? What was this poor girl doing here in the Tent of Orange Mist, whose lewd prettiness re-
viled the fools who entered it? Something jarred in his mind.
He froze, knowing that he would never advance toward the re-
cumbent form in the lunar overcast. Even the gentleness he intended seemed gross. Yet why be exquisite? The girl (he almost
thought child) had been ruined, and there would always be an
ache in her life as she tried to reconstruct what had been denied
her, impulsively living backwards out of a sense of justice
fouled. She would never be the girl she was once going to be.
He loathed the thought but remained a soldier, able to think appalling things without surrendering to them. He cared, but he
did not abominate himself; rather, at moments such as this, he
cast over himself a tiny dust of dried-up ovaries, a graphite powder akin to the powder in guns, that dried his throat, needled his
mouth, clogged his nose. Needle-sharp tears ran down his face
as he tried to work out what he had become to this girl.
Guardian? Pimp? Tutor? He was all these, but also her destroyer
in spite of everything. Had he let her flee into the streets, she
would be dead by now; so in a crude sense he had rescued her,
but he had maimed her to save her. It was the imperfection of

this outcome that jarred him; he still, for all his military experiences, retained a shred of law, and longed for a tidy, designed
life: not improvised, but ordained. He was tired of having to
make things up as he went along. The impromptu sickened
him. Perhaps he was coming apart, at the outset of a monstrous,
huge campaign. He wanted nothing more than to become a
Nankinger, stuck in a wasteland of blood and etiquette, passed
over for promotion, but allowed to pursue his own fancies. The
cup began to rattle in the saucer. He began to back away, telling
himself he shrank from almost everything now, having used
himself up in trying to pass for a regular soldier, a weekend
samurai.

Now she was stirring, calling out to someone called Shu.
Who remembered anyone's name? He continued to back away,
sipped some tea, then turned around and continued downstairs
without seeing Hong, who, placed in a dark corner, stood poised
but helpless with his carefully built garotte: a length of baling
wire, two wooden handles, shoulders and arms of pent-up ferocity. Hong may not have known everything, but he knew
enough; and he was going to kill Hayashi on the synecdoche
principle: the part for the whole, the whole for the part. Hayashi
he would kill for only some of his deeds. Yet the man was already downstairs. Hong looped the wire experimentally around
his own neck and began to tug, getting nowhere until he pulled
with his hands behind him, near the middle of his back. He felt
himself failing and choking, but it was Scald Ibis who released
his neck, scolding him with an embrace that sealed his cough
with a kiss.

Back in the chimney, Hong could hardly believe he had not
murdered Hayashi; from the quivering in his limbs he thought
he had, but as he quietened he began to feel inordinately glad he
had survived to garotte another day; Hayashi had survived to be
strangled later that week. There was no going back on that,
whether it cost Hong his own life or not. He could adjust the
corpse into precisely the place where he was sitting now, and

leave him there forever, bound, gagged, apertures plugged, swathed like something from a Pyramid. Actually, it would not matter if Hayashi were alive or dead, so long as he got him in there, keeping him secret, warm from the coal fires beneath (thanks to Chinese fuel looted by the Japanese). It would be almost a shrine, to those in the know, as the well was down below, crammed with son and ice. He called to Scald Ibis to thank her, but she sat there invigilating him soundlessly, knowing not what to say to him, sensing he was a time bomb now, doomed to explode. Part of her wished he would somehow delay things, even in the teeth of his grief for Shu, long enough for a month to elapse, although what else could happen in the villa was beyond her. Years of the same, she thought. It will never happen. When you have lost a son and a wife, you have a clear right to imperil your own life with whatever expressive gesture. Sometimes the excess emotion had to run out of circumstances, never mind whom it splashed.

She thought that way about Hong, at daughter-father distance; but when she altered the words *son* and *wife* to *brother* and *mother*, she broke down altogether, certain that she, too, could not maintain her pose. They would be beheaded together, no doubt thrashed beforehand for insulting and deceiving the Imperial Army. It was their destiny, like something composed by evil forces in the universe: a devil's doctorate in F major. Her mind wandered, into and out of music, emperors, cooking, sport, the fake characters her father added to calligraphy, the paper car in which two literary lovers might drive away together, the Nazi with his armband and Iron Cross who had burst into the four-and-a-half-mat room, the origami birds Hong said he had affixed to the chimney wall to keep him company. Why, she wondered, have I not caught some disease down there or become pregnant? I have heard about these things. Do they not apply to me? When would Aki and Fuyu, the geisha tutors, return?

Try to see it empty as she did, she found her universe adequately full. There were things in it which, once capable of confusing her, now sustained her; she had come to count on them, unworthy as they were, and she added Hong's bubble gum, always the same piece, to the list; then the movie projector he had never had at his parties, the canned goods looted from other houses in Nanking and rickshawed here into the storeroom that was always locked. This was her world, unrequested, unsavored until now, like Chinese read as Japanese and making only intermittent sense. What else, then? Had she already exhausted her minor realm? If so, it would hardly sustain her long. She sought around her memory, delighted to find anything to itemize:

Anna May Wong's round-faced pertness

the *Xīan* character with four hands and a lozengelike head

small presents kept in the folds of her kimono

slips of old bamboo

the night-soil man with his mule cart

October, her birth month

Moth Wing, Meng, Cixi, Qiu and the missing Dé, ever willing to be told the Chinese army was coming to rescue them: an army from a newly united China. They would be given jobs in the movies or as bar girls in glossy hotels. It would all come all right, and each girl would get a brand-new wardrobe. "With velvet to stroke my face on!" Dé had been thrilled, moving Scald Ibis no end. Oh, Dé, what's become of you? She had to stop. Hong was stirring.

After she patted his palm, Hong, moaning softly, pulled his hand back through the slit. He was better off in his bedroom, she thought, if only he would behave; but one glimpse of Hayashi and he would be off, avenging, slaughtering, his garotte flying like a relic of some kite whose panels the wind had ripped away.

What truly worried her, though, was love, about which she had thought a good deal before the invasion. A woman who finds a perfect love must spend the rest of her life in ponderous grief—because love ends. A woman who finds a less than perfect love will grieve less at the prospect of a life's end. Never, she thought, envy those who find their perfect mates, for conjoint ecstasy serves only to sharpen the barb of parting, he before her, she before him. Better, in some ways, to find nobody at all but a series of temporaries or substitutes, whom you never mourn, who never mourn you. She had come to call this defense mechanism the visor of the economical heart, knowing that such affairs were not often a matter of will anyway. So she would abstain, eschew, forgo, all those denying words, seeing that she was already making the best of a bad job. How could she do otherwise, marooned in the Tent of Orange Mist? What was this doctrine of the lukewarm lover except something half-hearted, half-baked? People arrived at such attitudes more through temperament than through logic. What logic told her, she who had lost a brother and almost a father, whose mother still rolled on the bottom of the Yangtze, hair undulating like a water plant, was that the so-called *délectation* should be inspected, for it told her not that men were depraved dogs but that they adored women's uncontainable profundity so much so that they would make a perverse feast of their waste. No one in her right mind could imagine *women* sitting at a table thus with silver plates and silver spoons; *they* would screech derisively at the very idea, even at the cannibalism that ate a man's rump steak. Men, however, knew how to abase themselves, and with reason; they, who did most of the abominable life-destructive things on earth, made up for it by groveling before their complementary opposite's least estimable product. This made sense to Scald Ibis; it was better than nonstop grieving, and as a woman she came out of it rather well, no longer a party to loathsome deviancy but an altar whose myrrh taught men their proper, awful place.

Thanks to discriminate looting, the room of four and a half mats had started to look Arabian rather than Chinese. Checkerboard screens came together at right angles, almost too busy for the eye to look at them, and polished brass tray tables held coffee pots close to the ground. On one big velvet cushion sat a purloined leopard-skin, and above a low divan made of nothing but cushions there was a painting of two headscarfed peasants talking together while one allowed a green bird to take flight from her hand. What this bric-a-brac did to the room was immense, making it look almost respectable, like the enormous study of a poet-traveler such as Pierre Loti, whose red leather boots were the only things missing. A pasha had joined forces, and tastes, with the pseudo-Mikado of the old salon, and Hayashi, whose tastes were far from pure, felt irritated at the motley; but what could he do, with staff officers sending him booty by porter from the best houses in the city? In no time, he thought, the place would be a warehouse, through whose contents admirals and generals would have to walk elaborate routes, unable to see one another. There was hardly the right amount of open space around the tea ceremony, whose austerity depended on an absence of clutter, the vision of a space into which you might fall. He did not have the rank, however, to fend off the officers' largesse, though he consigned much of it to the upstairs rooms, now leaving the storeroom unlocked because it was in constant use; he had arranged things around the cache of canned goods, so that anyone fetching supplies of meat, crab, tongue, or peaches plucked them from a hoard that evoked the horn of plenty. As the food went out, the things around what was left changed position and slid, making a dry mineral sound that upset Hong's nerves: each time, he thought someone was coming to get him. He cleaned less and less, half inclined to shift his role, under the impress of grief and rage, to the compensatory one of clown. Now, when feeling worse than usual, he would enter the four-and-a-half-mat room with five or six chairs perched on his back, all carefully meshed together, wobbling but temporarily secure. When they fell, he laughed hugely and had the girls help to carry them out again.

"Not funny," Hayashi would bark in Japanese. "Please desist." But Hong took no notice, almost hoping to offend them into killing him.

"No more chairs, Hong."

"As you say, Colonel," Hong would answer, reminding himself of the garotte he had almost applied to Hayashi's throat. One of these days he might be able to crucify him on a chair, spread-eagle him, and then do a painting of the result. Each time the chairs clattered down, Hong had disrupted the specialized peace of Hayashi's room, evoking the chaos outside, demonstrating the uselessness to Japanese of chairs.

"Kindly remove them and do not, please, perform any more chair tricks."

"No tricks," Hong said always, "I am always looking for the right place for them." On he chewed while Hayashi wondered at the fatigue in Hong's jaws; it was such an American habit, especially as Hong had begun to blow bubbles when he entered fraught with chairs; it seemed part of the act. One day he would open his mouth wide and a huge bubble, big enough to encompass his head, would loll out, gradually engulfing him, deep-sea-diving him at the expense of calligraphy. Hong was beginning to crack, Hayashi thought; therefore work him even harder so as to watch his disintegration sooner. He was a flunky with a knack for languages, that was all. What would happen if he were promoted to sergeant? Would the strain show even sooner? Hayashi appointed him sergeant then and there, warning him to live up to the dignity of the rank: no more chairs, and no more wearing of shoes (Hong rarely went barefoot unless reminded, and then he just shuffled out of his shoes, leaving them where he stood). People had fallen over his shoes but had cursed Hayashi.

"You, an educated man," Hayashi said.

"Educated for death, sir."

"Where was that?"

"Nanking and Shanghai universities, Colonel. I was a slow learner, so it took longer."

"So why this?"

"Come down in the world, Colonel, sir, mostly from gambling and whoring."

So he belonged here, after all, Hayashi thought, and complimented himself on discerning the man's demeanor: he spoke smartly enough, but he had a hangdog, loutish stoop, a way of looking at you that suggested he already knew your price. Educated for death? How did one achieve that?

"Nuns, sir," Hong said. "English and Scottish nuns. The object of religion, they teach, is to prepare you for death. Nothing else matters. Once you have learned that, once you have drenched your mind in what the ancient Greeks used to call *deinosis*—things seen at their worst—you need fear nothing. The French author, Pierre Loti, sir, he made a postcard for his friends, putting a profile of a mummy from 1225 B.C. next to one of himself. Now that takes Pierre-like balls, doesn't it?"

"A samurai without knowing it," Hayashi said with grim smugness. "I wonder at a man such as you in such a trade. You are surely not a very good cleaner."

"But at dying, sir," Hong sneered, "I might be found quite satisfactory. One day I will know."

"Would you like it to be today, Hong?"

The sword swished and, like a wing of flat airfoil, took tiny flight, whizzing above Hong's head. He had not flinched. There was some applause, but not from Scald Ibis, looking on horrified.

Again Hayashi swung at him, and again Hong held his stance with opened eyes. "See," he said, "those nuns had what it took, sir." Did he care? No, he did not. He would care only if Shu could be put back together again. Anyone who had seen and mystically absorbed the profile of Ramses II on Pierre Loti's postcard would discern in the old potentate's bearing the duplicitous humility of a head waiter, a pout of excruciated obedient forbearance that had not wilted with time, the eyebrows mounting high while the chin drooped, thrust by aversion.

Hong remembered, and he knew what people talked about
when they talked for the sake of talking, which, he had heard,
was the sincerest thing they could do. It would only be days before they figured him out; he was no longer being discreet, he
was showing off as if this Japanese *conversazione* were one of his
own parties, and the Tent of Orange Mist a tableau from his
mind.

Hong was not loved in his own department; he was too creative and inventive for that. He published and exhibited more
than the rest of them put together, and he spoke out against all
institutions, sinecure lickers, title fanciers, idea stealers, formula
mongers, of all of whom the department had too many. After a
singularly outstanding year that even the department had to ad-
mit was almost beyond belief, he received a bronze medal about
a foot in diameter, fitted with holes so that he could lace it to
him or hang it stably from his backbone. With it came (an ironic
touch from the department) a small trolley to carry it on in his
old age; but he loudly declared the medal a cang, best split down
the middle and sawn to accommodate his neck. He was willing
to wear it, but only as a means of subjugation, so everyone might
see how he thought about the university. One of his jokes, orig-
inally coined at the enormous party with which he celebrated
the award, was that he would have to cut out his intestines and
dry them to provide an adequate and appropriate ribbon. One
thing they would not do, however, especially after the medal's
bestowal, was grant him the title of distinguished professor,
which he was nationally and throughout the world; the title
brought nothing monetary, but was being used locally, at least
until the Japanese arrived with a new system of incentives, to reward gifted social climbers and yes-men who had the demeanor
of distinction without any of its hazardous mental attributes.
Hong had spoken harshly of calligraphy parasites, who infested
the committees; he had no hope of advancement, so he re-
signed, to the chagrin of the two or three honest souls in the department. His letter, done in exquisite whorls and curls on a

gigantic screen requiring four students to bear it to the department, had ended as follows, in a series of militant innuendos:
"Plagued with overtures to become a distinguished professor
elsewhere, and not only in China, but along the Isis, the Cam,
and the Thames, not to mention the Hudson and the Missis-
sippi, I feel obliged to take my leave of you; I may not respond
to these overtures, but I prefer the perpetual delight of honor
deferred at my own instance to the degradation of waiting to be
tapped by a tribe of mendicant mediocrities whose tongues
from long use have acquired a khaki tint." There was more: he
was laying about him with broadswords and axes, sparing none.
His few friends, however, managed to get his resignation re-
jected, so he now swam, like a goldfish engorged with plums, at
Medal rank, both feared and revered, awaiting a direct call from
heaven, where the finest calligraphers ended up.

Perhaps this brush with Hayashi was precisely the apotheosis
he was waiting for; he just had not recognized it yet for what it
was. Asked to provide letters of support when he applied for an
endowed chair, he produced encomiums from Jacques Maritain, Bertrand Russell, Henry Moore, Henri Matisse, Frieda
Kahlo, T. S. Eliot, and Anna May Wong, who wrote in Chinese.
Accused of name dropping, he was told that humbler support
would be more convincing—this was a streak of behavior ever-
strengthening in China, and it said the best men were extolled
by the least worthy, that true virtue was seen most clearly by
those who worked the land. What the department did not wish
was a dandy-virtuoso in a golden chair, subjecting the less flam-
boyant of his colleagues to his whims. Hong scoffed and peeed
on the medal daily, having installed it under the lid of the dry
well in the garden. Watching his yellow spritz bounce off the
corrugations of its banal legend, he would nod and feel sorry for
Jacques Maritain and the rest, those deluded nonpareils who
had taken him into their company at a distance. He was an out-
sider-insider, wholly incapable of being institutionalized, but he
had what is sometimes called historical courage; he may have

dithered, but he sooner or later followed a clear line into intransigent originality. As a houseboy speaking both Japanese and English, he was priceless really, as the invaders were beginning to recognize. His fame had spread among the butchers, and he was soon to become palpably distinguished.

"Dare we?" Hayashi was murmuring in the hallway as Hong plied his filthy duster of a shirt.

"*Toujours l'audace*," Hong answered, without halting his stroke.

"I have the power to do anything: line of duty," Hayashi said. "It would be only a matter of minutes."

"I am willing," Hong said, feeling his hair prickle inside his sergeant's cap.

So it was done. Hong became an official interpreter, revested in an equally shabby uniform and badly cut open-necked white shirt, but now allowed to wear on his collar the divine emblem of the translator: the multiple mouth, a whole series of pairs of lips surrounding the central hole, the mouths moving through three hundred and sixty degrees to demonstrate mobility. There was no salary, Hayashi said.

"Oh," Hong quipped, "then it's just like being a distinguished professor." Could this be happening to him, who had still not cut the knots of grief within? Shu was dead out there in the winter cold; his wife had vanished; his daughter had been raped, and here he was aiding and comforting the enemy after deserting. He would be shot twice, once in the front, then, after a twirl, in the back. Wherever he went, he would be Japanese, cloaked in Japanese. He suddenly saw the sun rise in the future as he and his geisha daughter came into their own, marveling at their luck and smarts. If he wished, Hayashi told him, he could avail himself of the services provided by the girls: Scald Ibis, Cixi—ah, God, Hong thought, the bourgeoisie: ever on the mend, always keeping things nice: a splash of paint, a cruel word bitten back. Or was that liberals?

EXCLAMATION OF SANDRO SOMATTI, S.J., MARCH 15, 1582

TO WHOM IT MAY CONCERN, I AM BEING THROTTLED NETHERLY no doubt some vengeance of my *confessi* yet what ill did I ever do them I am festering have been unable to move the hood even in salt water *o questa sterilità* of this country this far-off desert this *remotissima gente* among whom I am *bottato* big hats like cardinals borne in palanquins on men's shoulders all of them popes guarded by uglies with Roman fasces

tell all this to Orazio or Fuligatti

how I itch and flinch

SO THIS, HONG THOUGHT, IS WHAT IT IS LIKE TO LIVE IN A COUN-try with no stickum on its postage stamps; minus a bottle of glue, you can't write anyone. For some reason he could not forget the old hotels of his adolescence and early manhood: cavernous bare rooms, furnished with cloth-patch armchairs strewn with lace armrests and antimacassars, the carpets threadbare, the soap made of congealed sawdust, the feather pillows oversized, the bar green and gloomy, with three huge billiard tables. Now he understood: these were memories of life with Ah, as they scuttled about together trying to avoid the eyes of household spies. They used to drink rice wine together, *hsa hsin*, hot in tiny cups, almost nonalcoholic, but ideal for the rituals of lovers' rendezvous.

Ah was coming through from wherever she was, using the paraphernalia of courtship to startle him. Not that they ever followed prescribed sequence. As a student she had presented herself at his shared office, exposed her bush, and told him in the bluntest terms how lubricated and swollen it was, how much it throbbed, and what it would take to put it right. He had locked the door and applied his hand, certain she was telling the truth. Never having been thus propositioned in his life, he almost committed the deed in his office there and then, but he finally took her off to one of those echoing, drafty hotels and stopped her throbbing with what she later told him was something between a cavalry charge and a plunge in swimming. Rough tactics for a coarse situation, he said, thrusting his way through, bundling her labia upward, such was his haste. Even on that singular day, they lost count of how many times they did it, until he was too sore to continue. "You're like a toffee apple," he told her, "boiling until dunked into cold water just before being eaten!" She came like a man with one harsh, despairing, downward cry of relief, and in no time was talking about Symbolist poetry before he became flaccid again.

The trouble with hotels, though, was the way the staff just walked in, at whatever time, unlocking in a trice what was locked, wandering into that paradise of lacquered walnut as if they, too, were staying there. They liked hotels, though, mainly because they didn't feel obligated to them: eminently leavable, a hotel room made no demands and extorted no loyalty, but it did brew nostalgia and pain, as they realized many years later, aching to renew a certain feeling near a glass-covered desk that had an ink bottle on it, pagoda on a sward of sheen. Or they longed for that particular feeble lighting, yellow-brackish, moldy-mellow, just the right degree of intensity for voyeuristic shadow play. Flyblown lampshades shielded their moist eyes from puny bulbs, turning their gaze inward, and upon each other, enforcing privacy even in the clinch. They looked at each other, then past each other, knowing the questing gaze could not escape that room and would eventually settle back where it had been before, enervated by its travel, whetted by separation.

It was only much later that Hong saw the likeness between Ah and Anna May Wong and, from then on, assumed he was married to the movie star. His lovemaking became sharper and more urgent, much to Ah's delight, at least until he met the real Wong and decided that American women were the best of all, made sexier for him because of all their aromatic soft leather, their straps and rubber patches, their perfume and powder and mascara. He loved tweed and gloves and silk stockings, the flash of a traveling (and much traveled) thigh. And, indeed, in the manner of certain hypersensitive men, his love for Ah increased because rid of lust, except that he could not work his lust on Anna May Wong. So his lust went out the window to become an abstract thing, applicable to a distant icon while Ah rejoiced at his newfound tenderness, his considerateness, his precisian's care. Hong almost fainted when he met the real thing, Anna May Wong treating him seriously as a bright Chinese mind when what he really wanted was to sniff her and have her. He had not reckoned with her Art, of course, and he spent the time fuming as she took his calligraphy seriously, putting intelligent questions while he strove to mask the excitement in his pants.

And now Ah had assumed forever her position on the river bottom, one arm flung into a derelict chicken coop in a final abandoned reach for something that was never there, her fate utterly unknown, better knowable now than it would be in a week's time as lampreys and the river dismantled her for no particular purpose. In the realm of copious possibility, there is always a chance that someone down in the silt will be unearthed and fished out by a meandering swimmer or some hook-and-rope contraption. Stranger things have happened. But during an invasion and what used to be called a sack, people keep ending up in the river on top of those already there, splayed in the downward float, eerily bleached by the brown in the current.

Who is watching anyway, from where, with what in mind?

The novelist? The reporter? Neither is there and, like whoever is left above the surface to look on, becomes obliged to imagine the worst, having nothing to go by. The novel is possible that recites Ah's gradual transit downriver and, shred by shred, her decomposition over the next few months, but it would be a courageous novelist indeed who tracked her thus, for such is not a popular thing to look at: true to life, of course, or at least to what a diligent scuba diver with nothing else to do would bring back from the depths. How the dead break up may achieve the status of obbligato, based on hourly reports, but readers need something brisker, which is to say the novel can only intimate certain happenings while the busy vaudeville of the world hogs attention. We do not ask for weather reports on behalf of our dead; we look away; but we can never deny the impact of the dead on the supposedly motivated living who close their minds, numb their memories, given over to the stale proposition that a live one is what we want to hear about.

Hear it for the Ahs, then, whose slowcoach metamorphosis from 1937 to 1938 deserves fanatic witness. We will not offer that here, but, out of honor to the principle of the novel's underground, we will report her onflow from time to time since she was loved, mated, made quick with child once, twice, and only then ruined beyond all prose's power to recover those longed for. She makes all the noise of a clipped toenail dropped into a wastepaper basket, but she will not fall out of sight, she will not, she will remain what she has been made. Hong will recall her forever, a man doomed to be enclosed in memory as the Chinese are by their language, and not by that Wall.

In their next conversation, Scald Ibis challenged Hong with open mouth. "How's atrocity, Father?"

"How's whoring, daughter?"

Were they coming apart that much? Not really; the entire family had lived on and through rhetoric, thanks to Hong's influence. None of them could resist saying clever things. Hong was less a sergeant now than he was an incipient officer, more an officer than Scald Ibis was a geisha. Or so she thought, wondering if her father was moving up the Japanese ladder fast; if so, it was because he was older than she. Would it eventually come out that they had cooperated, played into the enemy's hands for gain? Was that what had happened, or did a slaughtered brother and son, a missing mother and wife, justify their entire performance? The gist of the matter was unprecedented circumstances in which there had been no conventional way of behaving. *On Mars*, she thought, abandoning the thought as too woolly. *In Japan*, she went on, but that notion went nowhere either. Here, then, she decided, nobody knew what to do save run, scream, plead. There is no etiquette for such goings-on as these. It's like the first man and the first woman. We are the pioneers. If life's worth having, worth keeping, then who's to say what you should and shouldn't do? After all, I'd much rather be reading poetry and looking at Old Masters, learning how to appraise them. All we are doing is making do: amateurs at this, scratching up just any old scheme. So it's no use being harsh with each other, we who are left.

"Nearer the center of power," Hong whispered.

"You're *still* the houseboy."

"Only as an affectation," he hissed sternly. "I can drop it whenever I want. Languages for me, girl. It's the old calling come to life again."

"Well," she sighed, "maybe there's a reprieve in it for me, too, Daddy. A real geisha."

"You're not Japanese."

"You're not exactly part of the Rising Sun."

He stood erect, on parade, his body trim inside the shabby uniform, under the crumpled hat. He was an interpreter with a beautiful daughter still among the living; it wasn't all bad, yet.

"You're respectable, then," she said. "I ought to bow."

"As you say, you ought to bow. It wouldn't mean much, anyway."

She could hardly credit it that her brother lay mutilated in the old well, that she was motherless, which made her feel like someone traveling in foreign terrain while blind. This could go on for years: the currying of favor in the same instant as horror multiplied. How could the mind fend for itself without coming to pieces?

She had begun to feel a little smug about herself. How much more of it she could stand, she had no idea, if pushed, she might manage a month, but the war could last for years even as she grew into hesitant maturity, her body defiled, her mind infested, her studies—well, forget her studies. Her father was playing his roles with high style, but she knew enough about him to watch for the first signs of his high-strung nature taking him over the edge. When he cracked, she would fall apart, too, geisha or not. When he advanced from interpreter to lieutenant, as he might well at this rate, she would have to retire, for it was the lieu-tenants who had made predominant use of her. Too tense to feel disgust, she parlayed her anger into numb defiance, certain that life would not always hammer her with gratuitous enigmas. Life was only testing her out: this was not the final examination or, as that pompous British ass from Oxford said, the *viva voce* ex-amination. She heard herself posing in the manner of Hong: yes, I am the born survivor, *soi-disant*. Her self-parody evinced a finesse no one had ever seen.

Game as she was for a sixteen-year-old, she felt sapped by the absence of Ah; all she did, in that bewildered improvisation of her day-to-day, she felt it twisting and rotting under the impact of Ah's disappearance. She felt inauthentic, unperceived, redun-dant, unable to call out or confide. Hong was approachable, to be sure, but they could converse only in secret, and, besides, there was always that giddy, dandyish side to him. He could be broken by grief, but a prank uplifted him more than it would most men. The day would come, soon enough, when Hong fi-nally rid himself of his facetious self-rejuvenations, but it hadn't come yet and it perhaps wouldn't until Hayashi made him a colonel. That was when, she supposed, either Hong could be-

head Hayashi or vice versa: a favor you never allowed someone
inferior in rank to do for you. Obviously, it would have to be
Hayashi who would have to go, but it might well end up being
Hong. Some fatuous game of equivalence was going on between them, and Hayashi didn't even know who Hong was.
Cleverly enough, he was making himself useful to the Japanese,
as he had to the department, the university, and even Nanking
itself. Hong had the happy knack of making and holding on to
powerful friends. It had saved him time and again, and he didn't
even seem to know it.

His daughter was more sullen than that; even she thought
so, but she made up for it by moments, or bouts, of intense
inwardness. It was as if awareness were an acid she poured
over the object of her regard, and all steamed before her, open
to her ruminant gaze. They were quite a pair, a model duo
in survivorship: gifted actors in their way, but also enlight-
ened, it would seem, about when to release a garotte or not even
apply it.

Scald Ibis would surely one day inherit Hong's remarkable
knack of sensing in people things they themselves knew nothing about. He read from the text that occupied their blank
minds. He looked in their eyes and discerned how they phrased
to themselves the yearning not to die, not to be cut off at some
miserable point. He saw the quavering mind behind the bon-
homie; he saw this in everyone, without their saying anything,
and he knew how they were on the issue: blustering, craven,
stoical, arrogant, vengeful, paranoid, and he felt sorry for them
all, knowing that none of them deserved to die. There was always something worth preserving in even the least fetching human; he spotted it in a glance and cherished it, sometimes
wishing for a mode in which he could add these somethings together, thus creating a monument to human virtue. He loved
people for being people, for being diverse and undulant, as the
French essayist put it, or for being immitigably touched with
wasted divinity. Part of his philosophy of life depended on hu-

man vulnerability, not that he sucked on it or fed upon it. Rather, it made him feel tenderer about the universe, its maker if any, and the prospect of leaving it behind to equally vulnerable creatures. Had he been a god, he would not have insisted he be prayed to, but he would have made his humans just as easily wounded, for that quality tamed them and made them sociable. In his day he had tried to take over the Department of Sociology because he felt the university needed serious studies of friendship; sociology, he said, was how people got together, nothing more.

Scald Ibis was less gregarious than he, no doubt because she feared people more; she might not have been dragooned into Chiang Kai-shek's army, but she *had* paid her dues in insult, and if she ever did anything again she was going to armor-plate herself against the knocks of history. Was she capable of murder? she kept wondering. She thought not, but she knew her father was, that one day soon he would reach the brink of the abyss and would stride over, on his way to a different human tribe of those who had killed. The question was: if they never found out who killed Shu, did Hong need just any Japanese? A scapegoat? If so, he might commit more than one murder, unwilling to entrust justice to some hypothetical war crimes tribunal held by Chiang Kai-shek or whoever would be running things by then. Anyone intending revenge would do better to do it soon, while the chaos went on. Once he killed Hayashi, though, their chances would be nil; Hayashi was their protector, and, as time went on, he might even come to like them so well he wouldn't flinch when he found out they were father and daughter. He might even be glad.

The girls kept up their habit of clinging to one another, upstairs in a single bed (a tangle of shuddering limbs) or, downstairs, flinching when they touched, but trembling when out of contact.

"Well, hug me," Cixi said, "before I get whisked off to some sickening Japanese rendezvous. I try not to think about it. I do

as I'm told, it's just like school. One of these days," she told
them in her hoity-toity city twang, "I'm going to be a famous
lady. No more of this rough stuff, my loves. Nothing but *pleases*
and *may I*'s. You'll see. Just use my mouth for kissing and eating.
Nothing but decent ways."

"You'll end up where Dé went," Qiu growled. "Dé was a
country girl. *They* crack first. You may take forever, but you'll fall
to pieces, and nobody to stick you together again."

"Only me," Scald Ibis murmured, "always picking up the
pieces." They had no idea that the new corporal was her father,
or anyone's at all.

"Clever bitch," Meng said, gesturing toward something invisible: a pattern in the air of a midge with ragged speed: "Scald
Ibis is the only snob in here. Always self-righteous, between her
legs a disinfected rose."

As the four girls one by one began to bear the brunt of the young
lieutenants' sexual onslaught, they began to fade, tire, and catch
diseases. Moth Wing got pregnant and vanished. Cixi and Meng
were taken for a drive to the river, to see the ice, and they did not
return. Hayashi provided condoms, and little penis bowls like
shaving mugs, but he never insisted on hygiene. The main
problem was that since the first day of the city's rape eligible
girls were in short supply. For a moment he had considered a
new taste: dead girls, exquisitely cleansed and painted, laid out
for knife- or swordplay, but no one took much interest, so he
had the streets and attics scoured for fugitives, who were then
brought petrified to the villa, made ready and launched into the
fray after being sprayed with whitewash and an odd British disinfectant called Izal that looked like milk and stank like ammonia. With more troops moving through the city, there were more
clients: young, fresh officers who had seen no combat, chirping

and singing, drawing their swords across their exposed toes before going upstairs with the latest batch of girls. Somehow, Hayashi knew he should hold onto the best and train them for extended service; but for that he would need a nurse, a doctor, and neither was available. That was what headquarters told him, so after a while he got on with venereal business as best he could, doubled his charges, quadrupled them, and wondered what he had to do before anyone took the slightest notice. Besides, the officers knew they could get food here as well as a woman, even if not the kind of food they were accustomed to.

Now, looted like everything else, books began to arrive, but he had no use for Chinese books, or musical instruments, trouser presses, tie racks, gramophones and radios. As each client left, he got a present culled from the heap: a toy to be buried with or to take to the next brothel as payment. It was all too much. The inanimate plagued him, so he gave Hong the vexing chore of stacking things away in such empty rooms as there were, and Hong got the weird sense that he was stashing stuff away against the outbreak of war, moving back in time even as events outstripped him. One day soon, he began to hope, his journey into the past would bring him to the day on which his son had died, and he would intervene. He would see what had happened to Ah, and he would undo it. If the unbelievable could happen once, it could happen twice. Certainly he and Scald Ibis must be the only two surviving Chinese already moving up the Japanese hierarchy for doing jobs they knew nothing about.

Was it only on December 3 that a peace initiative had started up, devised by the Vice Chief of Japanese Staff, Hayao Tada, proffered through the good offices of the German ambassadors in Tokyo and Nanking? Chiang heard none of this until the fifth and consented to discuss a cease-fire a day too late: the march on Nanking had begun the day before. In twelve days the city had fallen; or rather it had fallen down. Perhaps this was why, Hong thought, the Japanese lingered, amazed to have done it, reluctant to leave the scene of so appalling a barbarism. They were proud of it, and fornicating on the premises gave the officers a pernicious thrill. It must have been like peeing on the dead. All those sandbags and huge timbers at the city gates had been no use. More than half the city's police had deserted. The place was done for before it was attacked, so perhaps that debility attracted the Japanese and held them there.

One day, Hong told himself, they will count up the Chinese dead, maybe even the Japanese dead, but there will only ever be estimates. Some people will never even merit the dignity of being counted, of causing one hundred to become one hundred and one. We run the planet in an approximate way, in round handfuls, never heeding the private agony of the individual, as if people were wheat, rice, sand. He had often wondered at the two mentalities: the one that made the other obey like sheep, that got its jollies by domineering; the other that somehow never got its refusal together and could be counted on to kill its opposite number on the enemy side. Wars happened, he thought, for lack of a conversation between both teams of goats, of victims. All they had to do was exchange views, which turned out to be the same views, and the war would never begin. All that remained would be the lynching of the generals. He, who had been at the point of strangling Hayashi, would have gone through with it but for Scald Ibis. No, he had not thought it through, but there was no need for that. Somebody had to pay for Shu, in that preposterous system of vengeful weights and measures murder brought about. Were there equivalences? He thought so: an eye for an eye, but what was the equivalent for a missing wife? What, if she were never found, would be the equivalent of Ah? How would he convert Hayashi into a missing person? Garotte him until he was unconscious, and then plant him in the chimney, bound, gagged, and blindfolded?

The ironic and destructive part of all such thinking was that both he and Scald Ibis needed Hayashi; he was their passport. So they would have to kill him later. The main thing was to keep close to him for as long as was necessary, and then, quick, the dynamite up his nose on some quiet, corrupt afternoon when half the Tent was dozing from the ecstasies of the previous night. The mess was beginning to make sense, he thought. The next thing to do, if possible, was to develop a successor to Hayashi, who would continue to favor them afterwards. So far, no deputy had appeared, no captain, say, unless that person were himself. Perhaps Hayashi, suspecting Hong's plan, had decided on the only way to thwart him: deputy Hong, whose only burden would be to favor himself. It could never be as simple as that: there was always bound to be an overseer held in reserve, a connoisseur of carnage fresh from Tokyo, a man no more committed to Hayashi than to Hong and Scald Ibis.

Thus his mind roamed and backtracked, wishing he had murdered Hayashi already and stashed him upstairs, sealing him in with best paper and strongest cow glue. His mind seethed with new-minted scenarios, none of which he felt able to follow. He and his daughter were running into a downward slope in Hayashi's affections; he had actually seemed to take a liking to the pair of them, perhaps because he had no idea of their being father and child. Unless—no, Hong decided. There was no way of knowing. The man was responding naturally to collaborators, not to be too polite about it, one of whom spoke Japanese, while the other had evinced clear signs of wishing to be a geisha. Not bad going, Hong thought: two protean survivors mimicking the behavior of mutual strangers. One thing he had noticed: Hayashi had begun taking in much more money than usual, but without passing all of it on to headquarters. He now had another British biscuit tin for his surplus, which added up rapidly. The one-, one-and-a-half-, and two-yen fees went into the books, but none of the rest of it, usually four yen, for a Chinese woman. It might be possible to kill Hayashi and make a break for the Chinese lines. No, with a tin of Japanese money, they would have to run the other way. They would never get away with it. The best he could do was skim some yen each day from Hayashi's hoard, and save it against a day of constant forked lightning.

It was time to tidy up the four-and-a-half-mat room. One evening merged into the next. A day of life merged into another, and Hong shook his head at his capacity for being so blasé about matters dearest to him. As he saw it, life was going to go on being like this for an interminable time. He and Scald Ibis must be the only father-and-daughter survivor team in Nanking or Shanghai, alive by flukes, having improvised their fate. One day, he hoped, it would make an excellent story at the dinner table, full of aliases and masks, coincidences and hairbreadth escapes. Yet when the time came, and cognac, coffee, and smoke mulled the air, he would back down and be unable to tell his tale, because of Shu and Ah. Such horrors locked the jaw, wanned the sense of triumph, sapped the best revenge. His only postscript would be a glum taciturnity, not even a shamefaced smile; after all, the element of collaboration had to be explained away. What they two did while thousands were being butchered was hardly the acme of patriotism: best hidden away under a disused, stained tablecloth, expressed in the plaintive twanging of a samisen whose notes could never be exactly deciphered, certainly not for hints of treachery and deceit. He could feel the silence coming toward him, the sound of the sealed chapter—chapter of accidents—being locked away from civilized discourse. Or, with Ah regained, things might be different, and her benign gaze might get him off the hook. All that hypocrisy was worth it, just to have her back.

But how? There were no records. Hayashi kept none, nor did he have the beginnings of any such thing; even his tally of VD cases was as haphazard as his bookkeeping. Nothing was book-kept or -kempt. Those who had made Ah vanish had moved on, perhaps by now dead or missing themselves. The huge, many-clawed ogre of war had gone its way, eager for new exercise, leaving behind it a slew of corpses the Sociology Department would one day have to count, knowing from the outset the figure wasn't worth having. In the depths of his frustration, Hong tried to find the strength to soldier on, pulling hideous faces, kowtowing, playing vapid roles, cosseting his enemies, stiffing his daughter lest a clutch, a hug, give them away. He would manage it, he knew, because there was nothing else. To have choices, he needed a civilization to flex them in, and of that there was nothing: no papers, no phones, no coal (except for the invader), no light, no food, no schools, no schoolchildren, no tramcars, no cars, no police, no water, no night-soil man, no neighbors. Uniquely solitary: that was what they were, wishing it would snow to cover up so many things unbearable to look at.

Scald Ibis was addressing him from a great distance. "Full house," she said. "All kinds of brass. They have come to inspect. There has been a request for *délectation*. We will be up late tonight, you translating, me in my lime-green kimono. How much more can you take, Father?" He said nothing, but he knew.

At all costs, Scald Ibis knew, her father had to be kept out of the four-and-a-half mat room when she squatted to do her piece. If she went along, doing so exempted her from further activity; it was cheap at the price, though gross. The problem was to find him just before she made her entrance and despatch him elsewhere on a wild-goose chase. Even as she tried to plan it, she knew the deception wasn't going to last forever. Perhaps, when he found out, he would not care; after all, it was they defiling themselves, not they defiling her. Well, she could get him checking the canned goods in the no-longer-locked storeroom, or just taking a rest in the chimney, like a wild man now civilized but hankering still for his cave. Keep him out, she told herself. Get it right. There's no need for him to know yet.

She had a hunch that, once he knew, he would go berserk and topple the whole house of cards, strangling Hayashi in front of the senior officers. Perhaps they would be better off dead instead of catering to the bizarre tastes of sake-soaked killers. Many majors were being made into colonels because, as

Hayashi had told Hong, too many senior officers were dying off: two by sniper, one by stroke, one shot down, one drowned at sea, one from fatigue, one from pneumonia. "None by syphilis, yet," he quipped. "We can always hope. It takes years, but so will the war, won't it?"

SERMON PREACHED BY SANDRO SOMATTI, APRIL 18, 1582

DEAREST, WHAT WE ARE MADE OF DOES NOT BELONG TO US BUT takes us on from within, testing and blighting. Part of the miracle of being able to study the mind of God consists in our observing ourselves as if we were He, distanced from self-engrossed passion and happily noting the fate of His raw material as it chides and stings us. It was only ever on loan, you see, my brethren, and not guaranteed to become a permanent source of intellectual delight. Sometimes the flesh is a great ridiculer of men, and the mere fact of having been born gives us no rights to happiness or even minor comfort. We are all here to be boiled up, turned into a broth, which shall still be His, whose love embraces all forms and states, from the most beauteous to the utterly degraded. It is not up to us to degrade ourselves, though many do; our heavenly chore is to discern the wisdom and love in whatever affliction befalls us, as if we were trees, fish, languages. All comes from God and goes back glad to be rid of the fray. Now let us pray for our brethren in China, even as we yearn not to fall apart or taste with compassion the most grievous calamities of the bodies vouchsafed us. Let us pray.

FRIENDLY BY NATURE, SHE WAS HAVING TROUBLE HATING THE enemy; or, rather, shifting blame for Shu to some amorphous nation, some boiling army, to Hayashi himself. She did not habitually think in terms of nations, armies, least of all the invading army of some nation. Art was more real to her than the roarings of power politics. The oddest thing of all was to live in her own home like a stranger: at least, as far as anyone could see, though internally she felt an extraordinary, savagely homesick pang for the house as it used to be, especially in summer with all doors and windows wide and music trickling from the gramophone. Thanks to his eclectic tastes, Hong had created for them an esthetic plateau on which, if nothing else, to quarrel about their tastes. Now, day by day, she had begun to feel something of the old delight return: the horrendous blurred, the benign aura of the old days came back. She had settled down, though engaged in enterprises even Hong winced at, and without his knowing the full truth. Time and again, she caught herself going about the house in a retrospective trance, heedless of the present, rehearing bits of Bach, Scriabin, Delius, or a fox-trot called "Who Walks in When I Walk Out?" recorded in the Palm Court of some London hotel, where Albert Sandler violined as well. In a way they lived more in the great—though pernicious, corrupt, malign—world than in the house, more a villa than a house, but less a palace than they wanted it to be. Lord knew how Hong, all got up as a Japanese functionary, felt about the same problem; besides, he was harder-hearted than she, with a sense of the absurd so strong it almost reveled in the grotesque juxtapositions the Japanese takeover had brought. Scald Ibis had fewer illusions than he, but the few she had were firm, not so much shuffle-worthy cards as intact icons to live by. One side of her hoped the senior officers would manage to poison themselves; perhaps indeed that was what happened to them all the time, though word went out about stroke, suicide, pneumonia, and so forth. She was killing them off already, perhaps. But not enough: newly made lieutenant-colonels poured in, eager for the fray in their warlike fashion, but sexually like schoolboys let off the leash. She thanked the chaste souls of all the ancient emperors for having exempted her from service in the Tent of Orange Mist, though she was still Hayashi's on demand. He had not claimed her in some while, however, and was perhaps suffering from a certain soreness, about which she had not heard much lately. It was possible he was so ill he would be replaced, and then what? Time to escape? What were the chances of his successor's being another Hayashi? Better to keep him on the premises, stamps and all. His successor might gather up ears as trophies. Hayashi might be civilized even further, she thought, given time and heart.

Once upon a time she prided herself on her delicacy. Had that gone away, she wondered, or just deep-down? Could such delicacy ever die, no matter what you were subject to? Was she closer to screaming, cursing, raving? Was she farther from rapt adoration, tender rumination, wordless ecstasy? If ecstasy blazed you clean out of yourself, so much that for a brief time you were nobody at all, did she now remain more within the staid bounds of herself? She felt more sluggish, certainly, less spiritually agile, less deft. Stock responses got in the way now of her old questing finesse, the honed sensitivity she had always thought part of her natural good humor. Had something that had been growing gone sour? Would it never effloresce? She was hardly the girl of all girls who should be put to such a test by orgy as this. Millions of other Chinese girls were better adapted than she, knew more and could stomach more.

So she reversed it: if she were that refined, that preposterously far from brothel crudity, then she need not fret: she was invulnerable, untouchable, incorruptible, and it would all drain away from her like water once the Japanese withdrew and the surving bourgeoisie went about denying all: oh, no, that never happened to *our* daughter, she was lucky. Dip ivory into iron filings, she thought, as if resuming an old chemistry experiment at one of the teak benches in school, and it will pick nothing up, not a single filing. Now, who ever spoke of a filing? No matter how depraved she became, inadvertently or from inquisitive choice, she would always reclaim her old fastidiousness, pearl from sewer. So there was no need to shy away from the generals and admirals at their *délectation*; theirs was the demureness of butchers who knew no better. And indeed no worse. To be overcome by such deeds, you had to have an infected soul to begin with, and soon you came apart, whereas someone such as she would bounce back immaculate, almost like a nun reprieved from the destructive element.

In her way, singing, reciting poetry, all in Chinese, she had softened the antics of the evenings, restoring some of the customers to an almost lost sense of domestic decency. If they could think of the four-and-a-half-mat room as their home, or part of it, they might behave reasonably, doing little untoward and actually developing a new fineness of being that turned them, at last, against besotted swordsmanship. Did that make sense? Not quite: she was trying to polish warriors, and it wouldn't always work; some of them, capable of tender instants for poetry or song, remained uniformed savages, especially when they got upstairs. She was going to try, anyhow, placed here for incomprehensible reasons, to be tested like a saint. What a notion! What a piece of conceit! After this, the remainder of her life would be placid. Nothing more would ever happen to her. She would lead a sheltered life, with equally sheltered friends, no longer dangling from the fringe of her father's parties, no longer wondering about boys, men, fathers, babies, her mother's joy in bed. She was not pregnant, she was not going to be, she was no longer Hayashi's; indeed, if, as it appeared, he no longer wanted her, or could have her, he would see to it that no one else had her either. In that case, she was made, with less and less demanded of her even as worn-out girls vanished at regular intervals, not even responsive to what was happening to them.

31

REMINDER NAILED TO
SANDRO SOMATTI'S
BEDROOM WALL

BE NOT A WOLF UNTO YOURSELF. REMEMBER THE HABIT OF YOUNG boys in the Arabian countries who hold up a big round piece of bread so you shall not see their circumcision. Sandro: if all else fails, be snipped, and be noble about it. It is not the thousand cuts, even if it be the first.

Remember: do not leave interminable notes to yourself. Make them short. For example:

Suffer, Sandro.

Itch,

Writhe.

Cease praying for relief.

But, rather, use the power of God-given analytical mind to solve the problem.

(You behave as if your member had a lustful role rather than being a mere spout.)

Work on it, o Jesuitical one. Even if you fail, Japan will not suffer.

If all else fails, use sign language: two fingers in mouth are snake; two fingers astride index finger, a rider; circle against sky is morning; cupped hand leaping away is deer's rump. Get better even if you do not recover.

BECAUSE HE HAD DISCOVERED THAT BEING A HOUSEBOY GAVE
him more freedom of movement than being an interpreter,
Hong was wandering about the villa with a stick to which he
had fastened a ball of cloth. This did not pick up dirt, but
moved it to a different area. After a while the collected dust
mice adhered to the cloth, thickening and augmenting its surface, which gratified him; now he was able to polish because
dust mice were softer than the cloth. First he did the stairs,
then the kitchen, finally turning his energies to the four-and-
a-half-mat room, in which some kind of preparation was going forward. He saw a silver tray, the little plates, the tiny
spoons, and at once realized what was afoot. There was also,

something new to him, a low table with a plate-glass top: innocent at first sight, but you never knew. So he lingered as the girls twittered and simpered, and Hayashi flitted in and out in a dress uniform, motioning and harassing, as was his wont when important visitors were due and he had to tear himself from Tannu Tuva, the accounts he doctored, and the latest magazine from Tokyo. He saw Hong malingering and barked at him to finish. "It will do," he said. "Leave it. Polish another day." Hong pretended incomprehension and continued to swab, crouching near the other table on which the silver tray sat. Peering at the girls in a strained upward glance, he wondered which of them was going to do the honors. They came and went so fast he could not remember their names, so he dubbed them by names he already knew from the (now much dwindled) first batch: Xiao of the constant chilblains and emaciated legs he called Moth Wing; Lu-niang, whose exquisite voice roamed about in pitch, making delirious melodic shunts, was Cixi; Yuen, always trying to walk in a straight line as her ankles gave way, was Meng; and Lu, of the runny nose and perpetual dry-washing of her hands, was Dé. Such a habit enraged Qiu. Mindless mourning, she called it, but Scald Ibis disagreed, smokily arguing that if the new girls were not to last long, they might as well vanish under aliases. Their names would never die.

"Pure spew, that," Qiu grumbled. "People have a right to die or vanish as themselves."

Scald Ibis went on disagreeing. "There are no rights here," she said. "When anything can happen, nothing is appropriate. Can't you see?"

Qiu shook her head and shoved a handful of yellow silk into her mouth to gag herself.

"That's right," Scald Ibis railed. "Back off."

All she heard was a viscous mumble.

"Tell me then," she shouted.

Qiu ripped the silk flimsy from her mouth and threw it at

Scald Ibis, whose lips, taut and inflated-looking, made an ideal target.

"We'll be next," Qiu said.

"We *were*, you mean. Didn't you notice the change coming over us? We aren't who we were. We're here now because we tuned ourselves up into something different. Comfort women the Japs call them. That's who we are now."

Safer to keep your mouth shut, Hong was instructing himself, and then wrap your body around your mouth for good measure. Funny how all those girls go out into the snow and melt away. Perhaps they all get pregnant and go away to happy motherhood, full of toothy Nippon baby. If you believe that, old Hong, you'll believe anything. Whoever told you interpreters needn't have opinions? He wished he had seen what happened to them; the same thing had lost him his wife. Japanese sleight of hand, he murmured. Sleight of head, no doubt. The truth, he said: yes, the truth, you oaf, pounding himself, you're a professor. Figure it out. Well, then, he began, how about this? One of the girls is always informing on the others, and who likelier than Scald Ibis? If she has much of her daddy in her, she's the one. Yet surely she didn't inform on them all; it's too automatic. She won't. But she might have let one or two of them in for it, and the rest informed on her, with diabolical results. I wish I knew none of them.

He had taken to sleeping with his enormous ancient medal under his pillow, retrieved from the well in which the remains of his son lay. Somehow it made Hong feel safer: they could not behead him from beneath, at least. He felt the cool of its metal as he drifted off to sleep, wondering if he should give the thing to Scald Ibis as a souvenir—of what? Distinction or ignominy? He decided to keep it since it was just about indestructible.

Fuming with officiousness, Hayashi tapped him on the shoulder. His face issued the imperative. Hong stood erect, kowtowed, then left the room with grudging ceremony, pausing every now and then to observe a smudge he would have to wipe out later. Just so long as an interpreter did not have to do the dishes again, as before. No, they threw them away, or the evening's most ebullient deviants kept them as trophies of an extreme experience secondary to fugu, of course, but worth talking up later on. Out he finally went, tossing at the room a sardonic shoulder flick that seemed to launch an unsuspecting bird. He was not going to miss this, as the British said, for all the tea in China. He did his best in the hallway to become a piece of furniture, noting a guard at the kitchen door who could not quite see him for the angle in the hall. He just stood in what resembled an officer's uniform; he was a statue, a sentry, the keeper of the gate. Until Hayashi moved him on, he would stay, his mouth just brimming with useful phrases in several languages. Nothing happened. The girls, whom he could see, went through their usual motions, drinking more sake than the officers, trying to be suave but achieving only a barbarous leer. China was going down the sewers tonight.

He saw his daughter approaching, but looked away from her black kimono. Hayashi, coming out to collect her, shooed him away, but he responded with geological slowness, edging away so slowly he seemed to be advancing. He said the Chinese equivalent of G'nite, cousin of S'nice. She ignored him, turned around, and went back to the kitchen, past the guard. Once again Hayashi shooed him away, urging him upstairs. Then he went to get Scald Ibis while Hong hung over the banister for a final eyeful. This time, with his mind on courtly matters, Hayashi failed to spot him, not least because the light on the stairs was poor as it always had been when this was a family home. In went Scald Ibis, the officers gathered around the table, Hong saw the top of his daughter's head, then it sank out of sight as a huge gasp arose from the rapt officers, and then he understood, he realized why she had been so twitchy.

Up the stairs he went, his brow on fire, a triphammer beating his brain, and the message *Wait, wait* trying to gain his attention. Into the chimney he went, palpitating with shame, deciding to climb down the trellis that night and leave them all to it. Back to the front and certain death he would go. Once upon a time he had been a man of the world, but now he had become a cantankerous innocent again.

He could stomach no more. He did not need to witness the entire performance downstairs; he knew it as well as he knew some of Shakespeare's plays, the novels of Stendhal, the poems of Mallarmé. Out he came, gathered up a few tools from the closet, and went back into the chimney. He waited there, never dozing, with the poise of a man who has made up his mind and merely waits for the clock to strike the hour. No guffaws from downstairs, of course; their ritual was too solemn for that, at least until the last act, in which the seniors ridiculed the juniors for hanging back. Scald Ibis went to bed, trudging upward from the salt mines. Two girls arrived with some man. Several officers left, admitting a fierce wind and letting the door slam. Hayashi was last, weary of it all, but telling himself it was better than being at the front.

So there he sat at last, fondler of his own ciphers, arranging the books, shuffling the disease cards, splitting the money into Tokyo's and his. The wind made him shrug, chilling something in his insides the size of a grapefruit. Cold bolus in the bowels. He tried the stamp collection, recalling how the Tuvans killed their sheep by making a slit through which to grope for the aorta and squeeze it shut. An oddly invasive method, he thought. Now where had he read that? Certainly on no postage stamp. What would happen if a country brought out prettily shaped stamps that showed a farmer clamping the aorta of a sheep? What would collectors do? Buy them even more? You could never be sure of which way human taste would jump. So long as the human race indulged in hot, secret practices, it would find itself interesting. Once the race became wholesome, it would wither.

He was pleased about tonight: the senior officers, more than ever before, had been delighted, and, as if to parade their manhood to the hilt, had brought out fat, dark cigars to choke themselves on. Serious inroads had been made into the sake. The junior officers had received a bombardment of insults and ridicule, but had behaved well during humiliation. If only Scald Ibis, he lamented, had sung; but she felt she had done enough. You did not add a pigeon to an albatross, she had said in her cryptic Chinese way, curtseying before she took her leave, in fact backing out of the four-and-a-half-mat room without once turning her back on the bemedaled, white-suited company. Some etiquette learned in childhood was standing her in good stead. A naturally courteous girl, she had a distinguished career ahead of her; star here, she would dazzle elsewhere. The odd thing, he thought, was how fast she had taken to things, to being profligate with her body, even though she could not have known the elements of whoring when she began. She had a way of intuiting an atmosphere, a social code, that spoke well for her Nanking education, her parents, her own powers of common sense and observation. Once she had mastered the language problem, she would move ahead into the most beguiling purlieus, where older geishas gave costly tutorials, grooming and honing. And any bad memories, of things revolting and degraded, would vanish. She would rise from the midden of prostitution and become pure as a paper bird, adroit as a celibate crane. Hong stood behind him, acknowledged with an enervated wave of Hayashi's hand. Stand there and gloat, the hand said; be there and admire, but don't speak, you will snap the spell, don't move, you will set up all kinds of incorrect vibrations. Hong behaved, watching the opportunistic ringmaster type his page, make his mistakes, remove the page, type up corrections on another sheet, then clip the correct-sized slip with the finesse of perfect vision, apply a smear of glue to its back, smoothing the glue by trailing the slip over another sheet, and then laying it in place like a newborn vein in an anemic eye. A tender pressure anchored it, a smooth sweep with the cushion of the middle fingertip wiped away any lurking air. The task was done, almost as if the sheet of paper were a bicycle tire.

Hayashi sighed and began all over again, knowing a night of this sent him to sleep like a charm. In other words, Hayashi cheated, but the esthete in him played the game; his lies were elegant, hardly those of a berserk swordsman, and his expression during all this was one of puckering raptness. His mouth moved in abstract chew; his lips pouted this way and that like a parrot fish reading; he could look down and now and then actually see them, heaving into view thick and unsteady. Having watched himself do this, he had found a phrase for it, not that he intended to tell anyone about it; those who noticed, and some did, would have to do without the phrase that, for him, nailed it down: mental mastication. He liked it. His mind babied it. Such a phrase did not erupt every day, not from the recesses of *his* brain anyway. He caressed the sheets, tapping out some rhythm on them. He liked paper, the way typing scarred its blank gaze; he liked typing, which was like warfare in the snow.

Something he said to Hong failed to elicit a murmur from the houseboy-interpreter, who was not bound to translate Hayashi's most motivated sighs. He asked again, something about calligraphy and typewriters, but Hong was not listening, and Hayashi felt the caustic bite of the wire against his throat, at first imagining he had done something reckless to himself, as when doodling you pass a paperknife over your Adam's apple and nick it ever so slightly, bringing yourself up short. After his lunge, murmuring the name of his son, Hong crossed his hands and heard Hayashi's legs thrash under the light card table on which the typewriter had always wobbled and jumped. On went the legs, flailing up and down, then sideways, though sapped every second by the rigor up above while Hong saw himself starring in a film noir of his own direction, half-hoping his pressure would tighten the wire so much that Hayashi's head fell off and away. Gone the head of the invader, the enemy, the butcher, the pervert, the pimp. All of his heads humbled by a length of old wire.

Hong gave a final jerk, then let Hayashi slither off his chair to the floor, wondering how to tell Scald Ibis this.

Now he locked the door, laid Hayashi flat on his back, and began something else, fishing from inside his shirt the out-sized medal for excellence with which the university gifted him. On the chest he set it, slightly to the left, hammering it home with the eight-inch nails he had brought along, using the holes that had once accommodated laces. In a sense he had honored Hayashi, had emblazoned him. How easily the nails had gone in. How easily, he lamented, they would come out. The man's face had set in a pawnbroked sneer, his mouth scrunched together as if in mock refusal, disdaining to show his teeth. Perhaps that was a Japanese fetish. No one had heard his hammering, only Scald Ibis, now scratching at the locked door, calling in intimate Chinese, being admitted, standing in horror that he had at last done what he always intended. To the chimney, she said, and he went in a flash, dawdling on the stairs out of uncanny presence of mind, while Scald Ibis looked down at her protector, wishing him alive but not well, wishing him well but not happy, wishing him happy but not sane. Round and round her emotions went, making her feel alternately wooden and electrified, drenched and bone-dry; surely Hayashi, lying there contorted and more out of his clothes than in them, was beyond help, garotted by her mild man of a father, the esthete party giver who knew languages, including that of the throat. Now she knew: there was an internal jest in the murder—the men of Tannu Tuva sang in their throats, could sing with their mouths closed, emitting a bottled, claustrophobic baritone that put the teeth of foreigners on edge. Her father had told her this. Or Hayashi himself, who had sometimes attempted such a mode of song. Her father had created poetic justice where there was none. She stared in horror at the giant medal nailed to Hayashi's chest, miserably noting Hong's name inside the laurels: the year, the cause, the reason. He would not be getting away with this, perhaps his first murder, but one set amid thousands; he had not wanted to be left out.

She went upstairs to talk to him, having locked the door behind her, without closing Hayashi's eyes. When the drunken admirals and generals found him, or whoever had the luck, life in the villa would be over. From her snow-white cheek a few drops of scalding water would forever spill. She just knew it. Hong refused to speak with her, shivering there in the chimney with his hands in his armpits, his feet crossed, trying to close the circuit that kept him warm. In whatever time remained to him, he must think the best thoughts of his lifetime. Hurry, Hong, he said: be definitive and articulate for your soul's sake. But nothing came. The garotte sat in his lap, at last fulfilled, best used on himself perhaps. Daughter, he thought, come here and do it to me, too. Rather you than they, whom he heard roaring up the stairs to look for him.

33

PRAYER OF SANDRO SOMATTI, S.J., MAY 1, 1582

OMNIPRESENT ALMIGHTY MINE, CALM THIS SOUL, ACCEPT HIS thanks for the sublime accident of an index finger slipped within the hood and moving easily down and around to evict the rotting syrup. Lord, Thou hast found my way for me. I am clean again. The itch has gone. I no longer writhe. Beyond this miracle I ask naught save not to lose my fingers, Father, I who have been sore, and tried, given much to think upon in the midst of comparing nations. Let it never retract again so long as I can scoop with index or little finger curved to just the convexity of the thing hidden within, whose bulk has no force, whose yield matters not. Bless this part of me almost putrefying for Thee.

SMASHING THROUGH THE SLIT PAPER THAT SEALED THE FIRE-
place, they found Hong by just looking for him everywhere. No
one had come into the villa, no one had gone out. Those who
left the room of four and a half mats had been noted by the
guard. It had been almost as if they had set up the entire evening
to entrap him, he who had had the run of the building, most of
all as an interpreter in uniform. Having driven Scald Ibis away
with his silence, he had simply crouched there in the temple of
soot, waiting to be seized. The wonderful thing, so far, was that
they knew of no link between him and his daughter, who might
still go on having a career there if she wanted it. All the same, he
blustered, emphasizing his role, his job, protesting in Japanese

at being hauled downstairs. They confronted him with the blood-soaked Hayashi (those nails had sunk right home) and asked him what he knew. There blazed his name on the medal. He said nothing. Instead of "Hong" the medal said something more elaborate; but they were not in the medal-reading mood. When you have been manhandled by generals and admirals, you develop a sudden sense of proportion, knowing that as soon as they leave you be their juniors will take you apart just to impress. Other armies would have delegated the search and capture to the orderly officer, or the duty officer, since a well-run army works through delegation; but this was far from being a well-run army, and senior officers delegated too little or too much. Officers of middle rank took the initiative far too often, practicing the ambitious form of insubordination known as *gekokujô*. What exactly is my stance, Hong wondered as they bashed him to and fro, yelling questions so loudly he could not decipher them. I am a university man, an esthete, scholar and gentleman, with missing wife, beheaded son, who has turned houseboy and interpreter in my own home.

He could hardly believe it. All he had had to do was keep quiet and wait for Hayashi to be promoted full colonel, then float gently up the hierarchy while Chiang Kai-shek sought him in vain. It would have been simple, yet not as simple and outright as what they proposed to do with him, that old shirt tied around his forehead as a blindfold, with the ballooning rest of it tucked into a turban shape above, his hands thonged behind him, his head bowed in front of the silver tray, his knees grinding away on one of the mats. He heard nothing, saw nothing. No trial. No farewell. Not even an order read aloud. He fixed his mind on Anna May Wong, on all the sly bulges in her face, but she slipped away back to Hollywood or London, to be replaced by Scald Ibis, voicelessly dissuading him after the event, whispering *another of your erudite mistakes*, except she even now held back, refusing to be his daughter, spurning the predictable cry of *Father!* as some lieutenant poured unholy water on the sword's blade, his hands trembling with fused fear and excitement. There was a pause as someone took position, shuffled, flexed both arms, then did nothing. Now they must have been nodding among themselves. This moment between worlds, for the victim, was the moment they savored, these *délecteurs*. Yet they refused to look into his eyes, where the real truth fluttered. What they were savoring was not his dread but their power, over his (to them) unknowable past, his ancient idea of what his future was going to be. Nothing went on happening. It was a charade. They had forgiven him. No, they would not forgive murder, so perhaps they were going to do something preliminary to him, something appalling they had no words for, but more than enough hand signals. He heard a grumbling assent even as the familiar aroma of human waste assailed his nose; indeed, his daughter's scent, fresh-minted for these bullyboys, these teak-faced old stagers.

Hong imagined it so well he took his place in the ring surrounding him. His head would fall plop on the plate, or with a subdued thud, like a cabbage. He would not hear it fall, unless through some last little flurry of the ear nerves he picked it up on impact. A beefy lieutenant took aim with the sword raised high, did a practice cut, recognizing that an honor of average caliber had been given him, and still held back, tasting the moment while the target shuddered, then struck with an awful disheveled cry. Missing completely and plunged into condemned, table, and floor by his momentum. Another seized the sword, shoved Hong rudely upright again, and capped him like an egg. On it went, with number three at last, after several crude hacks, severing the head. It was the sake, turning them into tyros in front of senior officers. Or it was the presence of admirals, generals, getting more than their money's worth tonight as another interpreter bit the dust. Hayashi had not been that popular, and several had already suspected him of cooking the books, selling stolen canned goods, making himself only too useful behind the lines—so as never to arrive at the seething front. "A clean sweep," said Fujimoto, but the others did not answer, knowing that the Tent of Orange Mist was finished even as it began to shine. They would have to go somewhere else: easily arranged, of course, and perhaps best left to that Chinese girl whose expertise had begun to flower so well.

Hong's remains went into the garden. Hayashi was removed with stately ritual, left as he was with the big medal stapled to his chest. Scald Ibis, who had seen, and almost bitten off her tongue trying not to scream, remained upstairs, but was not called upon. The girls, weeping and tottering, cleaned up the blood and tossed everything into a big canvas sack. Once again the room looked hospitable, its atmosphere free of gruesome vibration. A small conference ensued, and the senior officers took their leave, cursing and blaspheming, as far from knowing who Hong had been as from knowing that his bubble gum remained in his mouth, trapped by chattering teeth before the lethal first stroke, undislodged by subsequent ones. It was a triumph to have something so American in his mouth from the beginning of the war to its end, almost like a boxer's gum shield. They had none of them managed to knock it out of him. There in the snow, sidereally apart, he in pieces lay not far from Shu in pieces, apt one day to be found, not by Scald Ibis, who never went near, but by a returning Chinese who had never heard of Anna May Wong.

In order to do something before she, too, was beheaded, Scald Ibis took over Hong's work around the house, finding another shirt, inventing additional chores just to keep her out of everyone's way. Sore-eyed, she tapped away at the winter dirt, the dead leaves, the sowbugs that rolled up doggo into a black ball when she approached. It would not be long, she knew, before *something*. She kept expecting Hayashi to come up the stairs after her, triumphantly crying, "I know who you are! I know who your father is!" No one asked her anything. It was almost as if the Japanese had been expecting something dreadful, and were rather glad, or relieved, when it came. The outside door into the chimney was nailed up, the fireplace was sealed with barbed wire. There were no memorials. Over the winter, and into the new year, the villa got dirtier with use, run now by a captain for NCOs only, some of whom were coarse-grained, thunderous men such as she had never seen before. She went on with her geisha studies, guided by Captain Mori, who provided her with books, but lacked the buried ascetic strain of Hayashi and could not fathom why she persisted in such an exotic longing when all she had to do was wait things out and then go whoring for the Chinese. Never once could she say, This is my own home I am defiling, my brother was beheaded in the garden, my father in the four-and-a-half-mat room. My mother is somewhere in China.

SOMATTI BATHING

THERE HE CROUCHED, ROCK OF AGES WAITING TO BE STRUCK BY lightning, hunched over his own organ, in hot water, scooping as gently as he could behind his foreskin with the small spoon from the tea ceremony, unable to see what he dislodged and removed (his belly in the way), but certain there was something, some milky syrup put to flight and at once diluted in the bathwater. He was seersucking the filth of the Orient for God, spoonfeeding his ungenial master who had inflicted this curse on him. Who would credit it, he moaned, who knows me? Surely it is not a punishment for not loving the Japanese enough? I would make a wondrous martyr, ungluing my member with a spoon, nailed to a cross but with my hands free so I could work the spoon. I could be doing better, even if using my mind only. Oh, to be clean without ever using a spoon, delving where I cannot see, as if my loins were the future. On he toiled, raving, but sensing in spite of all a relaxation down there, a lack of itch and fidget, knowing that if he left the acorn to its own devices it would burn and become fearsomely bony until the day he would have to let the Jews clip him, his own *confessi*, to keep him both pious and clean. He would rather scrape at what he could not see, convinced that of all Jesuits he had been chosen as the soil in which the seed of irony could burgeon best. Looking up at this bitterly un-Italian landscape, he started his usual ablution prayer and repeated it for another half hour, until he had finished, then climbed out of the water, newborn and pristine for a few days even as God's miraculous ways with the human body began to befoul him again, constantly proving to him he was alive and doomed.

ONE YEN

FIFTY-FIVE YEARS LATER, SCALD IBIS, MORE JAPANESE THAN
Chinese, still remembered how leaflets had rained down on
Nanking, promising decent treatment, how Chinese soldiers
had killed Nanking civilians for their clothing in which to
desert. We were dead before we died, she thought; we were
never meant to know. History had wafted her away from the
Chinese Communists who occupied Nanking as the Japanese
retreated, Scald Ibis with them, afraid to stay among those who
would certainly themselves have killed her father for being so
much a dandy, a self-engrossed hedonist. Over the years she in-
gratiated herself with successive waves of drug barons and began to belong, rising to a level that some called culture

consultant; and, as she did so, both horror and sex began to disappear, as did her passionate interest in art. Instead, she became an arbiter of silks, sashes, bow knots, obsequious smiles, slightly chiding commentary, the ways of a woman of the world with men of authority. After the execution of Hong, she soon regained her status: a fill-in, a surrogate whose professional expertise increased daily, so much so that she made several innovations sanctioned in the trade: the pensive mouth during recitation (when others recited), based on Hayashi's own mouth movements; the head toss, an almost Western piece of arrant flightiness that amused many a senior officer; and the tongue-peep, in which the tongue protruded a tiny amount like a single labium coming out for air. This last, both erotic and feckless, touched all who saw it; the little pointy thing could not help itself, it had to see what was going on. Her days with the *délectation* soon ended; she had too much intelligence, too much flair, for an antic so agricultural, best done by semiliterate girls. It was she who eventually ran the Tent of Orange Mist in her own house, that battered suburban villa, using Hayashi's old typewriter, continually revising the stock of canned goods, sifting the stolen furniture and bric-a-brac in the four-and-a-half-mat room. She kept better records than he, restoring the old prices and sticking to them, helping herself to nothing (she was well provided for), and maintaining order by gently easing the clientele up in rank, which she accomplished by cloaked persuasion and allusive propaganda: she let it be known how happy admirals and generals had been *chez* Scald Ibis, dropping names, nicknames, and even the names of wives. After a year or two, during which Nanking smothered in hardship, her Japanese had become good enough for banter and puns, and her techniques of conversation puzzled her clients; she seemed more Japanese than the Japanese themselves, having acquired—and here in their accounts of her they began to falter—a neat, scrubbed, perky diligence; no, a sturdy reckless ambivalence; no, a portable, learned dignity; no, ceremoniousness full of gusto and snap. No one knew quite what quality had surfaced in her, but it was not Chinese. It must have rubbed off on her from constant contact with the occupying power, and perhaps it was something like studied diffidence, an elegance in her credulity. She loved to listen and her replies were replete with erudite geography, references to Hokusai and Hiroshige, little runs of poetry that sounded familiar but had been improvised according to a wholesome model. "A sheet of paper, eternal," she might say, or, more concisely, "Deafening clouds," all apropos of something cruder and more ephemeral.

She was becoming a true geisha, not so much losing her Chinese culture as somehow appending it to her new one. And she read more voluminously than her father had, never loath to bring a volume to the tea ceremonies and float a little quotation toward her guests, asking their opinion. It was said she had even organized her own *oyakei*, an all-night wake, in the incessant absence of a *shasô*, public funeral in Japanese. She had even, under tutelage, learned how to make jokes of an excruciatingly palatable kind, saying, for instance, of a slow period in the Tent of Orange Mist, that it was *nippachi*, the February season in Tokyo when things seem to come to a virtual halt; of course, in military terms, this meant only a lull in reinforcements, a change in commanders at headquarters and the hiatus being felt all the way to the front as the new man picked up the reins. Her precocious worldliness made her attractive in a noncommercial way, as if she were some brilliant tutor or a messenger from the sacked empyrean advising them on how to survive gladly in a foreign country. Imagine, she once said, the little just-visible beasts that run across sheets of paper are the ones that made the run in Hayashi's time; they know nothing of us, who squash them if we are quick, nor should they. That kind of thing amazed them, for she uttered it with pertinacious innocence. From the supplies hoarded upstairs, she began to offer a buffet in the evenings, yet without the merest trace of vulgarity. The *tatemae*, the code of surface reality, mattered to her immensely, and none had a sharper grasp of how feet should behave: if someone found a *zabuton* (floor cushion of polished cotton) in his or her way, as in the room of four and a half mats, the correct way to deal with it was to slip the feet underneath it while taking care not to tread on the silk-embroidered fringes of the *tatami* or straw mat. Some junior colonels, promoted for brilliance rather than social *savoir faire*, did not know how to accept and deal with a *zabuton* on entering, so her lessons were most specific, delivered in the manner of a juvenile martinet, commanding them, first, to sit behind or alongside the floor cushion until she said, in her somewhat warbling accent, "*Dôzo oate kudasai*," meaning "Please be seated." "What you do next, gentlemen," she would say, "is to apologize, then accost the *zabuton* from behind, setting both hands with fingers undercurled upon the cushion, pushing the knees forward and sitting down on the middle of the cushion with your legs folded beneath you, your big toes touching." She insisted on these matters like an outraged pedant although with exquisite, nearly simpering demeanor. There was yard upon yard of this etiquette, like some casuistical replacement for life. She also began making her clients speak a little English, the acme of chic, thus introducing such expressions as *excuse me, bravo rather*, and *what-ho* into the casual chat of cruising gangsters whose Japanese lacked all subtlety. Sometimes, when she felt perverse, she taught them other phrases, such as *j'adoube*, from chess played in French (for when she adjusted someone's cup), or *saperlipopette*, obsolete for "My goodness!" An outsider would puzzle as this little circle of fawning officers lisped and tooted in foreign languages while waiting to do the deed of kind upstairs with the rumpiest girls in Nanking. Scald Ibis had become the place's Plato; the Tent of Orange Mist was her cave; and the business zone of the four-and-a-half-mat room, the *tokonoma* (alcove) and the *toko-waki* (side alcove), was her no-man's-land. She ruled here with all the pique and zest of a baby emperor, lecturing bloodthirsty men about which gifts to bring, all in a somewhat garbled version of

Japanese seasonal time: dried bonito, cakes, fresh fish, *furoshiki* (wrapping cloth), dolls, postcards, incense sticks, molded cakes, a tin of green tea, a tin of boiled candies. In so doing she trampled over the vital distinction between duty gifts (*giri*) and gifts from the heart (*ninjô*). The officers indulged her, though, without quite knowing her story, thinking they had on their hands a slightly crazed survivor who was doing her damnedest to be Japanese, but shredded their customs, categories, and words of elaborated courtesy. She stormed into their mental presence and brought broken tokens with her, anxiously sticking one word after another until she had a sentence no more like a sentence than a coral reef is an internal combustion engine. She was a ghost to some one of the social climbers (*nari-agari*) who had attached themselves to the upper levels of the Japanese officer corps: their only way of surviving the occupation but, if successful, requiring their departure from China as soon as hostilities ended. Scald Ibis knew she would have to leave, having acquired a skill not valuable in China, at least until pigs had wings. Instead of anticipating Japan in any detail, however, she thought of a future in Malaya, Korea, or the United States, having vaguely to do with silk, poetry, and hyperrefined etiquette, whose study she had almost come to put in place of anguished memory. Had she really, still sixteen, gone into the frigid garden and retrieved Hong's bubble gum, stark as flint, not trapped between his teeth but gently lodged as if poised for flight, his hold on it relaxed at the last, his teeth marks final as something from the Stone Age? Her memory stirred up by violence, she had thought of putting the gum in her own mouth and soaking up juices that had felt death, but she desisted, kept the gum in her pocket, to be held onto in moments of berserk trial.

A well-read girl, she had heard of Sir Thomas More's daughter and how *she* kept her father's head; but she was not that absolute a spirit. All she needed was to have it with her, as he had kept it with him, knowing he had invested in it something myth-inspired. It was historic gum, to be sure, and so winnowed of its flavor it might have done duty for the oversoul, the abstract lattice that all structures have within them. She was at the beginning of a long saunter in refined frigidity, to be counterpointed only by intense learning, an almost fanatical dedication to the miasmic world of butterfly women pigeon-footed on vertiginous sandals; gleaming ebony chignons, party games, ingeniously arranged sprigs of plum blossom, fans of gold paper, rickshaws, obis, and piled-up coiffures. Which is to say that, highbrow as she always was, she became a moonlighting geisha, granting favors every now and then for the right price. She kept her name, translated, but if she had ever become an American she might have renamed herself Velmanette or Doryanne: fancy enough without spilling over. From war to peace she went, never able to forget the war, in which, as she felt it, she had aged from sixteen to thirty, was it, in weeks, then slowing down somewhat, but rattling along to doomsday.

She was at the Tent of Orange Mist until 1945, when she left with two suitcases and an uncertain future at the hands of the Americans: yet another team of invaders. Until then, she walked in the garden by the graves; even in the dark the graves were ablaze with flowers. Her mind threw kimonos over the soil. No invader would breach that garden's wall. No monster lurked behind its shrubs. The garden had suffered all it was ever going to. Or I would have been Starlene, she thought; you heard such names in those days, with the peace. The men, though, had names truncated or circumcised: Harv, Merv, Orv, Shep, and so on, officers with oily hair and bloodshot eyes, and tanned like so many Japanese. She felt marooned in allusive introspection, telling herself that men, like deer, had strong scent glands in their rear ends. Their backbones were made of teething rings. The inside of her skin was all tattoos, and she had survived only because she had turned her life inside out as if searching for something. To Confucius, son and penis were one and the same, the same word: product and producer fused.

The longer she lived, the less chronological her life seemed.

An orphan changeling knew no time, no phases, hardly even cause and effect, but saw phenomena as a shower of dabs, a windstorm of confetti, the whole of her fast-mutating long life having no more architectonic than the blossom on a tree. She excelled at successive improvisations. At the same time her mind scooped up unconnected memories, from women reeling silk thread after plunging cocoons into boiling water to opium and heroin which, initially, prolonged erection and delayed ejaculation. She would always hear the noise of broken glass, the hollow cannon shot of a door flung back against its hinges and almost coming loose. Had it not been for the Americans, she would have become an utter geisha, but Americans had no need of geishas, not even made-over Chinese ones; they had cruder needs, though strewn about with sporty euphemisms. Looking at a snapdragon in any garden, she nearly choked; squeezing the flower to open its mouth, she saw her own minus its false teeth: a hapless oval, just a hole. After childhood and adolescence, she had bloomed in a fantastic paradise *perdu*, destined for chronic dryness like some diabetics. She became a functioning puppet with a flashy name, part of the lubricant of peace, an injured party made to pay the price exacted from those who had maimed her. It made no sense to flee, none to stay. All that had made sense to her was that "geisha" used to mean someone passionately committed to the arts, but how did you become a geisha in a time long gone? She became someone between a geisha and a talk-show host, ever willing to prattle or even to inquire, yet fractionally falling short of consummate snobbism, always having something in common with the exploitable common people (and therefore, perhaps, though in vain, a link to Mao when he came).

What a waste. Americans loved her, too much, too often. She always lacked that frisson of hauteur, that parabolical disdain, of the tried-and-true geishas who survived on as the last symbolist poets in the art of courtesy. Powdered sublimation was her goal, but what she arrived at was close to the name role in a movie she saw in her declining years: *The French Woman*, in which Françoise Fabian, sleek and erotic and wealthy, clad always in the muted grays of the off-duty geisha, ran a call-girl operation, swamped by vicarious longings she never catered to. Such a life of desiccated prosperity, Scald Ibis thought, was mine, in my juiciest years. I was long ago made marginal; all I wanted, with sexual ardor, was to be safe, wholly under my own control, as close to golf as to children, as devoted to sake as to marriage. Thank God I am living in Japan, a country where a woman of sensibility in early old age has a role, if she can sing, if she can play the samisen and recite—if she happens to be a geisha of some kind, whether superannuated or not. I am an *onsen* geisha, as they say, of the "hot-spring" variety. Once, in 1982, over two hundred of us stormed the local police precinct because foreign whores were snapping up our business. Whores are illegal whereas we are not. And we won the day. You have to look after yourself. You cannot go dropping atomic bombs on people you don't like. Only countries can do that. Ordinarily I despise people who divide everything into three (toadies and lamebrains), but I rather admire those who divide into four and five (originals and freethinkers), but I look back, I think, on three stages: Happiness, Horror, and Work. It is almost as simple, and bald, as saying the European Renaissance was based on Choice, Privacy, and Literacy. Layers of skin, added on like wetsuits. It's all in the way you dress things, present them, as with Hayashi, who bore the same name as his country's premier and, for a while until that premier fell, enjoyed a vicarious ascendancy over officers senior to him, though he was no relative. I forget. Was Hayashi out of office before his namesake died at my father's hands? In and out in 1937, both of them, the premier first. It was enough for him to have been, as long as he lasted, a Hayashi, at least if he could not be a Hirohito. An old woman does not need memories, but it is often all she gets. I am luckier than most, old hag smoking cigarillo, an American habit, small-lensed glasses slipped too far down my nose for me to read; done up in a thick quilt (it always seems to be winter), left hand grinding my ebony cane into the concrete. Here I am waiting my turn. They dare not speak to me, I look so weatherbeaten out of geisha garb. Small hands. Truculent eyes. A handkerchief of unsurpassable silk dangles from my cane-holding hand, but not a flag of surrender. No hat. I might be watching a cockfight to prove I have no emotions left. I am here to see my lawyer.

A few months later, Scald Ibis walked into a Tokyo courtroom to file suit seeking damages for having been shanghaied into prostitution at the age of sixteen, fifty-five years ago, in 1937. The Japanese military had recruited and organized tens of thousands of Chinese, Korean, and Japanese women, most of whom died after appalling pain and suffering. Known as comfort women, they numbered from one hundred thousand to two hundred thousand. The only problem, Japanese authorities said, was that hearings would not be possible because the testimony offered might violate the privacy of other victims, who might wish to remain silent and unexposed. It was clear, however, that the prices charged for a comfort woman had been as reported: Chinese, one yen; Korean, one and one-half; Japanese, two. Scald Ibis, who tackled each day like an imagination newborn, was the same person who at sixteen had begun to close her eyes before each kiss.

Paul West is the author of fifteen novels, including *Rat Man of Paris, The Place in Flowers Where Pollen Rests,* and *Love's Mansion,* for which he won the 1993 Lannan Prize for Fiction. The recipient of an Award in Literature from the American Academy and Institute of Arts and Letters, he has won numerous other honors. He has taught at Cornell, Brown, and other universities, and currently resides in upstate New York.